Bury
the
Lead

MISCHA THRACE

Bury
the
Lead

bhc
press™

Livonia, Michigan

Editor: Chelsea Cambeis
Proofreader: Jamie Rich

Bury the Lead

Published by BHC Press

Library of Congress Control Number: 2020937564

ISBN: 978-1-64397-219-0 (Hardcover)
ISBN: 978-1-64397-220-6 (Softcover)
ISBN: 978-1-64397-221-3 (Ebook)

For information, write:
BHC Press
885 Penniman #5505
Plymouth, MI 48170

Visit the publisher:
www.bhcpress.com

To all the Sherlockians who
dream of having their own mystery to solve

The Consulting Detectives Rules for Investigative Reporters

1. There is nothing more deceptive than an obvious fact.

2. The little things are infinitely the most important.

3. It is a capital mistake to theorize before one has data.

4. Any truth is better than indefinite doubt.

5. Dogs don't make mistakes.

Bury
the
Lead

Chapter One

INTERVIEW CLOTHES are the devil.

The starched white collar of my button-down squeezes at my throat like a noose, doing exactly nothing to assuage my nerves.

"Remind me why I'm doing this," I say, waving a leather folder at Ravi, who has spent the past ten minutes waiting for me to remove myself from his passenger seat. "This isn't even the kind of story we tell. We're better than this."

"Well, yeah. I'm better than most things." He offers me a goofy grin. "But don't you bring me into it. This is your grand plan, Captain Overachiever."

"This was a stupid plan. This"—I slap the dashboard with the folder—"is stupid. It's just human interest."

"It's what they asked for," Ravi says. "And it's good. You know that."

"It's boring." Sweat pools beneath my equally boring black blazer.

"It's a requirement. You're the one who wanted this internship, remember?"

He's right. He usually is, although even under the pain of torture, I wouldn't admit it, because I'd absolutely never hear the end of it.

"I just don't want to be pigeonholed. I don't want to report feel-good stories about cute kids overcoming obstacles. Anyone can do that. I want the stories that matter, that mean something, that are more interesting than my sister and her horses. There's no mystery there—no scandal. It's all rainbows and fluffy bunnies."

He pins me with a stare over the rims of his black glasses and holds it until I squirm.

I sigh. It's the outfit. It has me out of sorts. "Okay, fine. Obviously her life isn't all fluffy bunnies, but you know what I mean. I want to be taken seriously, and this doesn't exactly scream serious."

"This is your foot in the door. Stop trying to find a reason it won't work. You did what was expected. You told a story. A complete story, a unique story. This isn't some half-assed interview with an uncle who wants to relive his glory days of getting paid to shoot brown folk in other countries."

The assignment for the senior internship application was to find a community member to feature in a Profile in Courage. Submissions could be written or filmed, depending on which department the applicant hopes to be placed in. I did both, even though I know my chances of getting an on-air position are slim. Which is fine by me. On no planet do I want to read canned stories other people got to investigate. I want to find my own stories, write my own exposés, and present my own findings on my own terms.

This internship could be my ticket to those stories, and those stories could pay for my ticket out of Maplefield. Mine and Ravi's both.

BayStateNews covers everything from local charity events to national politics, and somewhere in there is the story that will help me win the Excellence in Emerging Journalism Award, a contest sponsored by the New England Journalism Association that awards $10,000 to a student journalist—money I desperately need if I'm ever going to get out of Maplefield.

"I'm dying here," Ravi says. The air conditioner in his car is on the fritz, and unless we're going over fifty, it only hisses vaguely warm air from the vents. Sweat plasters black curls to his forehead, and I'm glad my pixie cut is short enough to avoid that particular look. "The clock's ticking. You doing this or what?"

"All right, yes. I'm going." I gather up my stuff. He turns the car off and leaps out, running to open my door for me. I roll my eyes, even though it's cute. "You're such a dork."

He bows, offering me a hand. "Just reminding you that chivalry's not dead."

"No, but you might be if you keep acting like this," I say, but I let him pull me up out of the car.

"You wouldn't. You'd be lost without your cameraman." He trots back to the driver's side to retrieve his messenger bag and camera. "Plus, you'd never find a replacement as pretty."

He's right on both counts, though I care far more about the first point than his relative prettiness, even if it is objectively quite high. When we're on a story together, Ravi's like an extension of my own body, my own brain even. He knows just what to shoot and exactly how to frame it to convey the feeling I want, even when I can't put it into words. It's one of the many factors that makes him my favorite human.

I double-check that everything is in the folder: the memory stick, the story, a resume, and a stack of printouts from the online news site I started three years ago. I set my phone to silent, then drop it in my jacket pocket. I'm morally opposed to purses, and my backpack, with its myriad of pins and patches, isn't professional enough to bring in. The faux leather folder I nicked from Dad's study will have to do.

"Noodz in forty-five?" I ask.

"Noodz in forty-five," Ravi confirms.

Noodz, the city's best ramen restaurant, is the reason Ravi volunteered to drive the forty-five minutes to the interview in the first place. Well, that and to avoid the herd of friends his sister currently had visiting.

"Then here goes nothing." I turn to cross the street. The Bay-StateNews building is intimidatingly modern—all glass and metal angles, a world away from my cozy bedroom and homemade website.

"Wait, wait!" Ravi fumbles through his bag and curses to himself. "Ah, here it is." He has a wild grin on his face that I can't quite read. He grabs the edge of my blazer and fastens a small enamel pin beneath the lapel. It's a black silhouette of a hawk-nosed man with a pipe and deerstalker hat overlaid with the words *Weapon of Mass Deduction* in silver script. I burst out laughing.

"For luck," he explains, a flush creeping up his olive cheeks that I choose to attribute to the heat of the August sun. He flips the lapel to reveal a flash of the pin, then lays it back in place. "You still look all professional-like on the outside, but hey—secret Sherlock."

It's a perfect gift for someone who worships at the altar of Sherlock Holmes.

And I do.

There was a time when this would've been a strange choice of religion for an eighteen-year-old girl, but thanks to the BBC and Benedict Cumberbatch, that's no longer the case.

I wish I could say it started with Consulting Cheekbones, because that would at least be understandable, but it didn't.

It started in seventh grade, with a teacher who hit us with the best classic literature had to offer: the creepfest that was Edgar Allan Poe; Richard Connell's diabolical *The Most Dangerous Game*; and most life-alteringly, Sir Arthur Conan Doyle's *The Hound of the Baskervilles*.

Mr. Braxton's penchant for violent reading assignments didn't always go over well with parents, but I owe the man my life—or at least my mind.

I devoured the original canon stories like they were holy texts and spent months glued to my laptop as I worked my way through every film and TV adaptation I could get my hands on.

I wasn't just a fan of Holmes; I was a student. I dreamed of being a reporter the way other kids dream of being ballerinas and astronauts. More specifically, I wanted to be the Sherlock Holmes of journalism and still do. His science of deduction would serve an investigative reporter as well as it served a consulting detective, and I embraced his methods with the enthusiasm of a newly converted cultist, wallpapering my room with quotes from the stories and series, and studying everything I could find about his methods. For my fifteenth birthday, I asked for—and received—a $200 course in micro-expression training. I'm lucky anyone still talks to me after an obsessive summer of practicing lie detection.

Ravi, the one person in the world I know would never lie to me, pulls me into a fast, hard hug. "You got this."

"You know it," I say, relaxed and easy now. Something about the pin—and maybe the hug—works. I do have this.

I was expecting a panel interview, but the receptionist shows me into a conference room with only a single man seated at the large table, scrolling through his phone. He's about my father's age, with thinning brown hair and yellow stains on the fingers of his right hand that tell of far too many cigarettes. He looks up as I enter but doesn't stand.

"Welcome, welcome," he says, eyes back on his phone. He gestures to take a seat. "It'll just be a moment."

The silence drags on forever while he finishes with his phone, and I have to fight to keep hold of the confidence I walked in with. I tell myself to acknowledge the nerves and set them aside. After a couple of breaths, it works. When he sets the phone down, I flash him a wide smile and stick out a hand. "Thank you for meeting with me. Mr. Jacobsen, correct? I'm Kennedy Carter, from Maplefield High."

He looks somewhat taken aback and holds my hand for a beat longer than is comfortable. "Kennedy Carter? Like the presidents?"

I keep the smile pinned on and play into his question. "Indeed. I still think my parents should've named my sister Reagan, but alas, they went with Cassidy." It's just the segue I need. I pull my hand back and open my folder, removing items as I speak. "Actually, Cassidy is the subject of my Profile in Courage. I wrote up a feature-style profile of her experience with partial paralysis at age twelve—a result of a horseback riding injury—and her subsequent return to the sport. At only sixteen, she's poised to represent the United States at the Paralympics next year in dressage."

I pause to let him scan the article before continuing. "Dressage is like a dance between horse and rider and is difficult for the average able-bodied person to master. For Cassidy, it's even harder because she no longer has use of her legs. In addition to the article, I created a video that highlights Cassidy's commitment, dedication, and perseverance in the face of circumstances that would thwart most others."

I say a silent apology to my sister, who would crucify me if she heard me describing her in such overzealous tones. Cassidy uses a wheelchair, yes, but it's hot pink and covered in stickers, including one that says *Not Your Inspiration*. She only agreed to do the video to attract sponsors, which all the top riders have.

I slide the flash drive and a magazine across the table. "I've included the full fifteen-minute feature on here, along with a sampling of videos I've done for the *Maplefield Monitor*, the news site I created for my school. I also do a print edition at the end of each school year. That's the most recent issue."

From the look on his face, Jacobsen was expecting some kind of homemade fanzine—maybe stapled at the corner, with a clip-art title page—but that's not what I've given him. The print edition of the *Monitor* features glossy, full-color covers and is professionally bound, with advertisements for local businesses scattered among the articles, reviews, and photos. Jacobsen leafs through it, the edges of his mouth tugged down, and nods occasionally to himself. I bite back a grin. No one else could present such an application packet. No way. I have this in the bag.

When Jacobsen finishes perusing the documents arrayed before him, he says, "Miss Carter, you certainly are a solid candidate. I am very, very impressed. But I'm afraid there's been a misunderstanding. The high school internship has already been filled. The only position left is for a college student. I'm afraid I have nothing to offer you."

The Making of a Monster

The thing no one tells you about vengeance is how much self-control it takes. It's worth it though, in the end. I think people should know that. Just how worth it vengeance can be.

To make you understand, I need to go back to the beginning.

This isn't the story about who I am today—the one with the power, the one with blood on my hands.

It's the story about a little boy, one who grew up in a world that ground him down.

It's the origin story of a monster.

Chapter Two

"**YOU DON'T** have time to change it. Come on," I say. "It's the first day, and we're gonna be late."

"I don't care." Cassidy dumps her makeup brushes on the bathroom counter. "The purple was a bad pick. I blame you."

"Of course you do. But seriously. Late. Let's go." I couldn't care less that her eye shadow is the "wrong" shade, not when it'll take her at least fifteen minutes to redo it, and especially not when it looks perfectly fine the way it is. Cassidy's gorgeous, with the kind of looks that would be perfect behind an evening news desk. Her choice of eye shadow isn't going to ruin her. "Your adoring public won't care about your makeup."

"Yeah, but I will."

"And I won't. Let's go."

"You're the literal worst," she says, but she surrenders the shadow palette and wheels herself out of the bathroom.

I grab both of our backpacks, dump them on her lap, and snag the keys from the hook by the door. "Meet you out front."

Most days, Mom drives, but this year, she's taking the train into Boston a few days a week for work, so I'm on chauffeur duty those days. Not that I'm complaining. The blue Saturn might be older than me, but wheels are wheels.

I back the Ion quad coupe—affectionately called The Planet—out of the garage and am relieved to find Cassidy waiting at the edge of the driveway. It would've been just like her to turn around to change her makeup the minute I was out of sight.

I stash the backpacks while Cassidy transfers herself into the passenger seat, then load the chair in. With just the two of us, the titanium chair fits fully assembled in the back seat.

We leave with enough time to stop for iced coffees, which is a critical part of the morning routine, even in the dead of winter. We take it the same way: with enough milk and sugar to barely call it coffee, and with at least one flavor shot apiece. Ravi once tried to convert me to the wonders of tea—an addiction instilled by his British-born father—but it didn't take.

The school parking lot is already packed when we get there. The first day is one of the few times everyone actually makes an effort to be on time. I pull in to one of the handicapped spots, and The Planet is immediately swarmed by a group of shrieking girls who must have been watching for our arrival.

Cassidy's crew is nothing if not extra.

The instant she's wheels-down, Cassidy is swept away without even a parting wave.

"That was intense," Ravi says, appearing around the edge of the car. "Like a school of very peppy sharks converging on chum."

"You're not wrong." I offer him my cup, but he grimaces and shakes his head.

"Too early for diabetes."

"Your loss."

We weave our way through milling pods of students and smile at Ms. Larson, the principal, who welcomes us back.

"No Henry?" I ask, disappointed.

"Already inside," Ms. Larson says. "You think he'd miss the first day?"

Ravi holds the main door open, and we find the golden retriever there, sprawled on his back with all four feet in the air as a pair of giggling freshmen rub his soft belly.

Henry had been a bittersweet addition to the school, but a welcome one, and his arrival was featured both on the *Monitor* and in the local paper. He's even listed on the staff page of the yearbook as *Official School Dog*.

He arrived two years ago on the heels of the school's biggest tragedy, when Liam Mackenzie, a senior and gifted jazz pianist, committed suicide two months before graduation. Not a soul had seen it coming. He was what all the teachers called "one of the good ones," well-liked by his fellow students and looking forward to attending Berklee College of Music in the fall. He was found in the boy's locker room, although why he chose that spot was anyone's guess, since he was as far from an athlete as a 120-pound jazz band kid could get. His typed note, taped to a locker, had said *Sorry Now?*

In the aftermath, many students found Henry easier to deal with than the counselors Ms. Larson brought in, and he soaked up a lot of grief for the remainder of that year. Everyone was happy when Ms. Larson announced he would be a permanent part of Maplefield High.

Ravi and I give the dog ample pets on the way by.

I think schools would be happier places if they all had Henrys.

JOURNALISM IS a senior-level elective taught by an actual legend. Mr. Monroe is the real deal, a retired investigative reporter who broke several high-profile stories in his day. Admittedly, those days are long in the past, but he worked with Bob Woodward and Carl Bernstein at *The Post* during the Watergate scandal, and that alone makes him a rock star.

He keeps his classroom desks in a circle, and as the first to arrive, I have top pick. I take one with a good view of the board and drop my backpack on the one beside it to save for Ravi.

The next student in is Claribel Garcia, and she takes a seat one desk over from me. Claribel has her heart set on writing the next great Mexican-American novel and is one of few people other than Ravi I'm cool doing group work with.

The rest of the class trickles in, filling the circle of desks and trading stories of summer adventures. Ravi darts in just ahead of the bell and slides into his seat with a clatter. "Made it." He huffs. "Shit, this is a long way from Art."

"You're here before Monroe though. That's all that matters."

He nods, still catching his breath. "Not making that mistake again." Last year, when we had Mr. Monroe for Current Events, Ravi had once been late by less than a minute and was forced to spend the period in the hall, writing a ten-page essay on the electoral college.

The bang of a slamming door silences the chatter around the circle.

"All right, sports fans," Mr. Monroe says, deep baritone rumbling in the dying echo of the door. He strides to the center of the circle. "Welcome to Journalism. I'm Mr. Monroe, but you can also call me *sir, Your Journalistic Highness*, or *that hard-ass who assigns too much homework*. I answer to all them."

A quick glance around the room is all it takes to weed out who's taken a class with him before and who hasn't. The latter sits rigid and wide-eyed while the former try—and mostly succeed—to suppress grins. Monroe is a hard-ass, no doubt, but he's one of the best teachers Maplefield has.

"If you know you do not belong here in Journalism," Monroe continues, "then I suggest you remove yourself at once and stop wasting the time of those who are where they belong."

No one moves. Even those I recognize from Current Events seem uneasy.

"Those of you who believe you do belong here, which appears to be all of you, would do well to question that belief. Ask yourselves," he says with the intensity of television evangelist, "if you have what it takes to challenge yourselves. Do you have what it takes to look at the world around you and really see what's there? I'm not talking about those little Pokingmen or whatever is on your phone screens; I'm talking about the realities of the world we live in. Do you have what it takes to see the truth not just in the world around you, but in yourself? Ask yourself: are you willing to do the work?"

He lets the question hang in the air, and I can't tear my eyes off him. He's easily past seventy years old, with deep lines etched into his dark face, but he's electric in a way I can only hope to be. He's not handsome, but he is charismatic. He can hold an audience in the palm of his hand, and I bet he did the same with his interview subjects—

milked them like a cobra-charmer until he got his story. This is what I want to learn from him: presence and control.

"Because if you are not willing to do the work," he goes on, "you are wasting my time. Not only that, you're wasting your own time, and you're wasting your classmates' time, and I will not stand for it. If, by now, you have begun to wonder if this is indeed the class for you, leave now, because I expect nothing but your absolute best."

No one moves. No one even breathes.

A toothy grin spreads across the old man's wrinkled face. "Perfect. I always love it when I get a group that is here to work. Now, for those of you who don't know me—yes, I am quite literally older than dirt, and yes, I do this job because retirement doesn't suit me. I did not live this long by being stupid enough to tempt my wife toward murder by staying home and being in her way all day. Gentlemen, that is a lesson you'll do well to learn now: happy wife, keep your life."

Tentative smiles flash around the circle at this and even a few outright laughs.

"While I'm sure you probably all know each other, at least by sight, alas, I do not. So, indulge me; let's go around the room and engage in the diabolical torture known as personal introductions. Give me a name and something about yourself that will stick in my addled brain."

He points to the kid closest to him, who looks startled as a result. "Hi, I'm, uh, Jackson Tolliver."

"There's nothing memorable about that, son."

"I'm Jackson Tolliver, and I've broken twelve different bones in twelve different accidents?"

Monroe claps his hands. "Brilliant! Mr. Tolliver, accident-prone. Next?"

I sit through three more of these—Corey Roberts, who races dirt bikes; Natalie Franco, who knows ASL; and Isaiah Colon, who ate a spider on a dare—before it's my turn.

I turn on my reporter voice and say, "I'm Kennedy Carter, and I'm the creator of the *Maplefield Monitor*."

Mr. Monroe smiles. "Ah, yes. Ms. Carter. I remember you from last year. I'm a big fan of your site."

The introductions continue around the circle, ending with a tiny blond girl, clad in an off-the-shoulder romper, who stares straight at me and says, "I'm Emma Morgan, and I'll be interning at BayState-News this year, where my aunt is a producer on the evening show."

I almost choke on the shock before I can acknowledge it and set it aside. That's my thing, my superpower. Compartmentalization. A good journalist is nothing if not objective, and had it been anyone else staring at me, I would've managed it, no problem. But not Emma, one of the pretty, effortlessly popular girls who seem destined to have the world handed to them on a silver platter. Not Emma, who's been the absolute banc of my existence since middle school.

I landed on her radar in sixth grade, when we were partnered to peer-edit each other's argumentative essays. I realized I might've taken the assignment too seriously when I saw she had written about the unfairness of the school's cell phone policy, while I had lobbied for the importance of death with dignity on the platform that if we can do it for our pets, we can do it for our grandparents. Emma called me a psychopath in front of the whole class and since then has become the gnat in my ear—the voice that points out every real or imagined flaw I have. So no, I can't just *set aside* the fact that she got my internship.

But I try. I force myself to focus on Mr. Monroe, who is saying, "In addition to weekly assignments, I want you all to start thinking about plans for your final project. It will be a yearlong inquiry into a given topic, but there's no need to panic yet. Each quarter, we will build on it. The topic can be anything you want, but it must be approved by me and no repeats are allowed. Sign-ups will be open until October first, and anyone who doesn't sign up in a timely manner will be assigned a topic by me, so unless you want to investigate the ins and outs of the newest hemorrhoid treatments, I suggest you start thinking about a topic now."

"Are finals projects solo or group?" I ask.

"Up to you. But group members must clearly prove their individual contributions, and the quality should reflect the additional brains working on it. Rubrics for both individual and group projects are on the back of your syllabus, which we won't be going over in detail because you are all seniors and thus capable of reading a one-page document."

Ravi and I grin at each other, silently claiming each other as partners.

"Now, a show of hands. How many of you are here because you still need English credits?"

About half the class puts their hands up with varying degrees of sheepishness and more than a hint of fear.

"Down. And who is here because they have a genuine interest in pursuing journalism, in any form, as a career?"

My hand shoots up, along with Ravi, Emma, and a handful of others.

"Keep them up." Monroe points to Isaiah, spider connoisseur. "What branch?"

"Sports."

Monroe nods. "ESPN is about an hour from here. You should look into their internship program. You might be too late for this year, but they have a robust college program."

"I'll do that, sir."

Monroe points to Ravi. "And you?"

"Photojournalism."

"Any particular area?"

"Nope, I'm open-minded." Ravi leans back in his chair.

"Just don't be so open-minded your brain falls out," Monroe says. "Focus is important. Goals are important. Kennedy, what about you?"

"I want to tell the stories people would rather ignore. I want to uncover scandals and expose secrets the world needs to know." Goose bumps spring up along my arms. "I don't need to be famous like Lauren Wolfe or anything, but I need to be heard."

Monroe is silent for a long stretch, and I wonder if I was too earnest, too corny. But it was true, dammit.

"I am very interested to see where you end up, young lady," Monroe finally says. "Wherever it is, I expect it will be fascinating."

Chapter Three

NEVER mind driving Cassidy to the barn, because it means I get a minimum of three hours to do as I please with the car. Most days, I end up at The Donut Hole, Ravi's father's bakery, which just so happens to be located across from a medical marijuana dispensary. When Mr. Burman decided to quit his soul-sucking job as a bank manager to pursue his passion for pastry, he saw a golden opportunity to capitalize on the state's newly loosened pot laws. We tried to convince him to call the shop Glazed & Infused or Half-Baked, but he said they were too on the nose.

I adore the little shop, with its gleaming black-and-white tiled floor and retro display cases. There are counters that run along the front window, with a rainbow of brightly painted stools for people who prefer their donuts with a side of people-watching.

The tangle of bells on the door tinkle as I enter. One of the four tall tables is occupied by a lone girl with a laptop and a stack of textbooks that threaten to topple off the small surface. A cookies-and-cream donut, loaded up with a mound of mini-Oreos, white chocolate chips, and chocolate drizzle, sits atop the books like a conquering nation's flag.

Mr. Burman's head pops into the pass-through window to the kitchen, and he waves me back. "Kennedy, love, you must try the latest creation. Come, come."

I duck around the counter and into the tiny kitchen, where everything is stainless steel and packed in so tight it's a wonder he produces as much as he does.

Ravi is up to his elbows in soapy water at the oversized sink, his glasses foggy from the steam. "Nice, Dad. Kennedy comes in, and it's all, 'Oooh, try my donut, favorite child.' I come in, and it's, 'Go wash the dishes.'" He rolls his eyes. "Really feeling the love."

I bite into the donut and moan in delight. It's like eating the tropics. The coconut flavored dough is studded with pockets of pineapple curd and topped with a thick ring of coconut frosting that's been dunked in crystallized ginger, lime zest, and shreds of toasted coconut.

"Good?" Mr. B asks.

"Amazing."

"Not too much coconut?"

"Only for monsters who hate coconut."

He beams and takes the tray out front to feature as the afternoon special.

My father thinks Mr. B is a hippy and that he set a poor example for his children by walking away from a lucrative career on a whim, but I love him. And his wife. And their kids. When I was in second grade, I even went through a phase of claiming my last name was Burman because I wanted to be part of the family so much. It took a few more years to realize that I actually am—in heart, if not in blood.

When Ravi concedes defeat to the dishes, we pull two milk crates away from the delivery door at the back of the kitchen and sit down.

"So, any thoughts on the final project yet?"

Ravi props his elbows on his spread knees. "Truth?"

"No, lie to me."

He shoots me the V-sign with two fingers—his dad's UK version of the middle finger. "No idea. We could just use the *Monitor*. I mean, if we're already running our own news site, we might as well get credit for it, yeah?"

I consider this. There's no way anyone else will be doing anything even close to the site, which is not only well established, but well regarded. There's an app that makes it easy for students to access it from their phones, and even teachers visit the site.

The *Maplefield Monitor* is more than a gossip blog or a mindless rehashing of school events. It features original stories and is updated biweekly, with the idea that the quality of the articles is more important than the quantity. Because it functions as the school's newspaper and I rely on the school community to provide tips and leads, both the website and the app have a suggestion form where users can offer input on content.

"I don't think Monroe is going to approve the *Monitor* as our final project," I say. "But whatever our topic is, it should be something that we'd be putting up anyway. We need something big, something we can feature all year."

"Like?"

"No clue."

"Hmm." He steeples his fingers beneath his chin in a parody of thought and after a moment says, "Okay, I know you're not going to love this because it's human interest-y, but hear me out. What about an ongoing series of student profiles? Something like *I Am Maplefield*, where each issue highlights a different kid. Actually, we can do teachers too—maybe even something cute with Henry—and make it as diverse as possible. Like we try to showcase the real Maplefield, not just StuCo and sports and that usual shit. Hit up the detention kids, the overlooked kids."

I mull it over. "The secret life of Maplefield High? It's feel-good, but not terrible. I just wonder if there's something bigger, something that really matters."

He turns those dark eyes on me and quirks a brow. "If you haven't noticed, the world is kind of a dumpster fire right now. Feel-good does matter."

I relent. It's impossible not to. "Okay, you're not wrong. But you know what I mean. If it's going to get us a run at the Emerging Excellence award, it's gotta be something big." And nothing big ever happens in Maplefield. Except… "What about the curse? We could combine your profile idea with an overarching story—a mystery." I'm already planning how to frame it and what arc it would follow. "We could look into the origin of the curse and do a feature on each person who's disappeared. I mean, we've already done Liam, but if the curse is as real as people think, there must be plenty of cases we can research. I mean, if seniors disappear every year, that's not just some made-up curse; it's a goddamn epidemic."

"The curse." Ravi stretches his long legs out in front of him. "Yeah, that doesn't suck. Are you thinking print or video?"

"I think print, with photography for the profiles. They might just be reproductions of yearbook photos, but maybe the families will have kept mementos or something we could use as props. Maybe culminate with a feature-length article and a video story. I'm assuming you want video?"

He nods. "I think it could work. Interviews with those left behind and such. The photography will be cake. Stark and poignant. This has potential."

I slap his leg. "And just think, if the curse holds, we'll have someone from our own class to investigate. It won't just be a historical investigation; it'll be breaking news."

"You look way too excited about one of our classmates disappearing." He falls silent for a moment, and I can see his thoughts spinning. "I think we should do the *I Am Maplefield* profiles anyway, as a counterpart. We can have the missing people on one side—tragic—but on the other side, we have the graduating class with their lives still ahead of them."

"That's perfect. You're a genius. I'm in."

MONROE APPROVES our project, as we knew he would. He likes the juxtaposition of the two topics and that it reflects enough work for two people. Possibly more than enough work.

I want to dive right into the curse, but Ravi suggests banging out some of the *I Am Maplefield* profiles first.

"I was thinking about that actually," I say over lunch. "Maybe *I Am Maplefield* should be pure photojournalism."

"Yeah?" He looks excited.

"Yeah. We'll do a short article to introduce it, but I was thinking about those black-and-white 'Stop the Stigma' PSAs, where people hold poster boards with facts written on them. It fits that whole stark-and-poignant thing we were talking about."

"Okay, yeah. I can see that…" His whole face lights up. "Wait a minute. Wait. A. Minute. What if instead of doing select students, we do the entire school?"

I'm about to protest, but he holds up both hands and shushes me. "No, no, listen. It could be really, really cool. Black-and-white photos against a plain white backdrop. Strip away everything except the person. Everyone would be shot in roughly the same position, with the same lighting and a fill-in-the-blank *I Am Maplefield* sign. Something like this."

He pulls a notebook out of his bag, turns it sideways, and prints *I Am* across the top, after which he leaves plenty of room to write, then adds *I Am Maplefield* along the bottom.

"Right?" He spins the notebook so I can see. "And everyone could complete the sentence however they want. They'd have the same sign, essentially the same photo, but their sentences would be totally different."

To prove his point, he takes the notebook back and writes *the most brilliant photographer ever* in the white space and holds it up to his chest.

I grab my phone. "Don't move."

I snap a photo and place the phone on the table between us. His hair looks like he has animals living in it, but his grin carries the image.

"This could definitely be cool." I make the image his new contact photo. "Let's do it. What do we need?"

"Poster boards, markers, a location, lighting equipment." He ticks items off on his fingers as he goes. He has artist's fingers, long and elegant.

"And publicity," I add. "People need to know we're doing this. I'll put a call out on the *Monitor* and set a push notification so everyone with the app has to open it to clear the badge. We can see about having the office make an announcement in the morning and hang flyers too." I'm warming to the idea. "This has potential. It would be amazing if we could actually get the entire school."

We stay after school to scout locations and startle more than a few teachers in our search. Ravi shoots down all my suggestions, but I know it's not personal. He has a specific idea for how this needs to look, and I trust him to make it work.

We duck into the auditorium, and Ravi stands in the center aisle, considering the stage. He purses his lips, then bounds down the aisle to vault onto the worn-out stage. He tugs at the heavy velvet curtains flanking the sides.

"If we pulled these taut, we wouldn't even need to bring in a proper backdrop."

He tugs on the crimson fabric to demonstrate and unleashes a cascading crash from somewhere in the bowels of backstage. He drops the curtain and leaps back. "I didn't do it!"

"Evidence says otherwise," I say with a laugh. "Should we see what it was or pretend it never happened?"

"I vote pretend it never happened."

I'm prepared to agree when I catch movement rustling the long curtain along the back of the stage. I raise a finger to my lips and point.

"I told you I didn't do it. Let's go," he says, but I'm already ducking behind the curtain.

In the dark, two figures—a boy in a baseball hat and a petite girl—are silhouetted against the light of an open backstage door. The girl rushes ahead, gait rigid and quick, and I catch faint laughter from the boy as the door closes behind them.

For a minute, I consider following them but then realize that might seem creepy. I make my way back to the front of the stage, where Ravi stands waiting. "Way to come in after me," I say. "What kind of backup are you?"

"The kind that sees movement behind a curtain and assumes it's either ghosts or someone getting it on, and frankly, I'm okay seeing neither of those things."

"Ew, in school?" At least I'd only glimpsed retreating backsides and not *naked* backsides. I sometimes forget how at the forefront sex is for literally everyone who isn't me. I'm not completely sex-repulsed like some of the aces I've talked to online, but I just don't get the point. I like to think I'm like Sherlock in this regard—I just have better things to do.

Ravi gives me a grandfatherly pat on the shoulder. "Yes, at school. We are teenagers. We have of the hormones, and we partake of the sex. Or at least we try to partake of the sex. We're not picky about location."

I shove him away. "Nope, still nasty. It's school. It's public. I hope you don't do things like that."

He waggles his eyebrows and laughs. "A gentleman never kisses and tells."

"Ravi Burman, you're full of shit. You literally always tell. In way, way more detail than I care about."

"I never said *I* was a gentleman." He grabs my hand. "Come on. I want to keep looking. This is a possibility, but it's obviously not secure enough to leave my lights up."

I follow him out to the hall, which is shockingly bright after the dimness of the auditorium and pitch-black of backstage, and we nearly collide with Ms. Larson and Henry.

The principal puts a hand to her chest and gives an embarrassed laugh. "Oh, you startled me. What are you two doing?"

I drop to a crouch, and Henry presses his head into my chest for pets. I scratch his floppy ears and give Ms. Larson a rundown of our project.

"That's a wonderful idea," she says when we finish explaining *I Am Maplefield.*

"So, we're just looking for the best place to shoot," Ravi says. "If we do it somewhere outside of school, I don't think we'll get as many people, and we really want to make it a school-wide thing."

"And you want to leave everything set up somewhere?"

"That'd be best."

"I'll tell you what," Ms. Larson says. "There's a classroom on the third floor that isn't being used this year. It's on a corner, so there are windows along two walls. Would that work?"

"That would be perfect." Ravi looks so thrilled I think he might hug Ms. Larson.

She smiles. "Okay, then. If you want to come back to my office, I can get the key for you."

As we walk, we ask Ms. Larson about doing a morning announcement to promote the project, which she says won't be a problem. We also get permission to post flyers around the building.

She holds the door to her office open for us, and we wait for Henry to trot in first. He goes to his bed in the corner and flops down with a contented sigh. I grab a pair of the strawberry hard candies from the bowl on the conference table. They're the same kind my grandmother used to keep in her living room candy bowl. I hold one out to Ravi, but he grimaces and shakes his head. He still isn't over the explosive repercussions of eating an entire bowl of them freshman year. He'd spent a painful day glued to the toilet in the nurse's private bathroom, and Ms. Larson didn't even punish him for the theft, just said that sugar-free candies were a valuable lesson in self-control.

I pocket the extra while Ms. Larson unlocks a shallow wooden cabinet on the wall. She plucks a single key from a hook and hands it to Ravi. This he takes far more eagerly.

"Do not lose it," she says. "This is a privilege and not one given lightly. That key only works for that room, so don't go getting any ideas."

"We shall use our powers for good," Ravi says solemnly.

Ms. Larson laughs. "I'm sure you will."

Room 331 is exactly what we need. We spend the rest of the afternoon stacking tables and chairs along one wall to make room for the photography equipment. The open windows let in a nice cross breeze, but it's still hard work, and by the time we have the last chair tucked away, we're both sweaty and exhausted, but very satisfied.

Chapter Four

MS. LARSON clears Ravi and me to use the end-of-the-day Directed Study period for our project, and we spend the first few days setting up the studio, bringing in lights, and hanging the canvas drop cloth that will serve as the background. Ravi wanted a seamless paper one, but buying one is way out of our nonexistent budget.

We have to scrap the poster board idea. Even if we used both sides, we'd still be looking at over $200 before we even bought markers. Instead, we get four whiteboards and a box of dry-erase markers for less than fifty bucks online. The plan is to print the sentence starter and *I Am Maplefield* in permanent marker and have everyone use the erasable markers to fill in their signs.

While Ravi puts the finishing touches on the setup, I nail down the logistics of getting people photographed as efficiently as possible. I drag a table into the hallway, where we can have everyone sign in. Since we want the people being photographed to be as relaxed as possible, we're only letting two students into the studio at a time: the one being photographed and the one filling out their sign. We want honesty and a glimpse into the inner world of the average Maplefield student; what we don't need is people playing to an audience.

The sign station is set up in the corner where the teacher's desk used to be. There, the person writing can have a bit of privacy and avoid distracting the person posing. The extra whiteboards give us some leeway if there are people who want to fill them out in the hall.

"When you're done, come stand here so I can get this dialed in," Ravi says.

I finish writing *Maplefield* on the last board in careful block letters, then bring it with me to the middle of the room. I strike a series of ridiculous poses in front of the backdrop.

"Farther up," Ravi says, all business now that he's behind the tripod.

"You're no fun." I step forward and hold the board up to my chest like he's taking my mug shot.

"But I'm still your favorite human." He snaps a shot, checks the back of his camera, then fiddles with the settings. "Almost…"

I hold still while he continues to shoot, letting him get the camera dialed in where he wants it and not caring a lick how I look in the pictures. They're just going to be deleted anyway, and it would take a lot more than an awkward facial expression to embarrass me where Ravi is concerned. He moves behind me to adjust the angle of a reflector and returns to the camera, presses the shutter, and checks the screen.

A huge grin splits his face. "Got it. Don't move yet."

He grabs the roll of duct tape we used to anchor the backdrop and brings it to where I stand. He rips off a length, touches his toe to mine, and tells me to step back. He fastens the tape to the floor and stands, excitement in his eyes. "Okay, come see."

Even with just the camera's built-in black-and-white filter applied, the image, while not a great shot of me, is lovely. The background completely disappears, so it looks like I'm standing in a white vacuum. It's more flattering than any Instagram filter.

"You're amazing," I tell him. "I think we're ready to get started. You want to go first?"

Now that the settings are configured, I can fire the shutter while he poses, but he shakes his head. "I think we go last."

"As you wish. Cass said she's more than happy to be our first victim, of course. I swear, it's a good thing she's so into horses; otherwise, she'd be trying to go to Hollywood." I check the time on my phone. Twelve minutes until the bell rings. That should be enough. "Want to get her done now?"

"Let's do it."

I take the stairs down one floor and knock lightly on the door of Cassidy's Directed Study room before opening it. The room is completely silent. I smile at the teacher, who is busy putting the next day's agenda up on the board. "Would it be possible to excuse my sister? She's part of a project I'm doing."

The teacher nods, and Cassidy quickly gathers her things, hooking her backpack behind her chair even as she spins away from her table. She mouths an exaggerated *thank you* that the teacher doesn't see.

When we're safely in the elevator, Cassidy says, "Oh my god. That class is awful. She doesn't even let us whisper. We can't wear headphones or do group work or anything. It's like prison. Seriously. Can I use Directed Study to help you guys? Please? I'm dying in there."

"It's half an hour. I think you can survive being quiet for a half hour."

"No, I really can't. It's awful. And Mrs. Thomas watches us the whole time. It's creepy."

The elevator chimes as we reach our floor. "Go left. It's 331. Mom and Dad would kill me if I kept you out of a study hall. Or they'd make you cut back on riding, so you could use that time for homework."

Cassidy sighs. "Fine," she says, dragging the word out before moving on from the subject. "Am I posing today? Am I first?"

"Yes and yes," Ravi answers, stepping into the hall. He has a whiteboard and marker ready to go.

Cassidy grins up at him, a little more googly-eyed than I'd like. Cassidy once said if I didn't want Ravi, she'd happily take him, and I had to explain there would be no taking of anyone, for any reason, until she was at least old enough to vote.

I stop Ravi before he can give the board to Cassidy. "We should do a real run-through." He nods. "Cass, sign in first, then we'll do the board inside."

Cassidy fills in her name and grade on the clipboard and maneuvers herself into the room. She parks at the back table and uncaps the dry-erase marker. Ravi takes his place by the camera, and when Cassidy spins around with the board facedown in her lap, I direct her to the strip of tape.

Ravi lets her get positioned and launches into his speech. "Thank you for participating in the *I Am Maplefield* project. We know it takes a lot of bravery to sit in front of a camera and share something about yourself, and we're grateful you've decided to join us." He keeps his voice calm and even, inconspicuously firing the shutter as he does. He'll do this with everyone—shoot when they're not expecting it— because we're looking for the unguarded moments as much as the good poses. "When you're ready, flip your sign up and let me see who you are. Whatever you do, don't think about Mr. Crawford in his underwear."

Cassidy giggles—as she's expected to—and holds up her sign. *I Am UNSTOPPABLE.* She grins and pulls goofy faces while Ravi clicks away. When she's exhausted her repertoire, she lets the sign rest on her lap. "Is that good?"

Ravi hits the shutter a few times in quick succession, but his face says it all. It's more than good.

"Perfect," he says.

Cassidy beams and doesn't even notice that he takes one more frame.

"IF EVERY picture we get is as good as this, it's going to be incredible," Ravi says over FaceTime later that night.

He emailed me the link to the album of Cassidy's photos, and even though they're all good, it's the final picture that's the clear winner. Cassidy is absolutely radiant in it. Ravi has that effect on people— even people who don't have unrequited crushes on him. His enthusiasm is so contagious that I don't begrudge delaying the curse research.

"I sent out a notice on the *Monitor* announcing that shooting officially starts tomorrow during Directed Study. We'll have to see how long it takes to get through each person, but I feel like if we just power through, it shouldn't take that long. I mean, the Picture Day people get through the entire school in a single day. Granted there are like three photographers and the pictures are lame, but still."

"Plus after school. Enough people stay for sports and clubs that we should be able to get some traffic then too."

The following day, we're both stopped multiple times and asked about the project, and by the time Directed Study rolls around, we have more people than we can possibly get through in a single period. Part of it is probably the novelty of getting to ditch study hall, but that's fine. I don't care how we get participants, just that we do.

I climb up on the sign-in table and hold up a whiteboard. "Listen up!" I shout, although most of the crowd has already turned to watch me tower over them. "Thank you all for showing up today. I doubt we're going to get through everyone here, but we're going to try. If you can stay after school, try to let those who can't go first. These are the boards you'll be writing your messages on. As you've probably heard, this is the *I Am Maplefield* project, and we're not necessarily looking for your deepest, darkest secrets—though you're welcome to share them—we just want to know who you are. It can be one word; it can be a sentence; it can be anything you want. This is about you. The only thing it can't be is wildly inappropriate."

"What counts as inappropriate?" someone asks.

"How about anything that would get you arrested," I say. "You'll be photographed in private and will be able to fill in your boards without an audience, but you are being photographed. Be honest, but don't be stupid. Show of hands, who already knows what they want to say?"

Several hands go up, and I move them to the front of the line. Up first is a bespectacled freshman named Anita Graves, whose board reads *I Am A Whovian* and has a drawing of a TARDIS.

Ravi gives his intro and starts shooting. I tell junior Jeremiah *I Am The Next Paul Pierce* Wiggins that he's on deck while I wave the next one in. We make it through six more before the bell rings. Most of the crowd in the hall clears out, but a few remain, including— much to my disappointment—Emma Morgan, along with her two best friends, Lily Caruthers and Victoria Melendez. Owen White, Emma's boyfriend, trails behind the trio.

"Can we do our boards together?" Lily asks. "We have soccer practice to get to."

I agree, just to get them in and out. I pass out boards and markers and join Ravi at the camera. His hair is disheveled. He bounces between his camera and the laptop tethered to it, completely in his element. "This is bloody great," he says. "They're killing it. Look at this one of Mariella." The senior's sign says *I Am The First Person In My Family Going To College.* Mariella is studious and shy, but she glows with pride in the photo.

"I stand here?" Lily asks before I have a chance to comment.

"Yup, perfect." Ravi returns to the camera.

I watch as he clicks away, capturing the girl's slightly horsey smile and a sign that says *I Am Studying ASL.*

Victoria goes next, with an *I Am So Excited To Become A Doula* sign, complete with a smiling baby face. I force myself not to roll my eyes. I can't imagine a worse job.

When Emma takes her spot on the tape, she pastes a practiced smile on her face and poses with the automatic ease of a model, angling her body just so, bending a knee and leaning into a hip. Her sign declares *I Am Going To Be Famous.*

"I want to pick the one you use," she demands when Ravi's done.

"They're all very flattering," he assures her. "You won't be embarrassed."

"Of course I won't be embarrassed," she snaps. "But I still want to choose."

"Em, we gotta go."

Emma waves Victoria away. "Let me see them." She reaches for Ravi's camera, but I shoot forward to grab her arm.

"Don't you dare."

"Let go of me." She tries twisting away.

I don't let go. "They're not even processed yet." No way in hell am I letting this girl dictate how things get done. "And if you put your hands on that camera, not only will your pictures magically vanish, but I'll break every last one of your fingers." I smile sweetly and release her grip.

"You're fucking crazy," she says. "This is exactly why I'm working at BayStateNews and you're not."

Ravi steps between us like a boxing ref. "Emma, soccer practice, remember?"

"Whatever." She jabs a finger at him. "I still want to approve my picture. It doesn't have to be today, but it will happen." She storms out, throwing her whiteboard onto the table as she goes.

Ravi squeezes my shoulder and returns to his spot behind the camera.

Owen White stands in the doorway, looking bewildered with a whiteboard at his side. I acknowledge and swallow the urge to murder his girlfriend. We have work to do.

The Making of a Monster
Continued

Once upon a time, there was a boy who was cursed from birth, who was ripped from the womb blue and silent and far too small. He grew slowly, always skinnier and weaker than his sister, who was pulled two minutes before him with the same poisoned blood but none of the curse. Where the girl had wavy auburn locks, his own hair sprouted in carrot-colored coils that would mark him as different, even when he finally shaved them off. He was narrow like a carrot too, easy to snap in half, which was what they started doing to him even before he reached middle school.

Like his sister, he was scary smart—the kind of smart that meant you could skip grades and become a doctor at fourteen, if only the evil parents would allow it. Instead, they said the twins needed to interact with children their own age, so they progressed through school as prescribed, always sitting together and playing together at recess because the other children were simply too boring for them.

And really, his sister was all he needed. The boy could've lived like that forever, happy in a world where they were together.

But by fifth grade, the teachers decided it was unhealthy for them to be so attached to one another and banished them to separate classrooms. The boy cried and begged his parents to change the teachers' minds, but the parents, like all good villains, refused and thus condemned the boy to his undoing.

Chapter Five

I KNOW the future of journalism is digital, but I firmly believe there is magic in good stationery. I assemble a rainbow of rollerball pens and consider which of my many notebooks to assign to curse work. The oversized red one with silky smooth paper and dots instead of lines will do.

The first few questions flow quickly:

When did it start/who was first?

Has there really been one per year? Who are they?

If the curse is real, why hasn't it been reported yet?

I tap the teal pen on the paper and add:

Are there connections between them? Common characteristics of vics? (Check gender, GPA, income? Or...)

Any common factors in their disappearances? (Time of year? Precipitating factors? Etc.)

I leave room at the bottom in case I want to add more and turn to a new page to start the list of what I already know.

I know without having to research that last year's disappearance was Elsie Borke, who had emailed a spectacular rant to everyone on her contact list about how the town was inbred, the school a joke, and that she was better than it all. She was in love, so the email claimed, with someone she had met online, someone older and worldlier, and she wanted to be with him without the judgment of small-town minds. Her parents were devastated, but because Elsie had already turned eighteen, there wasn't much that could be done.

The year before was Liam, but I'm not positive he counts because it wasn't a disappearance. I add his name and basic info anyway, with a note to check if there was anyone else that year who didn't graduate.

The year before that it was Brianna Washington and her unborn baby. Rumor had it that she left to have the baby somewhere private, like it was the 1800s or something. No one had been all that upset to see her go. Brianna could be abrasive and downright bitchy, and it only got worse once word was out about the pregnancy.

Counting Liam, that's three. Three seems enough to justify consideration that the curse might be a real thing.

Researching something as nebulous as an urban legend will be difficult, but even if nothing comes of it, I figure I can spin it into a school culture piece about the power of collective beliefs or something like that. Even a meta piece reporting on the reporting could be interesting, especially if Ravi films the process and I do video journals. I scribble a note to ask him his thoughts on doing something like that for backup in case the research goes nowhere.

The next page is for brainstorming people who might be helpful. Ms. Larson and the guidance counselors could provide graduation data, but something tells me they're not going to be the most cooperative sources. If there really is a school curse, it won't reflect well on the administration to admit it.

Class advisors, then. Every graduating class gets two teachers assigned to them to assist with planning things like prom, senior trips, and award nights, and teachers are the biggest bunch of gossips I've ever seen. They talk about students, their coworkers, and their personal lives probably more than they even realize. If I can figure out who they are, I know I can get the class advisors to spill some dirt.

Tracking down old students shouldn't be too difficult either, thanks to social media and the tendency for families to stay in town for generation upon generation. Elsie's rant about being inbred might've had a grain of truth, given how long some people have been here.

I'm about to start a new page when my phone chirps with an incoming video call from Kylie. I almost ignore it, but Kylie is the closest thing I have to a Baker Street Irregular and is one of my best sources for student news. Everyone knows that it pays to keep sources happy.

I don't even have a chance to say hello before she ambushes me.

"You'll never guess what's happening." Her eyes are wide and excited. She's outside, and her face glows an eerie blue from the light of her phone screen.

"You're being chased by hyenas?" Judging by the way the image bounces and jostles, it isn't completely implausible.

"What? No. We don't have hyenas in New England." Her voice ticks up at the end like the statement wants to become a question.

The urge to convince her that we actually do have a rare miniature species native to western Massachusetts is real. Somehow, I resist. "What's up, then?"

"The police"—she whispers and pauses for what I assume is dramatic effect—"are at Emma Morgan's house."

I drop my green pen. "What? Really? Why?"

"No idea," Kylie says, and I wonder why she even bothered calling if she doesn't have actual information. "But I bet it's something newsworthy, right?"

"I don't know. Maybe. Wait, how do you even know this?"

"Victoria was having a party, but it ended up being lame. Jacob was supposed to show, but he didn't. I have homework to do anyway—I can't believe how many problems we have in Calc—so I left and saw the cop car parked right in front of her house when I drove by. I noticed it because I was scared about getting pulled over. I only had one beer, but still. You know how the cops can be. So, I got home, left my car, and walked back over. Just being nosy, you know? All the lights were on in the house, and I could see her mom and her brother in the living room with a cop—the big bald one. I don't know where Emma or her dad were." Kylie stops to breathe at the end of this monologue, and I have to admit, I'm intrigued.

"Did it seem like maybe the cop was visiting? Like maybe they were friendly?"

"I don't think so. They have that big window in the living room, so I had a good view. Emma's mom kept shaking her head and covering her face like something bad was happening, and her brother wouldn't sit still."

I prop my phone against the desk lamp so I can still see Kylie and pull up Facebook and Twitter on my laptop. "Huh. And you know nothing else? Did you see anything else out of the ordinary?"

I check the police department's Twitter and Facebook accounts next. Both are updated regularly and make good sources of information—particularly once the comments get rolling—but there's no mention of the Morgans on either feed.

"Other than the police car in the driveway, no." Kylie steps into a pool of light that illuminates the phone screen, and her face disappears from the frame as keys jingle in a lock.

I scroll through my own Facebook feed, searching for any mention of Emma, but it's all cute animal videos and memes. Typical. Everyone has a Facebook, but no one really uses it.

"Okay, home now," Kylie says. "You want me to call you if I hear anything else?"

"Yeah. Thanks, Kylie."

"You know I keep you in news." She waves goodbye before ending the call.

I try Instagram and Snapchat but only find pictures from Victoria's admittedly lame-looking party, two artsy shots of Ravi's cat that I like, and absolutely nothing remotely newsworthy. The BayStateNews app gives me plenty of news, as always, but nothing I can conceivably connect to the Morgans.

I check the time, then FaceTime Ravi. He answers looking distracted, clad in his ratty red Manchester United tee. I will never understand boys and their unholy affinity for falling-apart T-shirts. I've offered to replace this particular one multiple times since he practically lives in it, but he refuses. Says it wouldn't be the same. Which I say is the point.

"'Ello," he says, then drops the phone in his lap so I'm forced to stare straight up his nose. I've grown accustomed to such a view. "Hold on. I gotta—yeah, I see you hiding. Oh, come on, you right awful bastard!"

There are muffled pops of gunfire in the background, and Ravi curses.

"I didn't call to listen to you play video games," I say. "Pause it. Or let him kill you or whatever. I need to talk to you."

"I will not…go gently…you fucker." The controller flashes across the phone, and he whoops in victory. The image on the screen tumbles around until he's properly framed. "Okay, sorry, things were happening. What's up?"

"Things are happening." I recount the conversation with Kylie.

"Mystery and intrigue," he says. "I like it. What's your theory? Robbery? Drug smuggling? Illicit gambling ring run out of the garden shed?"

"I don't know yet. There's nothing on any of the news or social media apps. Nothing in the *Monitor's* inbox either."

"So, we investigating? Covert night op? I can be your Watson."

I laugh. "It's almost midnight, and this is real life, not a video game. I'm pretty sure if we go stalk the Morgan house in the middle of the night, we'll be the ones ending up on the news. I just wanted to keep you in the loop and see if you'd heard anything."

"Not a peep."

"All right. I'll let you get back to your war, then."

"Breakfast date?"

"Hell yes." It'd be a cold day in hell when we skipped Sunday brunch at Bennington's—news or no news.

"Cool. I'll scoop you around 9:30. I'm thinking tomorrow is going to be an omelet day."

"Every Sunday is an omelet day for you," I remind him, because ninety-eight percent of the time, it was. Not that I can fault him. Bennington's does amazing omelets.

I take a final scroll through my feeds, but there's still nothing about the Morgans. I set the alarm for 8:30 and crawl into bed, wondering about the logistics of getting a police scanner. That would really come in handy.

THE BLARE of an alarm pulls me from sleep, but it isn't my usual *Doctor Who* theme song. The tone is harsh, persistent, and impossible to ignore. I fumble for my phone and mute the screeching alarm. Centered on the screen, over a cascade of notifications from the *Monitor* app, is an Amber Alert.

Emma Morgan, straight A, all-American soccer player, is officially missing.

Chapter Six

HELL MUST be chilly, because there's no way we're making it to Bennington's.

I call Ravi four times back-to-back while I get dressed, hoping the prolonged ringing will cut through his dreams, but it doesn't. I'm not surprised, given how many rounds of his screeching chicken alarm it takes to wake him up.

So I do the only reasonable thing left: show up on his doorstep and knock loud enough to wake the neighbors.

Mrs. Burman opens the door, looking like she's been up for hours, and pulls me into a warm hug. "Oh, honey, have you heard? Isn't it terrible?"

"That's why I'm here," I say when she releases me. "Ravi up yet?"

"Not yet." She bustles me straight into the kitchen. "Can I get you some tea? Juice? I have a casserole in the oven, and the muffins just came out. I thought I'd pop round with some food and see how the Morgans are holding up. I can't even imagine if it were my Priya missing."

Priya, as if hearing her name, pads into the kitchen in a pink polka dot bathrobe, black hair bundled in a messy bun atop her head. She waves a sleepy hello. "Oooh, muffins," she says, brightening. She pours a glass of juice and butters a muffin, and I see no reason not to follow her lead.

"Honey, go get your brother up," Mrs. B says. "I want to talk to you both."

Priya freezes with a muffin top halfway to her lips. "Whatever it is, I didn't do it."

I know the fourteen year old well enough to bet there's a whole host of things she did that her mother has no idea about, and she's probably trying to figure out which is about to bite her in the ass.

"I know. It's something else. Just go."

Priya, muffin still in hand, shuffles over to the bottom of the stairs and yells, "Ravi! Ravi! The house is on fire! We gotta go! Come on!"

A thud sounds from above, and I burst into laughter, spraying muffin crumbs across the table. Priya returns to the kitchen looking smug.

Mrs. B shakes her head, not quite hiding a smile. "You're a horrible child."

"But efficient and still the favorite," Priya says, hopping up to sit on the edge of the counter.

Ravi staggers down the stairs, looking bewildered and more than a little underdressed in just a pair of crooked glasses and plaid boxers. He takes in the sight before him—all muffins and females and a distinct lack of fire—and mutters, "I hate all of you."

"Lies," I say. "And can we talk about how much I wish we had a whiteboard here? This should be your picture. *I Am Gullible.*"

"I hate you the most," he says and heads for the fridge.

Priya sticks a bare foot out to shove him back. "Ew, Ravi, no. Thou shalt not pass. Go put pants on."

"I need a drink."

"You need pants."

"You need to rethink how you start people's days."

"You do need pants," I say. "Shirt and shoes also required. Things are happening."

"Hate you all," Ravi grumbles again, but he disappears to get dressed.

"Ah, teenage boys," Mrs. B says. "Just wait until you're both parents, then you'll understand. We all deserve sainthood for not killing you."

Priya and I exchange horrified looks.

"Yeah, I think I'll stick to pets." I have zero intention of having kids. Ever.

"Oh, you'll change your mind." Mrs. B opens the oven to check the casserole. Whatever it is, it smells saucy and amazing, even at eight in the morning.

Priya's phone chirps, and she jumps off the counter, hazel eyes wide. "Holy shit," she says, ignoring her mother's tutting. "Did you see this?" She turns the phone around to reveal a missing person flyer with Emma's photo and contact information for the police.

Ravi reemerges, clad in jeans and a T-shirt over a long-sleeve thermal. "What's that?"

"What I came to drag your carcass out of bed for," I say. I run down what I know, which isn't much, but still more than they do. "They'll be organizing searches for her this afternoon. I think we should go." I know it's crass, and I would never say it out loud, but this has the potential to be the most newsworthy thing the town has ever seen. There's no way I'm not getting the story from the front lines.

Ravi rakes a hand through his hair. "I'm in."

"Me too," Priya adds.

"I don't think so," Mrs. B says. She pulls a bubbling casserole smothered in melted cheese from the oven. "You can come deliver this with me if you want to help. You're too young to be getting involved in search parties."

Priya looks like she's about to protest but Mrs. B keeps talking.

"I was friends with Chad Morgan when we were in high school, you know. He was my winter formal date. I can hardly imagine what that poor family is going through right now." She sounds on the verge of tears. "They're going to need all the support they can get."

THE FACT that it's Emma Morgan who's missing and not someone I actually like is probably why I'm finding it so easy to approach this like the story it is, but I also want to believe I've gotten better at being objective in general. For a journalist, objectivity is everything. It's impossible to report the story or take the photo effectively without it. Emotion can't play into it. The country, the world even, looks to the news for facts, not feelings—at least not feelings from the source. The feelings should be the audience's. The content, the stories themselves, should be evocative, not the reporter. Journalists are the conduit; the content is what matters.

On the drive into the center of town, I set up a Google Alert for "Emma Morgan" so that any story mentioning the case will land in my email. I'd rather have too much information than risk missing something.

The town is already swarming with news trucks. Crews are stationed at the town common, which is serving as command central for the search organizers, along with the Morgans' house and outside the police station. The church parking lot is overflowing with cars, which spill onto the lawn and sidewalk. Something tells me they're not all worshippers.

Ravi parks in front of the delivery bay behind The Donut Hole. According to the police Facebook account, there will be a brief press conference at ten and search teams will assemble immediately following. Just enough time to acquire sustenance.

We go in through the back door, and Mr. B immediately puts us to work. Weekends are always a whirlwind, and Saturday and Sunday are the only days Mr. B pays for extra kitchen help. The college students who came in at three in the morning to start frying donuts are still working, splattered in chocolate and flour. The counter girl sticks her head in to say they need more maple bacon ASAP.

Mr. B hands me a huge metal bowl full of freshly fried donut holes, kisses my forehead, and says, "Sugar them and get them out front."

Ravi is put on dipping duty even as he explains we can't stay.

"You're staying for now. Help us through the rush," Mr. B says. "Then you go."

We don aprons and do as we're told. While the older workers cut and fry the donuts, we fill and ice them. The work is repetitive and automatic and offers us a good place to talk, which is all we wanted anyway.

"Okay, I gotta ask." Ravi shakes the excess glaze off a chocolate-covered donut with a purple-gloved hand. "Are we thinking curse?" He whispers the last word like it has actual power.

"No," I say. "This is different. Definitely. From what I've heard, the curse kids always disappear at the end of the year, right before graduation, and there's never been a response like this. Ever. We would've remembered something like this, even if it happened when we were in elementary school. No, this is something new."

Ravi raises an eyebrow—an expression I can never quite master. "You know, when we actually go join the search, you might not want to look quite so pleased that you have a story."

"But I am pleased." He gives me another significant eyebrow lift. "What, too honest?"

"Bit too honest, yeah."

"Tact is just not saying true stuff," I say. "Your eyebrow is going to stay that way if you keep looking at me like that."

"You're incorrigible," he says. "So, not the curse, then. What are your theories?"

"Not sure yet. The stories that are already up don't have a lot of details. We should learn more at the briefing. On social media, it seems like everyone is genuinely shocked, so I don't think she lit out into the night on some grand adventure."

"Maybe she fell down a well? Or is in a ditch somewhere. Mom always thinks I'm going to drive into a ditch. It's like she thinks ditches have some kind of dark mystical mojo that lures unsuspecting drivers into their abyss."

"Wait, I wonder if her car is missing. I don't remember any of the reports mentioning it either way, but they would've included a description of the Mazda if they thought she took off in it, right?"

"You think kidnapping?"

"Abduction more likely. Kidnapping usually indicates there's a ransom request, and while the Morgans obviously aren't broke, I don't think they have ransom amounts of money."

"Never know," Ravi says, which is true. You never really did know what went on in other people's houses.

We finish three trays of donuts before Ravi ducks out front to make a large iced coffee and tell his dad we have to go.

"You're joining the search?" he asks.

Ravi nods.

"You two be careful. I know how you can get."

"Cross our hearts," I say and snag a white chocolate raspberry donut from the tray.

Ravi fetches his camera from the trunk of his car, and we go around to the front of the shop and cross the street. People are already gathering on the common. Two police officers arrange a podium in front of the gazebo steps, and a younger guy wearing too-short khakis makes sure the microphone is working. The press are assembled to one side, flocked together like birds of the same species.

We stop short of the crowd, and I turn my back on it, handing my phone to Ravi. He steps back, raises the phone, and gives a three-finger countdown.

When he gives the final nod, I square my shoulders and say, "This is Kennedy Carter, live from the Maplefield Common, where police and citizens are gathering for a press conference regarding the disappearance of Emma Morgan, senior at Maplefield High. As always, the *Monitor* will be bringing you the news as it happens, so stay tuned as we find out more."

I upload the video through the *Monitor's* app and send a Breaking News notification. I'm not going to scoop the professional news outlets, but I can at least keep up.

Instead of joining the press, I lead Ravi to the side opposite, knowing that every photo taken from the press pool will capture the same scene. It's a good call, because what we get is visceral enough to make my objectivity waver just a fraction. From where we stand, we have a clear view into the shadowed recesses of the gazebo, where the Morgans sit huddled together with their backs to the cluster of press. They look utterly broken.

I nudge Ravi and nod at the scene. He raises the camera without hesitation and captures them sitting there, waiting to tell the world their worst story. He might give me shit about my acknowledge-and-set-aside mantra, but he knows about objectivity too, and really, this is nothing. Not really. This isn't squatting down to take a photo of an orphaned girl covered in napalm, the smell of burning flesh hot in the air as she flees her burning village. This isn't documenting someone as they burn alive.

We've talked about what it would mean to be the one to take those pictures, to record the atrocities of humankind without interfering, and Ravi agrees that telling the hard stories is important, that seeing that girl in real life might be heartbreaking, but to not immortalize her agony, to not share it with the world, would be tantamount to pretending it didn't exist. That is a far worse crime than taking the picture. The suffering deserve to have their stories shared so that maybe such horrors won't happen again.

To us, taking a photo of a scared and broken family isn't sacrilege. It's documentation of a horror that no family should have to experience. It's something the world should see.

It's also something only we have.

Chapter Seven

CHIEF OF Police Angus Liddell is a middle-aged white guy with a paunch that indicates he spends more time in his office than on the streets. While I don't fault him for this, it's a reminder of why I never want to be a managing editor somewhere, chained to a desk and supervising the people who are actually out there getting their hands dirty.

He taps the microphone to check that it's on and waits for the murmuring crowd to quiet.

I pop the last bite of pink-frosted donut in my mouth, lick the sugar from my fingers, and take a pull from my nearly empty coffee.

Showtime.

I set my phone to record audio as Ravi raises his camera to get the requisite still images as the Morgans emerge from the back of the gazebo to join Chief Liddell on the steps.

"I would like to thank you all for coming here today," the chief says. "This is going to be brief, as we are still in the earliest stages of the investigation and have a search to get started. I ask that you hold all questions until the end. At approximately 10:00 p.m. last night, police were summoned to the home of John and Melissa Morgan, who reported that their daughter Emma, seventeen, failed to return home from her shift at Uno. The Morgans had not seen their daughter since Friday evening, when the girl left to spend the night at a friend's following a soccer game. Melissa Morgan received a text Saturday morning that Emma would be working a double shift at Uno and would return home that night. It has since been confirmed that Emma did not make it into work and hasn't been seen since early yesterday morning. We are working on tracing the location of her cell phone and obtaining phone records as we speak. According to friends and family, Emma routinely goes trail running on Saturday mornings, and we will be concentrating a physical search on the areas she is known to frequent. It's possible that she has fallen and is injured or unconscious somewhere. There has been no evidence of foul play, but we are also not ruling anything out at this point. If anyone has any information, anything at all that might help us find Emma, we ask that you come forward at once. For those of you planning to participate in the search, I would like to thank you in advance for your help. Everyone who is participating will need to register at the green tent behind the gazebo, and your locations and search leaders will be assigned from there. Now, let's get out there and find Emma."

The press erupts in a volley of questions, and someone shouts, "Can we get a statement from the family?"

Mrs. Morgan turns toward her husband, who wraps an arm around her. On her other side, Michael Morgan, Emma's brother, stands pale and rigid.

"At this time, the family would like to thank the community for their help and support in bringing their daughter home," Chief Liddell says.

"Could this be the work of a kidnapper?" someone else from the crowd calls.

"As I said, at this time, there is no evidence of foul play, but we have not ruled anything out and again ask the public to come forward with any information they may have."

A redheaded reporter pushes her way to the front to ask, "Has Peter Vernon been questioned?"

"We're doing a thorough canvas, but no one has been implicated in the disappearance yet."

I shoot a look at Ravi. Peter Vernon is a registered sex offender who moved to town to escape a scandal in Maine, where he was caught sending and soliciting naked pictures from underage girls. He'd tried to argue that he was only nineteen at the time and that made it okay, but it didn't. He'd been prosecuted and forced to register as a sex offender—a fact the local paper had announced upon his arrival a year ago. The tiny article contained hardly any information beyond that, so I'd taken it upon myself to dig up the details. I'd even talked to one of the girls whose pictures he had. She was a multi-sport athlete, petite and blond and full of confidence.

Just like Emma.

As Liddell fields the final questions, people make their way to the green tent set up on the far side of the common. Ravi and I join the lines, listening as people speculate about what could've happened.

"Well, that was not terribly informative," Ravi says. He steps away to take a few photos of the crowd, which has swelled beyond the number at the press conference with people who are more eager to join the search than listen to speeches. It looks like half the school has shown up.

"We know they don't know much," I say, "so we need to find our own answers—like who the friend is that she stayed with Friday night. It sounds like that was the last person to see her."

When we reach the front of the line, we add our names, birthdays, and contact information to the tablets that are set up to register searchers. The lady behind the table asks if we have a car or need a ride. Ravi tells her we have wheels. She hands us each a map printed on flimsy copy paper and circles an address.

"You can join the group at the reservoir. That's going to be the biggest group since that's where most of Emma's run went. Meet at the parking lot and check in with the bearded guy in the fluorescent green jacket. He's the leader. He'll have an email with your names on it."

We thank her, retrieve the car from behind The Donut Hole, and join the parade of cars heading for the reservoir.

On the way, I check my phone and find social media flooded with pictures from the common, more than half of them selfies with dramatic captions and a #FindEmma hashtag. The bigger news sites are already posting coverage of the press conference, and the usual tide of thoughts-and-prayers comments are rolling in.

We pass Peter Vernon's house before turning onto the reservoir road, and I slap Ravi's arm, cursing myself for not making the reservoir connection earlier.

"Hey, driving the car here." He shakes me off. "Gonna make me crash and kill us all."

"Ravi, what about Peter? Do you think it's a coincidence that we're on our way to search the reservoir, which is right in his backyard? Which puts his house right on Emma's jogging route? When we already know he has a thing for tiny blond girls?"

"I think…it might be?" He glances over. "Why? You really think he graduated from dick pics to chasing girls in the woods?"

"It's possible."

"We still don't know there's been foul play. You know better than to write the story before the facts."

I hate when he's the reasonable one. We park and join the crowd gathering at the edge of the parking lot. Their division of the search party assembles quickly, organized as promised by a mountain of a man in a highlighter-bright windbreaker.

"Okay, people. Listen up." The man's voice booms, and everyone shuts up instantly, though Ravi manages to take a quick photo before turning his attention over. "We're going to be doing a grid search, which means everyone needs to get in lines and stay in lines. Do not wander into your neighbor's section and do not fall behind. We don't want this to turn into a search for you too. If you find anything of interest, do not touch it. Stop, alert your line-mates, and wait for me to come to you. Do not move whatever you find. We hope this is a rescue mission, but if it turns out that it's not, we need everything documented in situ, as it's found. Disturbing the evidence could delay the search and put Emma in danger. Anyone caught doing that answers to me directly, got it?"

We got it.

The reservoir is surrounded by acres of wooded trails, conservation land, and an observatory atop a hill so steep it has delusions of mountainhood. People are guaranteed to be stationed up there already, using the mounted binoculars to search the trees for signs of life.

We take the main trail into the forest, though the path is only wide enough to accommodate three people walking abreast, and even those ones end up bushwhacking before long. The trees blaze with autumn colors, and the air is brisk enough to make the hike comfortable. A task as grim as ours seems better suited for a gray day, but Mother Nature has her own agenda.

Every few minutes, someone bellows Emma's name, and everyone tries to step a little softer in hopes of hearing a reply, but none ever comes.

Ravi shoots several photos of the line of searchers but mostly keeps his attention on the ground before his feet.

After maybe a half an hour of walking, a cry goes up from down the line. "Think I got something!"

Everyone turns to the kid who's spoken—a junior I recognize but can't name—and crowds in to see what he found.

"No one move," the leader barks, and people freeze mid-step like a game of Red Light Green Light.

"Piece of fabric," the boy announces, pointing at a broken branch. "It's purple."

"Is it hers?" someone asks.

"Is it bloody?"

The search leader doesn't answer, just uses a small digital camera to take photos of the tree branch where the fabric hangs and the ground beneath it. He removes a paper bag from one of his jacket pockets and uses a twig to nudge the shiny scrap of fabric into the sack. He folds the top down twice, writes something on it, and zips it into his breast pocket. He extracts a plastic flag from a different pocket and sinks it into the dirt before unclipping the black walkie-takie from his belt to radio in the report.

Ravi documents him documenting the find.

We continue on, and any thought of this being just a sunny Sunday walk vanishes. That scrap of fabric might be completely unrelated to the search, or it could be concrete proof that Emma was here, but the fact that no one knows one way or the other casts a pall over the entire group. It feels like everyone is looking a little harder now, and shouts of Emma's name ring loud and often. In the quiet between calls, we hear the crashing of other waves of searchers elsewhere in the woods. I wonder if they're having any luck and then have to wonder what actually counts as luck in this situation.

As I scan the land in front of me, part of my brain spins the sentences that will become the story. This isn't a story I can sit on, and doing the rough draft in my head like this makes the actual writing of it so much faster. The big sites already have their versions published, but I know the Maplefield community will turn to the *Monitor* for my account because I can give them something the big channels can't: a Maplefield perspective. No matter how this turns out, I'm positive that the news hitting mainstream media is going to be vastly different than the news we'll hear in the halls, and neither are likely to have the whole story. I need to be the link between the two versions.

"Everybody stop!" a woman at the end of the row shrieks.

"Sounds like she tripped over a severed arm or something," Ravi mutters.

"No shit."

This time, everyone knows not to move, but necks crane to get a glimpse of what halted our procession. The news of what's been found travels through the search group like a lit fuse: a tangle of what looks like human hair, long and blond, is snared on a branch.

Speculation bubbles up and down the line, and I curse my poor positioning. I need to see it—or at least hear what the leader radios in.

"It could be horsehair," I say to Ravi. "Riders use these trails too. Cass's old barn has direct access to a ton of entry points."

"Could also be Emma's hair."

"We need to find out."

"They won't know until they DNA test it, and you know that's not as fast as *CSI* makes it look."

"I'm going to see if I can get closer."

"You're gonna get caught."

"So what? What's he gonna do, send me back alone? I don't think so." I drop behind the row of searchers and ease my way up the line. The leader is busy photographing the hair and doesn't see me slip in between two older women. He tugs on a pair of the same purple gloves Mr. B keeps at the bakery and cracks the branch far enough back to remove the entire tangle, as he put it, in situ. He bags it, branch and all, sticks a flag in the ground, and radios in a report of "hair, possibly human" and our GPS coordinates before asking, "Should we proceed or hold?"

"Proceed," the staticky voice on the radio says.

I jog back to my place by Ravi as the leader gives the order to move out. "Definitely blond," I tell him as we march forward. "But still can't rule out horse. Horses can be blond too. Looked like it could've been tail height."

"Listen up, people," the leader bellows. "Up ahead, the terrain is going to drop off steeply on one side, and we're going to collectively shift left to follow the trail. We'll spread back out once it widens. Everyone needs to pay attention to where their feet are, because I don't have time to chase you down a cliff."

He isn't lying about the drop-off. It's like the entire right side of the woods disappeared. The right-hand side of the line falls in behind the others, and no one loses their footing. One look down the cliff makes me glad we're not the group searching that ravine.

Everyone squishes together to get past the drop-off, and we bottleneck, slowing almost to a halt. I consider the likelihood of Emma falling into the ravine during her run and almost crash into Ravi when we do stop completely, although there is no shout of evidence this time.

I pull my gaze from the depths and realize why.

We've found Emma Morgan.

Chapter Eight

THE SILENCE that follows the discovery is longer than I would've thought possible for a group this size.

All around us, hands fly to mouths, to hearts, and over the eyes of the younger searchers in shocked horror. Ravi's hands rise automatically, muscle memory propelling the camera up to create a barrier between his brain and the horror before his eyes.

My hands do not go to my face, or my chest, or my eyes, but they do shake—just a little. I acknowledge the tremor and will it away.

Emma is sprawled at the base of a large evergreen, a purple satin gown spilling out around her in shimmering waves. The hem of the dress, torn in one spot, has ridden up her calves, revealing the curve of slender ankles and bare, manicured feet. Emma's toes are painted a shocking shade of lime green.

The tremor in my hands returns, and for a wild moment, I want to rip off my Converse and put them on the dead girl's bare and vulnerable feet.

Ravi threads his fingers through mine and squeezes to the point of pain.

Someone retches, and that's the thing that breaks the spell. I tear my eyes away from Emma's green toes, slam the lid on my emotions, and acknowledge the rest of the scene as chaos erupts around us.

Sherlock dictates that we must not simply see, but observe, so that's what I do.

A single sheet of paper is tacked to the tree at eye level where it's impossible to ignore, with a single sentence typed in large font: *I am sorry this had to happen.*

A suicide note? It doesn't seem possible. Not from Emma Morgan.

Nothing about this scene makes a scrap of sense.

Only the unnatural stillness of the girl convinces me that we haven't stumbled into a bizarre high-fashion photo shoot.

Which means it's staged. It means everything here matters.

My pulse is galloping, but I know the great detective's methods. If there was ever a time to apply them, it would be now.

Still squeezing Ravi's hand, I start with the note because it's the easiest to look at. The paper looks like generic copy paper, and there's nothing special about the font. There are no obvious flaws that I can see in the actual letters that could link it to a specific printer. The objective part of my brain wonders if Maplefield PD even has the know-how needed to compare printer inks.

No matter.

The note is anchored to the tree with a single shining thumbtack. It could be the perfect surface for capturing a fingerprint, but it is also easy to wipe clean.

Next.

Next is hard.

I want to be strong and stoic like Sherlock, unmoved by the human morass around me, but when I drop my eyes to Emma, it's like Earth's rotation speeds up and everything becomes unbalanced.

So I break it into manageable bits, isolated parts of a whole too overwhelming, and work in sections—quickly, because wailing sirens split the mountain air, and our guide is already pushing us back, trying to preserve the scene.

She doesn't look like she's sleeping because dead bodies never do, not really. But she does look peaceful. Her expression is neutral, eyes closed and mouth slightly open. There is no blood, no bruising, nothing to indicate head trauma or strangulation or anything remotely obvious. No froth at her mouth or vomit on the ground to suggest poison. Her dress has tiny spaghetti straps, which are intact, and a snug bodice with small tulle butterflies along the top, almost like something a child would wear. Her arms are bare and free of lacerations and blemishes. No, not quite free. There's a slight smudge around the bicep of her left arm. A bruise? Dirt? I'm too far to know for sure.

I keep going. Aside from a single tear at the hem, the dress is intact and clean. One leg is bent at an awkward angle but doesn't look swollen. No bloodstains anywhere I can see, but the full skirt could be hiding anything.

There is shouting from the path behind us and the sharp crack of breaking branches as the police swarm the area, jarring me out of my objective trance and back to the horror I've been cataloging. They shout orders to clear the scene and assign escorts to take us out of the woods, and I'm forced to leave with more questions than answers.

CASSIDY AND I are silent on the way into school, and for once, I'm glad it's Mom doing the driving. There's too much noise in my brain to be responsible for my sister's life today.

"If you girls want to come home early, you call me. I'm home all day," Mom says as we wait in the drive-thru at Dunkin'. She doesn't even give us a hard time about our froofy coffee or ask if we want something extra; she just orders without question from years of knowing what we like. Though had she asked, I might've opted for a couple dozen shots of espresso.

I barely slept last night, and I hate myself for it, because I can only blame part of it on getting my story posted. The rest was pure nerves—a complete failure in objectivity. It's not like I've never seen a dead body before. I have two dead grandparents after all and an aunt who died of breast cancer when she was only thirty-two. I went to all the funerals, knelt by all the caskets, scoffed at all the makeup. The fact that Emma's body had been unexpected and in the woods shouldn't have rattled me like this. How could I ever hack it reporting from a war zone if a single corpse has me this shaken?

An all-call went out last night, alerting parents that a student had died under unknown circumstances. Counselors would be available throughout the day, and any students who opted to stay home would be marked excused. Mom had tried to get us to stay home, but neither of us could face the thought of stewing in a quiet house. It's better to go out, be among friends, and pretend things are normal.

Cassidy's morning crew is already waiting when we pull in, and the girls sweep her away before she can utter a proper goodbye. I don't see Ravi's car in the lot and worry he won't show. He's the one I need to get through this day.

I'm about to go inside when I feel a hand on my arm. I turn and my mother wraps me in a hug that I first resist, then allow.

"You don't need to be the tough one all the time," she says. "Just remember that."

"I'm good," I say. "It's not like we were friends or anything."

Mom smiles, but it looks sad. "My strong, brave girls. I don't know where you get it."

"All the spinach," I say, needing a joke, needing to not remember Emma's pale, naked feet and empty eyes.

"All the spinach." Mom nods and climbs back in The Planet. "Call me if you want a ride. Really."

I wave goodbye, forcing myself to acknowledge the feelings—*the feelings suck*—and set them aside. With that, I lift my chin and start across the parking lot.

"Ken, wait." Ravi looks as haggard as I feel. I stop to let him catch up, and he throws his arms around me with such force that I nearly spill my coffee on us both. I adjust and squeeze him back, feeling my brain finally start shifting into order. I may have zero desire to jump his bones, but his hugs are pretty spectacular. I might've stayed here indefinitely if not for the sound of the warning bell calling us inside.

Ravi plants a chaste kiss on the top of my head, then pulls back, taking my coffee and draining half of it in one long pull. I don't even protest, because if he's drinking my cavity-inducing coffee, he must be even worse off than he looks. As we head in, he pulls a white paper bag from his messenger bag and hands it to me without relinquishing my cup.

The bag is stuffed to the brim with slightly crushed but still warm cardamom donut holes. They're not my regular menu item, but he knows I adore them. "This is why you're my very favorite human."

"Couldn't sleep," he says. "Went in early with Dad."

"Same, only with fewer donuts." I pop one in my mouth.

Ms. Larson is still standing at the front door when we get there despite the warning bell having rung, and she sends Henry trotting over. I drop down so he can press his head into my chest, and I consider asking Ms. Larson if we can just walk him for the day instead of going to class, but I know other people will need his snuggles more than me. Emma's actual friends, for instance, of which there are many.

Ms. Larson gives us a sympathetic smile as we get closer, and I worry she's going to try for a hug, but she just says, "I understand you both were there when Emma was found. Please don't hesitate to let me know if there's anything you need or anything the school can do to help."

The principal looks like she's aged a decade since the previous week, and part of me is struck by an inappropriate urge to ask if it's easier this time or harder. Liam was more than anyone should have to deal with, but now it looked like he had only been the dress rehearsal. I don't envy Ms. Larson's job at all.

"There's going to be an assembly after homeroom," she says, "and the counselors will be here all week. There's no shame in talking to them."

I don't say anything to that, because I most certainly won't be talking to the counselors. I need to set the feelings aside, not wallow in them. But I don't begrudge anyone who does differently.

"Do you want to take Henry?" Ms. Larson ushers us inside. "I need to do the announcements. He can stay with you until the assembly."

"Yes, thanks," I say and mean it. Ms. Larson points at us and tells the dog *go*, and he stays with us while she disappears into the main office.

I sink onto the bench outside of the office, and Henry lays his blocky head across my thighs. Ravi plops down next to me.

"Skip homeroom?" he asks.

"Skip homeroom," I agree.

We lean into each other and pet Henry while a truncated version of morning announcements runs: basically, there has been a tragedy over the weekend, and everyone should report to the auditorium at the start of first period for an assembly.

"Article looked good," Ravi says. "Lots of comments."

I nod. "The shots from the search really helped."

"I have to tell you something." Ravi's knees piston up and down, and he clasps his hands on them to steady them to no avail. He won't look at me, and it makes me nervous.

"Okay," I say warily.

"I took her picture. When she was dead, I took her picture. I didn't even think; I just did it, and now it's on my camera, and I keep trying to delete it, but I can't decide if that makes it better or worse."

"I know." I press my thigh into his. The jackhammering slows, then stops, but I keep my leg there. "I was with you."

"Does that make me some kind of pervert? I feel like a pervert. A ghoul." His voice is tight, and he shifts away from me.

"Oh god, Ravi, no. Of course you're not a pervert. You reacted like a journalist. That's nothing to be ashamed of."

He shakes his head hard, like he might dislodge the image through sheer force. "I didn't react though. I panicked. It just happened."

My heart physically aches for him. He's not as good at compartmentalizing as I am. He might never be, but that's part of why I need him. He's my reminder of the human cost of what we cover. He's my heart.

"Maybe I'm not meant to do this," he says. "Maybe I need to stick to happy, mindless portraits of kids with funny signs; shoot some weddings; take corporate headshots. I'd still make a—"

"Stop." I can't bear to hear him tear himself down like this. "You are so much better than corporate headshots, and you know it. You are the most talented person I have ever met."

"Then why won't this go away?" Ravi thrusts his hand out, palm down, where the shaking can't go unnoticed.

The vise on my heart gets tighter. I hold my hand out next to his. I thought my tremor had gone last night, but it began again, just a little, when I got to school. And it's worse now, in the face of the raw emotion radiating off Ravi.

"Same," I say. I take his hand, ease it down to Henry's waiting head. "Pet the dog. You think I didn't sit up last night picking apart my own reaction? I did. And you know what I decided?"

He doesn't answer, but some of the tension has left his body.

"This, the shaking, the self-doubt, it's normal. And it's not a sign of anything other than the fact that it was our first violent death. And it was someone we knew. Of course reporting on something like that is going to be hard. It's supposed to be. It's not something you should even have to do. It's like when they don't let doctors operate on their relatives because they think they can't be objective. News flash, they can't. This whole thing is the journalistic equivalent of that."

I scratch Henry's ears. "We want our stories to make people feel things," I say to the dog as much as to Ravi. "I think that means we have to feel things too, even if we don't want to. The feelings just can't get in the way of the story, and they didn't. We told the story objectively, without making it about our own reactions, so that's a win."

The corner of his mouth twitches up. "Remember that talk about not sounding quite so pleased to have this story?"

"Doing it again?"

"Doing it again." He hovers his hand over Henry's head. The tremble isn't gone, but it's lessened. He stands and offers me his not-quite-steady hand. I take it and let him pull me up.

Chapter Nine

WE BRING Henry to the auditorium, sit him on the stage, and take seats in the back where we can watch everyone come in. I'm in journalist mode, already planning a story about getting back to normal after unthinkable tragedy.

As classes pour in, Henry trots down the stairs at the edge of the stage and positions himself for optimal pets.

"We should get some shots of Henry doing his thing," I say. No one will complain about extra dog pictures, and I need to give Ravi something to remind him that he's still a photojournalist.

He nods. I watch as he extracts the camera from his messenger bag, looking for any sign of hesitation, but he steps into the aisle and drops to one knee to shoot at Henry's level. When he returns, he scrolls through the images on the camera's back panel: a wide shot of somber-faced students, four different hands petting Henry's head at once, a girl hugging the dog around his fluffy neck. All the images are razor-sharp; his hands did not shake at all.

There is none of the usual pre-assembly raucousness that marks most gatherings of the entire school. Even the teachers look apprehensive as they stand along the walls near where their classes are seated.

Ms. Larson enters without fanfare and steps behind the podium. I switch my phone to record. She stares out over the quiet crowd for what seems like forever before speaking.

"As many of you already know," she says, voice steady but hoarse, "we suffered a terrible loss over the weekend. One of our seniors, Emma Morgan, was found in the woods at Stone Reservoir. It's still too early to have all the answers, but a note was found at the scene that indicates she may have passed away from suicide."

Whispers and sniffles erupt around the echoing room, and Ms. Larson waits them out. I jot her phrasing "passed away from suicide" in a notebook in case we're too far back for clear audio. I hate that phrase—*passed away*. It dances around the truth, the way all the euphemisms do: crossed over, called home, departed. It's like no one wants to say the D-word, even though died is exactly what they did.

"I tell you this not to upset you, but to inform you. I know rumors and gossip will be rampant in the coming days, and I want to remind everyone to keep their focus on what's important: that we have lost a valued member of our school. My heart goes out to all of you. It is never easy to lose someone you love, especially when it is so unexpected and the person is so young. Emma was a vibrant light in the Maplefield community. She was an honor roll student, a talented soccer player, and a good friend. Her loss will be deeply felt by everyone who knew her. No one is expecting the next few days and weeks to be easy. Emotions are going to be running high, and you may feel things you don't understand. We've brought in specially trained grief counselors who will be available for anyone who wishes to talk, and they will be available for staff as well as students. There is no shame in reaching out. If Emma had reached out, perhaps she would still be here today."

"Whoa, victim blame much?" I whisper.

Ravi doesn't answer but raises his camera in time to catch Ms. Larson strike the podium with an open hand. Several students jump in their seats.

"Suicide has become an epidemic in this country, and we need to stop being afraid to talk about it." Emotion makes her voice raspy. "Do not stay silent. If you are suffering, say something. If your friend is suffering, say something. This is not the time to turn inward, but a time to reach out. Maplefield knows how to deal with hardship. We have been here before. We will find strength in each other, and we will hold each other up and hold each other close. Do not take anyone for granted. Be kind to each other. Be kind to yourselves. In the days to come, be there for each other. You are only as alone as you make yourself be." Ms. Larson's voice breaks, and she pinches the top of her nose.

Ravi gets the shot as students shift uncomfortably in their seats. And then something happens that I would never have predicted. Victoria Melendez rises in the middle of her row, climbs over the legs of several students, and flies up the stage steps, where she wraps her arms around Ms. Larson. Ravi's shutter clicks as they hug and cry for all the school to see.

THE REST of the day passes in a sort of haze. Bells ring, classes are attended, but there's a pall on the school that makes it hard to concentrate, and it seems, hard to teach.

In Journalism, Emma's seat is conspicuously empty, and Mr. Monroe opens the class by asking if anyone has anything they want to say.

Natalie Franco raises her hand. "I don't think it's right that they're even reporting on this. It's not anyone's business how she died."

"Nah, that's bullshit," Jeremiah says. His head snaps around to Mr. Monroe. "Sorry, sir. Didn't mean to say that. But don't the people got a right to know if someone's dead?"

Natalie answers before Mr. Monroe can. "But not the details. Not that it was suicide."

"Suicide is one of the most contested areas of reporting," Mr. Monroe says. "As you've just demonstrated. On the one hand, there's the issue of the deceased's privacy and that of the family, but on the other hand, there is the desire to sell papers, to get clicks, to pull the most viewers. Oftentimes, relatives don't want to publicly admit that a loved one has taken their own life. Then again, there can be cases when the act is committed in a public manner, which puts it in the public domain."

"Or if they're celebrities, right?" Jeremiah says. "Like that dude who ate the crazy food. Anthony something."

"Bourdain." Mr. Monroe nods. "Yes, when it's a celebrity, the public often feels they have a right to know."

"Doesn't that make more people kill themselves?" Claribel asks. "Like they make it cool?"

"There is often a spike in suicides following reports of celebrity suicides, that's true. But does that mean they shouldn't be reported?"

"Of course not," Jeremiah says. "If people are gonna kill themselves, they're gonna kill themselves. You can't force someone to do it."

"Not true though," Ravi says. "What about that girl from Wrentham we talked about in Social Topics? She was convicted of murder for convincing her boyfriend to kill himself. And they were our age."

Jeremiah leans back in his seat. "Shit, you're right. Still doesn't mean it shouldn't be reported though. News is news. Even more so in that case."

"So, do we agree there are some cases that should be reported and some that shouldn't?" Mr. Monroe asks.

I say, "I think the issue is less about whether or not we report suicides, but how we report them."

"Go on."

"I think the problem is when the reports are unnecessarily graphic or sensational," I say, still planning the words as I speak. "I mean, the original one back in the nineties was Kurt Cobain. He cultivated a whole emo image while he was alive, had legions of fans who wanted to be like him, and when he killed himself, they did too. Would all those people have done it anyway? Maybe, maybe not. The nonstop media coverage of his death wouldn't have helped though. Same thing with Robin Williams and Anthony Bourdain and all the others. I think it's possible to report suicides without giving every single article an over-the-top, click-baity headline, and the coverage doesn't need to be so excessive. People die, even famous people, and it's a tragedy, but the world doesn't need to put it under a microscope."

Ravi kicks my foot. I ignore him. Journalist mode has taken over. I researched this very topic last year, and the stories practically begged to be told. "On the flip side, there was a rash of youth suicides a few years ago that were the direct result of extensive bullying, and I absolutely think those need to be reported to the fullest extent possible, because those are the cases where, yes, the victim took their own life, but the world around them handed them the gun. One of those kids was only ten years old. Ten. Of course the world needed to know what he went through, because the people who did know failed him, and the world needed to see what the consequences of bullying and abuse can be. Those stories led to the anti-bullying laws, which aren't perfect, but they're something. So yeah, sometimes sharing the details is important, even if it feels salacious."

"Comments?" Mr. Monroe asks.

"I agree," Ravi says. "You scream the stories that have the potential to stop a tragedy from happening again, but you don't linger on the ones that might cause more tragedy. You try to break the cycle, not perpetuate it."

"Well said." Mr. Monroe nods approvingly. "Anyone else?"

"I just don't think it's the world's business to know how you died," Natalie says, refusing to budge.

"Not even if it's murder? Or a shark attack? A new strain of Ebola?" I ask.

"That's different."

"So, it's only suicide that's the problem? It's so shameful that we should pretend it doesn't happen?"

"Suicide is a sin, okay?" Tears well in Natalie's green eyes. "We shouldn't act like it's not. It's selfish and stupid, and everyone left behind isn't only missing you, they're having to worry about you burning in hell because of a stupid decision you made without thinking about it or asking anyone for help." Natalie pushes her chair back from the circle and flees, slamming the door, but not in time to block the sound of her weeping.

For a moment, no one moves, shocked into silence. Then Claribel gets up, chair screeching against the tile, and says, "I'll check on her."

Mr. Monroe nods. When the door closes again, he surveys the class. "Emotions are difficult, messy things. Your stories will evoke emotion, and it may not always be the ones you intend. You can never know what baggage someone brings to your work. It's important to be sensitive to the emotional needs of others, but not crippled by them. We live in difficult times, and it's important to shine a light in the darker corners of the world while remembering that goodness exists too. Seek a balance not only for your audience's sake, but for your own."

Chapter Ten

THE STORY about the brief search for and discovery of Emma's body becomes the most-viewed and most-commented article in the *Monitor's* history in a matter of days.

The outpouring of grief is real, with the vast majority of the comments expressing some variation of *We love you, we'll miss you, fly high!* Then there are the people working through the seven stages of grief, with most of the posters stuck hard on denial, the ones who claim Emma wasn't suicidal at all, but that's understandable. No one saw Emma's death coming any more than the previous classes had seen Liam's. I don't think anyone ever really sees suicide coming. It's like the more obvious candidates for such a death would rather talk about it than act on it, while those who follow through come out of nowhere. Maybe the difference really is in the talking. Maybe, sometimes, having someone know that you're hurting enough to want to die can be enough to stop you from doing it.

The comments that are a problem are the ones attached to pseudonyms. The *Monitor* allows anonymous comments, but many people opted for their real names because it's such a Maplefield-centric site. The app isn't available for public download but shared through the school's email list. I thought the ability to submit tips anonymously was important enough to outweigh the drama that occasionally erupted in the comment sections, but I'm starting to rethink that policy.

Buried in the comments below the article about Emma are a handful of users taking advantage of their anonymity to take their final shots at a girl who had probably made their lives hell at one point or another.

I'm glad she's dead.

She deserved to die.

Why won't anyone talk about what a bitch she was? Part of the reason we're all getting along right now is because she's gone.

The only nice thing she ever did was die.

Out of the hundreds of comments, the vitriol makes up only a fraction, but it's enough to make me consider closing the comment section completely. I could delete the offensive remarks and leave the rest, but the thought of targeted censorship rankles me. The first amendment is sacred to journalists, and I can't bring myself to violate it.

Besides, the comments aren't completely wrong.

Perhaps it's the constant monitoring of the comments that did it, but that night, I dream of walking through the woods in a purple dress, rocks and twigs stabbing the soles of my feet as I try to stay one step ahead of something I can't see. Birds caw from high in the trees, a chorus of avian accusations that follows me all the way to the big evergreen.

I wake not with a pounding heart, but rather the uneasy realization that I overlooked something. I check my phone. There's still an hour before the alarm is set to go off, but I know I won't get back to sleep. It's too early to call Ravi, so I stare at the slowly brightening ceiling and try to piece together the images from the dream, to put my finger on what I'm missing. The feeling of grasping for something just out of reach is real, like when a word gets trapped on the tip of your tongue. It's not the leftover confusion of my dream—I'm sure of it.

The alarm sounds before the answer comes. I roll out of bed annoyed and tired. The feeling clings on the drive into school, and I'm irrationally irritated by the ceaseless perkiness of Cassidy's friends.

"Punch me," I order Ravi on the walk in.

"Or not," he says. "You okay?"

I'm going to have to be, tired or not. I have interviews to do, and no one wants to open up to a cranky journalist.

Emma's funeral was two days ago, and while I have no intention of reporting on the actual event, I thought a profile piece, with quotes from friends and teachers, would be a thoughtful way to close the coverage on her death.

"Just tired." I shake my head, swallow a gulp of coffee, and try to set aside the crabbiness. "Let's do the long way."

Instead of heading straight inside, we veer off onto the grass to walk around to the teachers' entrance in back.

"Well, I have good news," he says. "I was going through the *I Am Maplefield* pictures last night, and we have almost three-quarters of the school done already."

"Nice." We're still spending Directed Study in the studio, but since Emma's death, we've only seen four students: three freshmen and Jacob Harris, who had been high and sporting an impressive black eye. We gave him a whiteboard anyway, since being high at school was pretty much Jacob's entire brand, and he wrote *I Am A Disaster* in huge bubble letters. We couldn't disagree.

Ravi offered to reshoot him when the shiner cleared up, but Jacob just smirked and said, "This is who I am, man."

The photo didn't turn out as awful as I'd expected, given the state of his face. Ravi, being the master that he is, managed to make it look ironic and funny instead of sad and pathetic. Everyone knows Jacob is practically raising himself since his father is a long-haul trucker who leaves for weeks at a time. It's an open secret that he deals, and rumor has it that his dad not only knows but encourages it. The only reason he's still in school is because that's where his clientele is.

"What are you thinking about your end of things?" Ravi asks. "With the curse. Do we keep pursuing that or should we talk to Mr. Monroe about switching topics?"

I've barely thought of the curse since everything that had happened with Emma. "I think we keep going," I say. "We obviously leave Emma out of it, and probably Liam too now, but the other disappearances are still relevant. I can shift the emphasis to the origin of the urban legend rather than an investigation into each person. Or not. People die, even students, and the world goes on. By the end of the year, if the curse strikes again, we're going to regret not being ready."

"I should've brought you donuts today."

The warning bell rings from inside.

"You really should've." I exhale a hard breath through my nose and kick at a patch of mulch. I gotta get over myself. "Okay. Acknowledge and set aside. Acknowledge and set aside." I plaster on a smile in an attempt to trick my brain into believing I'm cheerful.

"That working?" Ravi asks, a skeptical look on his face.

"Enough." And it is, right up until something punctures my foot and deflates my zen. I bite back a yelp, but not the curse that follows it. "Dammit!"

"What? What's wrong?" Ravi snatches the coffee cup from my flailing hand before I spill it on either of us.

"Something stabbed me in the friggin foot." I grab his shoulder for balance and yank my shoe off. A shard of bark protrudes from my sock. I pluck the offending splinter out and freeze.

This is it.

This is the thing from the dream that I missed. It wasn't the birds that triggered the feeling, or the incongruous dress.

It was the walk.

I drop my socked foot to the ground, barely feeling the cold asphalt through the thin cotton, and clutch Ravi's arm. "Her feet," I say, waving the piece of mulch at him. "Ravi, her *feet*. Holy shit."

He looks more than a little concerned about my sanity, but I know I'm right. I shove my foot back into my shoe, exhaustion a distant memory now. "Do you still have the photo? The one of Emma? From the woods?"

He nods warily. "Yeah. Why?"

"Is it on you?" I'm already reaching for his bag. "I need to see it."

He shakes his head. "No, it's at home. I switched to a new memory card. It was too weird to be walking around with that on my camera all the time."

I grab his sleeve and pull him back the way we came. "We need to get it. Now."

"What's going on? We can't just leave school."

"Says who?"

"You drove Cassidy, remember? You need to take her to the barn later."

"Yeah, that's later. It's fine. We can be back by then." I'm practically jogging now that his car is in sight. "I need to see the picture."

"Larson's gonna catch us," Ravi protests. "I'm all for skipping, but this is a little blatant."

"No, she won't. Bell already rang. Let's go."

He unlocks the car doors. "If they call my parents, I'm blaming you."

I don't fill him in on what's going on yet, not until I can back it up with proof, but I keep turning it over and over in my head, all the worst details from the scene, and I know in my bones that I'm right about this.

I don't even bother raiding the kitchen at Ravi's like I normally would. I march straight upstairs before he even has the door shut.

"You know, I have no idea what you're on about right now, but you're kinda pissing me off." Despite the words, his tone makes it clear that he is more intrigued than angry.

"Show me the picture and I'll explain. I need the picture first." I sit on his unmade bed and wait while he boots up his laptop. He rolls his desk chair over to the bed and sets the computer beside me. I don't remember it being so unbearably slow before.

Ravi straddles the chair backward, slots the memory card in the reader, and hesitates. "You sure you want to see this?" The look on his face says he definitely does not.

"Yes. Open it up."

The scene is less shocking on the computer screen than it had been in real life. I've had enough time with the image in my head to know what to expect, but the shimmering purple fabric looks like liquid in Ravi's photo, light glinting off the folds, and I'm again gripped by the surreal thought that I'm looking at a fashion shoot.

"Zoom in on her feet," I say. My heart is pounding, but my finger is absolutely steady as I point to the spot I need to see. Journalist brain is in full control.

Ravi does as I ask, magnifying Emma's bare feet until I can make out a slight chip in the polish of the pinky toe on one foot and the faint lines on the sole of the other—the one that twists at such an unnatural angle.

"Holy. Shit," I whisper. This is huge.

"What? What's so important about her feet?"

"Look at them." My mind is positively racing. "What do you see?"

"Feet," he says, starting to sound annoyed. "Girl feet. Nail polish, smooth skin, no scaly bits like I have."

"Exactly."

"Exactly what?" He's clearly sick of being one step behind.

I laugh—a short bark of a sound that could almost be mistaken for distress. Almost. "You see, but you do not observe. Her feet are smooth. They're clean. The polish is intact."

"Yeah, and?"

"And where are her shoes? She's got this fancy dress on—totally impractical, by the way—but where are her shoes?"

"I don't know," Ravi says slowly. "She was barefoot. I don't remember seeing shoes. Maybe she didn't wear any?"

"Then how are her feet so clean? There's not a speck of dirt on them. If you walked through the woods barefoot for even a few steps, the soles of your feet would be caked with dirt. But hers look like she just had a pedicure."

Ravi stares at me, and I see the moment it comes together for him. He goes to lean back in the chair, realizes he's sitting backward, and flails for a moment before regaining his balance. "You mean—"

"I mean." I can't help the grin that starts. "Emma didn't kill herself at that tree. She was left there. This isn't a suicide. It's a murder."

The Making of a Monster
Continued

Once separated, the boy grew terribly jealous of his sister, who was more like a chameleon than a girl at all. While they were in the womb, she had stolen all the charm and sucked in all the confidence and left the boy with nothing. He knew she loved him—when they were little anyway—but he also knew she was tired of him. She never said it out loud, but she didn't have too. They were twins. They didn't have to say things to know they were true. Not like other people.

She thrived in their separate classrooms, even though she liked the same things as the boy: Star Trek and rockets and entomology. It was just that she knew how to hide it. She could be whatever anyone wanted. The boy could never figure out how to do that. It felt like a betrayal of his very self, and besides, passion wasn't meant to be contained. There was nothing better in the world than being so excited about something that your face hurt from smiling. He couldn't understand why that joy made people uncomfortable, but he knew it did, and he came to hate the things that made him happy.

That hate grew to be his constant companion, filling the spot his sister belonged in. He hated his face, with its too many freckles and too-close eyes. He hated the hard lumps that sprouted on his injection sites—lumps he never saw on his sister despite using the same brand of needles and the same insulin. He hated his parents for cursing him and hated the teachers for ignoring the kids who picked on him. But most of all, he hated the pair of effortlessly graceful and athletic boys, with their loud shouts and dirty jokes, who fouled him so hard during gym that he had to hide the bruises beneath long sleeves and jeans, even in the heat, just so his parents wouldn't ask questions.

Those boys, with their straight hair and strong arms, were the monsters.

Chapter Eleven

"**W**E NEED to take this to the police," I say.

"And say what? We think it's weird her feet are clean? They ruled it a suicide. She's already buried."

"It doesn't make sense though. Her feet couldn't be that clean if she walked through the woods and somehow killed herself without leaving any evidence."

"The note is evidence," Ravi says. "And maybe she took her shoes off and an animal took them. Or they could be hidden under her dress. We didn't see them move her."

I shake my head. "I know I'm right about this. Think about playing in the woods when we were little. The dirt would live in our feet for the entire summer, but hers are pristine."

Ravi studies the image, still zoomed in tight on her feet. He pans back out, and we scour the scene for signs of her shoes but find nothing.

"I'm going to report it," I say. "I'll go alone if I have to, but I have to do it. I can't knowingly conceal a crime. That's a crime itself."

"You're not knowingly concealing a crime. You're concealing a theory," Ravi says. "Listen to yourself. You're so desperate for this to be more of a story than it is that you're grasping at straws."

The accusation stings, perhaps even more than he intended, but I set it aside. "That's not what this is," I insist. "Look, imagine I'm right, just for a minute. Imagine she was killed. That means whoever did it got away with it. She's buried and branded a suicide. We can't let that stand."

"Ha!" He points a finger at me. "So it is about the story." He doesn't look jazzed about it.

"It's not only about the story. But okay, yes, there's a story there. A potentially huge story. And we might be key players in unlocking it." I close the laptop and slide off the bed. "So, are you driving me to the police station or am I walking?"

THE DESK sergeant does not look amused when we say we want to see the lead detective on the Emma Morgan case.

"There is no detective on the Emma Morgan case because there is no case," the woman says from behind the wall of safety glass.

"Then I want to see the officer in charge of the initial search." I channel every molecule of my on-air voice into the request. I'm not about to be brushed off.

The woman sighs, gives us a look that stops just shy of a glare, and says, "One minute. Take a seat."

Ravi drops into one of the hard plastic chairs that litter the waiting area, but I'm too wired to sit.

"You need to be nicer," Ravi says. "Pissing off cops is bad."

"I didn't piss her off. I was merely making a request, and she was being needlessly difficult."

"To-may-to, to-mah-to," he says. "I would just like to end my day without being arrested."

"We're doing our civic duty. No arrest imminent."

The door opens, and a man in his midforties appears. "Kennedy Carter?" He steps toward me.

I nod and extend a hand. He shakes it automatically. Most adults do. "Thank you for seeing us. Is there somewhere we can talk?"

"Sure, this way." He waves us back through the door he came through.

Ravi stands reluctantly and follows us to a small, gray-walled room. The chairs are padded, and the table is adorned with a fake flower in a plastic vase, so I doubt it's an interrogation room. Good sign.

"I understand you're here about Emma Morgan," the officer says after we're seated.

"Yes," I say. "I'm the founder of the *Maplefield Monitor*, our school's online newspaper, and I was part of the search party that found Emma. Something occurred to me that I thought I should share regarding the nature of her death."

The cop leans forward and props his elbows on the table. "Go ahead."

I sneak a glance at Ravi, who's starting to look a little gray himself. On my own, then.

"I believe Emma Morgan was murdered." No use beating around the bush.

I have to hand it to him, the officer has an ironclad poker face, because he doesn't so much as flinch. "On what grounds?"

"The state of her feet."

The officer regards me like he's trying to work out whether I'm joking. "Elaborate."

I run through the theory for him, not mentioning Ravi's photo. I'm almost positive it's not a crime to possess such a thing, but I don't feel the need to introduce it either.

"And why are you reporting this now?" the officer asks.

Heat crawls up my cheeks. I know the next bit is going to make me sound unreliable, but it's the truth. "It only just occurred to me. I had a dream about where we found her, and I realized her feet were too clean for having walked through the woods all that way."

The officer is quiet, but I know about interview techniques, and I'm not stupid enough to fill the silence just because it's uncomfortable. I've said my piece. Now it's his turn.

"Excuse me a moment." He rises from his seat, which is not the reaction I was expecting.

When he's gone, Ravi sits bolt upright and whispers, "We should go. This is ridiculous."

"Relax, it's fine."

"Says the not-brown-guy in the room. All things being what they are, police stations are not high on my list of places to hang out."

"Greater good," I remind him. "This is important."

"So is avoiding unwarranted arrest."

The door opens, and the officer comes in with a slim manila folder. The look on his face is bordering mighty close to pity, but that can't be right.

"This is Emma's file," he says. "I can't let you read it, but I can tell you what it says." He shuffles some of the pages around and skims over them. "We did a full autopsy on your friend's body, as is procedure in any unexplained death. There's a note about the dress—that dirt was found along the hem and in several spots inside. It's possible that she wiped her feet with it, for reasons we'll never know."

He closes the folder and places it on the table. It's a struggle not to reach across and grab it.

"What was the official cause of death?" I ask.

He's quiet long enough that I think he's going to ignore the question, then he sighs. "The manner of death has been classified as undetermined."

I sit forward. "Not suicide?"

He shakes his head. "Not not-suicide. *Undetermined* simply indicates a lack of sufficient evidence to deliver a completely concrete finding. In this case, the note does indicate suicide, but there were too many questions surrounding the specific cause of death to officially rule it as such or anything else."

"Like murder?"

The officer meets my eyes, and he suddenly looks too soft to be a police officer. "Or accidental. I have a niece your age," he says. "I can't even imagine something like this happening to her or one of her friends. I know it's hard to wrap your head around this, and I am very, very sorry for your loss, but please don't torture yourselves by creating ghosts that aren't there."

I take a slow breath and look down at my lap. *Steady.* I can't fight with a police officer. That will end badly. It will end extra badly for Ravi. "You're right," I say when I can trust myself to be reasonable. "You're right. I'm sorry for wasting your time. It was a stupid theory."

The officer smiles kindly; he isn't taking us seriously, but he isn't some fascist monster either. That complicates my anger in a way I don't like.

"I don't know if you're interested, but our desk sergeant can give you a list of support groups in the area. I know it's hard, but it can be helpful to talk to people who have experienced similar losses."

I thank him and let him get the list of meetings for us, then walk out into the bright afternoon sun. I wait until we're in the car and out of the parking lot before turning to Ravi, who looks more than a little relieved to see the station in the rearview mirror.

"Well, I don't know about you, but I think we're going to have to solve this one ourselves."

"You heard him. There's no case to solve. If there were, they'd be solving it."

"I'm not wrong about this."

We drive in silence for a few miles, and when we reach the stop sign nearest the school, Ravi sighs and turns to me. "Okay. What's the plan, then?"

"Just pull in. We'll wait for the next bell and slip in like we were there all along. Or you can drop me and go home, take the full day. I would, but I can't strand Cassidy."

"No, the *plan-plan*. For the investigation."

I regard him for a minute, but he seems sincere. "You believe me?"

"I believe *in* you," he says. "That distinction is important, at least right now. But I trust your instincts, so if you think there's something here, let's uncover it. I mean, we did find her body; we might as well see it through."

I grab him in a fierce, awkward hug across the center console before I can stop myself. "I'm right. You'll see."

"So? Plan?" He lets the car roll forward, and we creep toward the school.

"Interview witnesses and people of interest," I say without hesitation. "Same as we would for any other story."

"Do you have a list?"

"I'll start one. We need to talk to Owen, of course. Most murders are committed by the people closest to the victim. Which means we'll also need to talk to Victoria, Lily, and Emma's family."

"We can't interrogate her family."

"Not interrogate. Interview. Whole different vibe."

"How are you going to convince them to talk to you?"

"We're going to say we're doing a feature on Emma for the *Monitor's* print edition—that she'll be on the cover and the lead story. We'll say it's an in-depth memorial. People will want to help with that."

Ravi gives it some thought and nods. "It's not the worst idea." He parks in the first spot he sees, even though it means a longer walk to the door. According to the dashboard clock, we have ten minutes until the sixth-period bell rings.

"I'm thinking we can use 331 for interviews. Hardly anyone new is coming for pictures right now, so we can talk to people uninterrupted but without it looking like we're having clandestine meetings. I don't want people getting suspicious about why we're talking to them."

"Are we really going to run the story?"

I shrug. "Not sure. Some version of it, I think. I haven't planned out the feature stories for the print edition yet beyond what we're doing for Monroe, but it would make sense to run an article on Emma. And if we solve her murder, that will definitely be a lead headline."

"Just thinking out loud here, but what if we tweak the whiteboards for Emma's story? I mean, if we're really running it. We could have the interviewees do signs with memories or something."

"I like it," I say, but what I really like is that he's getting on board with this. I know in my gut that I'm onto something, but chasing it down without having Ravi on my side would be terrible. "I'll see who I can talk to today, but why don't we plan to officially start tomorrow? I'll come up with a list of must-talk-tos, and we can add to it based on what we find out."

Ravi agrees, and we get out of the car with two minutes until the bell. We slip around the back of the school, not wanting to risk the front door or a walk by the main office, and duck into the teachers' entrance as the bell rings.

We sneak into the building and into our last period classes so easily that I believe we're in the clear, right up until Directed Study, when Cassidy rolls into the studio looking impossibly smug.

"So," she says, stopping in front of me. "Do anything fun today?"

Ravi shoots me a worried look, but I ignore it. "Learning is always fun."

"Oh, please," Cassidy says. "I know you skipped, like, everything."

"And what if I did?"

"You'd be grounded, and Dad wouldn't let you drive. Or have a phone. Or any freedom at all." She's only exaggerating a little.

"Oooh, sibling blackmail." Ravi rubs his hands together like a cartoon villain. "Let the negotiations begin."

I ignore him. "And you're what, asking me to buy your silence?" I'm starting to think I liked my sister a lot better when she was younger and worshipped the ground I walked on."

"Let's say we enter into a pact of mutually assured destruction," she says. "I'll keep your secret if you keep mine."

I cock my head. "And this secret would be what, exactly?"

"You're going to bring Bryce to the barn with us today, and you're not gonna tell. Especially Dad."

"That's your price?"

Cassidy nods.

"Done."

Cassidy's face splits into a giddy grin and she squeals. "Yay! I already told him he could come. He's been wanting to for a while, but I didn't know if you'd keep it a secret, but then I saw you leave with Ravi—my homeroom faces the parking lot, you geniuses—and I knew I had my chance." She squeals again. "I can't wait!"

I'm a little hurt that she didn't automatically think I'd be down for pulling one over on the parental units. "Just make sure he's ready to go."

"He's already ready. Can I stay here for the rest of Study? I'm already done with my homework, and I want to fix my makeup, but Mrs. Thomas will never let me out of class."

Her enthusiasm is adorable, but I'm not about to let on. Give the monster an inch and she'll take a mile. "You don't need makeup to ride a horse."

"I do if I want to look fabulous doing it."

Ravi laughs. "The girl has a point."

"You're a damn traitor." To Cassidy, I say, "You can stay. Once. This is not going to be an everyday thing."

Cassidy salutes. "Aye, aye, Queen Skipper of all Skipdonia." She wheels over to the whiteboard table and upends her makeup pouch.

I turn to Ravi and roll my eyes. Planning will have to wait.

Chapter Twelve

I WISH I could just pull everyone I need in for interviews without having to be tactful or patient, but Ravi reminds me that those are virtues I'd do well to practice. So instead of stalking Emma's friends, I wait until I see Victoria and Lily at lunch to tell them about the memorial project and arrange for them to meet us in 331. Both girls are so eager to help that I'm almost embarrassed for them.

I spend the rest of lunch searching faces and trying to deduce who knows something they aren't telling. I'm not ready to go so far as to say someone at Maplefield killed Emma, but I'd bet money that someone from the school at least knows something.

The one thing I see at lunch that makes me smile is Cassidy, who's giggling and sharing a plate of fries with Bryce. Before yesterday, I couldn't have picked the kid out of a crowd, despite that crazy strawberry blond hair, but he surprised me by being genuinely interested in what Cassidy was doing with the horses and not just trying to get her breeches off. He was polite and funny, and it's only a matter of time before he's suffering through awkward family dinners with us.

I'm okay with that.

The rest of the day crawls by, and I wonder if I should've tried to separate Lily and Victoria for their interviews, but ultimately decide it would draw unnecessary attention to insist on different times.

Ravi and I do some quick rearranging of the tables in 331 so we can have a comfortable place to sit—as comfortable as a classroom can be at any rate.

Victoria and Lily are prompt. I thank them for coming and ease them into the interview by asking for favorite memories and tales of first meetings to establish rapport. They have stories for days. I let them ramble for a bit, jotting down notes I don't need, then ask, "Is there anything you can tell us about Emma's last days? Anything that stuck out?"

Victoria's knee starts jiggling, and she looks down, but not before I catch the sheen of tears in her brown eyes.

Lily shakes her head. "Everything was normal. That's why I just can't believe this, you know? I mean, yeah, there was some drama with her and Owen, but she wasn't, like, depressed about it. Or I didn't think she was anyway."

"What was going on?"

Lily hesitates, like she's not sure how much of her friend's drama she should spill.

"It's okay," I say, taking a gamble. "If you don't want to explain you don't have to, but I'm not going to print everything you say. I'm just trying to understand what happened."

Lily nods. "Right. Well, Owen was being a possessive jerk. He got like that sometimes—he can have a temper—but Emma thought it was cute. She liked a little jealousy; she said it's how she knew a boy was really interested. I don't know... I didn't really get it, but that's how it was. She likes drama. *Liked.*"

Victoria's leg pumps faster at the correction, and she sniffles. Ravi hops off the table he's perched on and fetches the box of tissues we've been using to erase whiteboards. Victoria takes the whole box.

I don't want to lose Lily, so I press on. "What was he jealous about?"

"He thought Emma was cheating on him," Lily says. "But she wasn't. We would've known. She told us everything."

I somehow doubt Emma would've told her friends about that kind of sneaking around, but who knows? It's not like dating politics are exactly my area of expertise. "Why did he think that, then?"

"I don't even know. Emma didn't know. He was just giving her a hard time, said he knew she was cheating and that he would prove it."

"Did he?"

"There was nothing to prove. She thought he was being ridiculous and said he'd get over himself. It's not like he could do better than her anyway, you know?"

I don't know Owen well, but I do know what Lily means. Owen isn't ugly, not exactly, but he's not in the same league as Emma by a long shot. They don't even have a lot of friends in common, or rather, Owen doesn't have a lot of friends, period. As far as I know, his life revolved around Emma and the wrestling team. They were sort of the school's odd couple, but I wouldn't be surprised if that had been part of the appeal for Emma. Anything for some extra attention. She would love the attention she was getting now. I don't bother feeling bad for thinking that because it's true.

"Do you think there was something going on at home that might've had something to do with what happened?" I try to keep the phrasing tactful, but it takes conscious effort. I want facts, and I want them yesterday.

Lily shakes her head. "I don't think so. They're as shocked as we are."

Victoria's head snaps up, eyes suddenly blazing. "Well, there was obviously something, wasn't there? People don't just kill themselves for no reason."

I shoot a glance at Ravi, who's perched back on his table, and he looks as surprised as I am. Neither of us had expected that kind of rage from Victoria.

"I think she must've been keeping secrets from a lot of people, not just you," I say. After our failed talk with the police, I don't want the world knowing I'm looking into a possible murder, but I can't help wondering if Victoria would feel better or worse knowing that was on the table.

Given her outburst, I consider the wording of my next question carefully. "The sleepover Emma went to before she…disappeared. That was with you guys?"

Neither answer at first, and I wonder if that was too close to an accusation.

Ravi leans forward and props his elbows on his knees. "No one's blaming anyone." His eyes are kind and his expression solemn. Both girls gaze up at him from their chairs like he could be their savior. We hadn't planned to do good cop-bad cop, but I'm not about to fight it.

"I wasn't there," Lily says. "Xavier took me to dinner after the game, and we went back to his place. His parents were away." She shrugs, like that explains everything.

"The sleepover was at my house," Victoria says. "I had no way of knowing I would be the last one to see her alive."

"Did she seem normal when she left?"

Victoria shrugs but doesn't look up. "I guess. She went running. I didn't see her after that. She runs right by that pedo's house though. She always does, like she doesn't even care that he lives there. Maybe he said something to her."

"That made her kill herself?" Lily asks. "No one could make Emma do anything she didn't want to do, never mind killing herself."

"Did something, then. I don't know." Victoria sounds close to tears again.

"It's natural to want to blame someone," Ravi says. "Had she mentioned anything about Peter Vernon before she died?"

Both girls shake their heads.

"But he is a sex offender," Victoria says. "He could've been watching her or something."

Peter is definitely on the list of suspects, but I'm not ready to share that yet, especially not with these two.

"Then she would've been naked," Lily says. "Not all dressed up like she was."

I seize on that. The dress was odd—no doubt about it—and any good Sherlockian knows that singularity is almost invariably a clue. "Had either of you seen that dress before?"

"No. It wasn't her normal style at all though," Lily says. "It was too princessy. And it looked retro, like from the nineties, but not in a cool way. Emma usually liked dresses with more slink. You remember what she wore to prom last year."

I don't, but I nod anyway. "Do you know where it came from?"

Neither girl does.

I think I've tapped them of all useful information, so I close by asking, "Is there anything else you'd like to say about Emma?"

Lily goes first, her eyes welling. "Emma was one of my best friends. I don't even know how to live in the world without her. I don't want anyone else to feel the way I'm feeling right now or the way she must've felt at the end. I think it's good you're shining a light on Emma's life so that people can remember her for who she was but also as a warning, you know? This isn't good. Two years ago, we lost Liam, and now Emma. I don't want a third name added to that list. Emma and Liam are enough. What Ms. Larson said in the assembly was right. We need to talk to each other. We need to be there for each other. The stupid friend groups and cool kids versus everyone else needs to stop. It's not worth it."

That last part is a little rich coming from a bona fide cool kid, but the sentiment seems genuine enough that I scribble down the key phrases, knowing they would make good copy.

"Victoria? Is there anything you want to add?"

Victoria doesn't look up from her lap, but tears drop onto her legs, staining her jeans dark in patches. She shakes her head. "I just want to know why."

KYLIE AUGER isn't on the official interview list, but when she walks into The Donut Hole after school, there's no way I'm letting her get away. If anyone has dirt, it'll be Kylie.

Ravi gives our favorite source a blueberries-and-cream donut and iced latte on the house and settles her in at the window counter.

"We're doing an end-of-year profile on Emma," I say by way of explanation. "You know, memories, stories, and stuff."

Kylie bites her donut and moans. "These are amazing. I could never work here; I'd weigh a million pounds." She sips her latte and refocuses. "Emma. Okay. What are you looking for?"

"Anything you can tell us. You always know what's going on." I'm not above a little ego stroking to get what I need.

"Oh, you mean like drama?" Kylie's all ears now. "You know I got you covered in that department. I mean, first of all, did you hear about her and Victoria?"

Kylie looks way too keen for this to be nothing.

"What about them?"

"Only that they had a massive fight the day before she died."

Ravi and I exchange a quick glance. This is the first either of us have heard of a fight between the two friends. "Emma and Victoria? You're sure?"

We have to wait for her to finish chewing before she answers, and I vow to stop feeding sources before they talk. "Yeah. Oh my god, I can't believe I didn't tell you. I only found out a couple days ago though, and I thought after the funeral, the Emma stories would be done."

She pauses for more coffee, and I have to fight the urge to take it away.

"Okay, so at the game—you know, the night before she died—Emma totally fucked up. She missed some kind of important goal kick—sorry, I'm shit at sports—and Victoria said she could kill her. Right out loud."

I drop my pen, disgusted. "That's the big fight? An offhand comment during a game?"

"No," Kylie says. "I'm not at the good bit yet. In the locker room—I heard this from Jodie, but don't tell her I told you—Vic practically dragged Emma into a shower stall and started yelling at her—in a whisper, but still all angry, you know?—saying she was done covering for her and that she didn't care if Emma hated her. She said she couldn't keep doing it."

Okay, maybe there was something here. "Couldn't do what?"

Kylie shakes her head, eyes wide. "No idea. I heard she was cheating on Owen though, so my guess is it had something to do with that."

Victoria hadn't mentioned any of this, but then again, why would she when we were supposed to be doing a memorial article? I'd have to circle back to Victoria—maybe talk to her alone.

"Any idea who she was cheating with?" Ravi asks.

"No clue," Kylie says. "It might not even be true. You know how Emma was: all drama, all the time."

I consider pointing out the obvious but want to keep Kylie on my good side. Instead, I ask, "Why do you think she killed herself?"

"Drama," Kylie answers without hesitation. "She always had to be center of attention, and no one gets attention like pretty white dead girls." She pops the last of the donut in her mouth. "Unless Victoria really did kill her. You never know, right?"

"I don't think Victoria killed her over a soccer game," I say, but I'm already making a mental list of follow-up questions to ask Emma's supposed best friend.

"You never know," Kylie says again.

Chapter Thirteen

THERE'S A lot I don't know, and I don't like it. On top of having a murder to solve, Mr. Monroe expects our initial research summaries in ten days, and I've barely looked at the curse notes since Emma died. I briefly considered changing the topic to something more straightforward, but I'm nothing if not good to my journalistic word. Stupid morals. I'll just have to uncover the origins of the curse, solve a murder, and win the Emerging Excellence award all before graduation.

No sweat.

The biggest stumbling block with the curse is data. It's not like I can google *Maplefield High senior curse disappearance*. I know; I tried.

I flip to the curse section of my red notebook and find the list of potential interview subjects. If the information doesn't exist on the internet, I'll have to find it the old-fashioned way: word of mouth. Beneath Ms. Larson's name, I list all the teachers I can think of who have been there long enough to see several graduating classes go through. Maybe Ms. Larson will at least point out who had been senior class advisors. I add a few more potential sources, including students I know that have older siblings, and by the time I close the notebook, I'm satisfied that I at least have a game plan, if not actual progress.

I'll use class time to pursue the curse, Directed Study to finish Ravi's project and conduct murder interviews, and somehow keep all these balls in the air and not keel over of actual exhaustion.

Which is exactly what's happening when I hear a tap on the door. Cassidy wheels herself in, clad in corgi pajamas. "I think Bryce is gonna ask me out."

I stifle a sigh that wants to turn into a yawn. "I think you and Bryce have already been out."

"No, not to the barn," she says. "Like a proper date. But Savannah likes him too, so I feel like I can't really talk to my friends about it." Savannah was one of Cassidy's enthusiastic morning crew and a force to be reckoned with.

"That's awesome," I say, even though the siren song of bed is making it hard to keep my eyes open.

"I think Mom and Dad are gonna freak out and not let me go. Should I even tell them? Or should I keep it a secret and say I'm going to Janice's?"

"Oh, man. This is so not my division," I say. "Okay. First, I think yay for Bryce having good taste. He's way less of a tool than his hair would lead you to believe. Second, I think lying to the parentals will end badly for all involved, and that includes me, because I don't want to be collateral damage of your love affair. Third, you do have some extra logistics to think about."

"Already figured out," she says. "Next time you're my barn ride, we bring Bryce and you can give him a lesson in the care and feeding of my wheels while I'm riding."

"You're diabolical."

"I'm prepared and think ahead." Now she turns on the puppy eyes. "Please? Please, please, please help this happen?"

I sigh. There's no way I'm getting out of this, and the fastest route to bed is acquiescence. "Okay, fine. I'll give him a crash course in traveling with an extra set of wheels." Cassidy looks ready to shriek in delight, but I hold up a hand to forestall it. "I will not, however, help you lie. If you're old enough to date, you're old enough to tell Mom and Dad. Or at least Mom."

"Deal," Cassidy says. "Can you drive me tomorrow? We can tell Mom you need the car to do something reporterly."

"Diabolical," I repeat. At this rate, I'm never going to solve Emma's murder, but there's something to be said for keeping my very-much-alive sister happy. "All right, fine. I'll come up with the cover though."

"Oh my god, you're the best!" Cassidy squeals. "Thank you, thank you, thank you!"

"Nothing says thank you quite like going away so I can sleep."

"I'm already gone! Sweetest of dreams, oh sister of immense awes—"

"Good night," I say, holding the door open.

Cassidy wheels herself out with only the smallest of delighted squeaks. I doubt that she'll sleep at all. I, on the other hand, am out before I even get the covers properly arranged, and it's blissful.

THE COVER story is simple: I'm going to drop Cassidy off at the barn so I can take The Planet to the library to do research. It's effective simply because it's true.

When the final bell releases us from school, I leave Ravi to finish up a few *I Am Maplefield* shoots on his own and meet Cassidy and Bryce in the parking lot. I start the lesson then and there, making Bryce watch how Cassidy transfers herself from the chair to the car and demonstrating how to fold the wheelchair for storage.

At the barn, Bryce gets a lesson in exiting a vehicle, along with assurance from both of us that Cassidy is completely capable of managing that on her own if someone fetches her chair. I hang out until Cassidy is tacked up and astride Mudd, the dark bay gelding she competes on, and then have to drag Bryce away from the fence so he can practice folding, stowing, and unfolding the chair while Cassidy isn't waiting for it. It's not rocket science, and he doesn't make it harder than it has to be. He's very matter-of-fact about it in a way that most teenage boys wouldn't be, and I like him all the more for that.

"Just so you know," I say, "I'm cool with the two of you doing your thing. I think my mom will be too. I like you enough that I'll warn you our dad can be kind of an ass, but if you're genuinely good to Cass, things will be fine with him."

"I appreciate the heads-up."

I nod. "And I have to add—clichéd though it may be—if you hurt or humiliate her, we're going to have a confrontation, you and I. And I can be way scarier than my father."

"Got it." He flushes scarlet right to the tips of his ears.

I burst out laughing.

"What I mean is, I would never hurt her. I think she's the coolest. This horse thing she does, it's crazy. You couldn't pay me to get on one of those things, and she does it like it's nothing. I've never met someone as dedicated as she is. I know being the crazy horse girl isn't usually cool, but she's got this passion, and I think it's awesome."

"It is," I agree. "And she can't really afford to be distracted right now, so keep that in mind. I'm not saying don't take her out. I'm just saying remember everything she's working toward. Don't derail her."

"I wouldn't do that," Bryce says, and he looks so sincere that I almost believe him.

I PICK Ravi up from The Donut Hole before I go to the library and regret it once I realize his eagerness has exactly nothing to do with the project.

"You don't understand, Ken," he says as we drive. "He's like a baby Giles."

"So stuffy, British, and way too old for you?" I'm kidding. Mostly.

"As in hot and smart and okay, yes, older, but sue me, I like it. It's not like he's old enough to be my parent or something." Ravi's infatuation with the new reference librarian is well established. Hot and smart pretty much sums up Ravi's type, regardless of gender, and the latest addition to the Maplefield Public Library is the poster boy for that.

"I don't know how this entire day has turned into me facilitating peoples' romances," I say. "Our goal is to fill in the timeline of disappearances, not get you a date."

"No reason it can't be a little of column A, column B."

"You're incorrigible."

"Also, your favorite human."

"Not for any reason that makes a lick of sense." I turn in to the library's parking lot and find a space close to the entrance, deciding to take it as a good omen. "Okay, we have an hour, hour and a half, to make this happen. Can we think about using your powers of charm for good?"

"No promises."

The Maplefield Library is housed in an old stone building that could double as a haunted house from the outside. Inside is a maze of narrow-aisled bookshelves and scarred wooden tables, and even though it's cramped and out-of-date, I love it.

We're greeted at the main circulation desk by an older librarian, who looks up from a book to smile and nod at us.

Ravi swerves to take the stairs to the second floor where the reference desk is located, but I don't. This elderly librarian spends all her time between patrons reading crime novels. She might be just the person we need to talk to.

"Hi," I say before she can go back to her book. "I'm sorry to interrupt you, but I was wondering if you could help us with a project we're doing for school."

"Oh, you're not an interruption." She places a bookmark into the novel. "What can I do for you?"

"We're journalism students at Maplefield High, and we're researching the Maplefield curse. It's an urban legend. The way it goes is that every year, a senior disappears from school and is never seen again. We're trying to figure out the origin of the curse and whether there's any merit to it."

"How interesting," she says, perking up. She may be gray-haired and bespectacled, but she's as keen as any Agatha Christie detective. "What is it you think I can help you with?"

"Well, we have a list of the disappearances we know of, but they only go back so far. We were wondering if there are any old newspapers we could look through or if there is anyone here who would remember rumors about local kids going missing. So far, most of the disappearances seem pretty mundane, but still."

"Well, off the top of my head there was that poor boy a couple years back who killed himself, poor thing. His mother was in here all the time—twice a week at least. Lovely lady. I can remember that boy coming to story hour as a wee little thing, and even then, he was so passionate about music."

Ravi nudges my foot, but I ignore him. I have no problem letting the woman reminisce about things I already know if it might lead to something I don't.

The librarian purses her lips, eyes fixed just beyond us as she searches her memories. "And there's Claire Mullroy, who took off maybe ten years ago now. A runaway. Her poor mother was another regular, always taking out the kind of paranormal romances Claire used to read, like she wanted to be ready in case the girl ever came back. I don't think she ever did. Mrs. Mullroy stopped coming in maybe five or six years ago."

I pull the notebook from my backpack and write *Claire Mullroy—Runaway—10 years*. A look through the old yearbooks will pinpoint what graduating class she was part of. I give Ravi's foot an I-told-you-so kick.

The librarian is on a roll. "And a few years after that, Martin Eckles dropped out of school to join the French Foreign Legion, of all things. His poor parents were furious because he didn't even say a proper goodbye, just left a note."

I note his name as well.

"Oh"—the librarian looks pleased at coming up with another memory—"speaking of notes. Madeline Archer joined the circus— the actual circus—just a few years back. As an acrobat. I don't know if you'd call that a curse or not, but she sent her parents a note on the back of a show flyer and has been traveling the world since."

I'm not sure that one counts since it sounds like she's alive and accounted for, but I add the name to my notes anyway.

"Those are the ones I can think of off the top of my head, but I'll keep working on it. Takes a while to get through all these memories when you get to my age." She laughs easily at herself.

"That's three more names than we had, so thank you. You've been very helpful. Is it possible to have a look at the old newspaper archives? I know I can search online through more recent issues, but I want to go back twenty or thirty years and see if there were any notable student disappearances or deaths back then. It doesn't look like they have back issues archived yet."

"My, you have done your homework." The librarian steps around from behind the desk. "Here, let me take you up to the research section. Silas can set you up with the microfilm. It'll be quite a different process from searching online, let me tell you."

She leads us up a curving staircase to the top floor, which houses the nonfiction. "You know," she says as we climb, "I think I do remember something else. A death though, not a disappearance. Four deaths, actually. There was a single-car crash maybe twenty-five years ago or so now, and no one survived. It was quite the tragedy, all Maplefield students. I don't remember the ages of everyone involved, but it seems likely that at least one was a senior. Would that count as your curse?"

"I don't know, but it's definitely worth checking out."

"It's so nice to see young people doing real research these days. You said this was for a journalism class? I would've loved a class like that in high school, but the best we got were Secretarial Studies and Stenography. I thought about being a court stenographer, but then I was hired here and well, never left! It might seem boring to you kids, but it's nice being able to serve a town, watch it grow up and change and, in a way, stay the same."

"That's exactly why we came here," I say. "You've really been very helpful."

At the top of the stairs, the librarian shows us to the reference desk. "Silas, these two need to look at some microfilm. Can you get them set up?"

The guy at the desk nods with a grin, gaze lingering on Ravi long enough to make me second-guess if the attraction is as one-way as I thought.

"Absolutely," he says. "What do you guys need?"

I'm about to explain, but Ravi steps forward, props his forearms on the counter, and launches into an explanation of our mission. Who am I to deny Ravi his moment when I know I can't give him the same?

Silas is easily ten years our senior, but his floppy brown hair and tortoiseshell glasses make him look younger—or at least less worldly. Plus, he's wearing a sweater-vest, and really, how threatening can someone be in a sweater-vest?

"Oh, yeah. I can definitely help you," Silas says. "This way."

He leads us to a room with a boxy microfilm reader and fetches the proper reels of film. "It can be slow going," he warns. "Even if you know what you're looking for, you're still checking each page manually. You'll get in a rhythm though, and it'll get easier. And by easier, I mean only marginally quicker."

"Any interest in staying to help?" Ravi asks hopefully.

Silas smiles. "Maybe next time. I can't abandon my post. But don't hesitate to come get me if you need something."

"Oh, I won't." When he leaves, Ravi is practically glowing. "He's hot, right? You know he's hot. And I think he's kinda into me. I know the age difference is odd, but I think it could work."

"Ravi, focus. We have work to do. And you know nothing about him except that you like to look at him."

"Which is important."

"Not as important as our curse."

Ravi knows enough not to argue, so he drags a chair over to the desk and watches as page after page of newsprint roll by on the viewer.

For want of something more concrete, we use the car crash as a starting point. We go back to the 1990s and started paging through, focusing mainly on headlines and obituaries. After a half hour of searching, we find the crash. Two seniors, a junior, and a sophomore had all been killed when their car crashed through a guardrail and sank into the pond. I note the names and date. Four deaths in one year could definitely trigger rumors of a curse.

We move forward, and two years later come across an obituary for another Maplefield student: seventeen-year-old James Henry

Blackwell, whose age could've made him a junior or a senior depending on his birthday. The obituary says he "passed away at home" but doesn't specify of what. I write down the name and date of death to cross-reference with yearbooks and take a photo of the whole thing, just in case.

We spend the rest of our allotted hour finding little of relevance but far more than we ever wanted to know about local politics, crime, and painfully outdated advertisements. It's not a waste though. If we can track down two more disappearances between the crash and James, we might have the origin of the Maplefield curse.

Chapter Fourteen

WITH THE curse research well underway, I'm able to turn my attention back to what really matters: solving Emma's murder.

Owen is next up, and I decide to approach him as if I have no knowledge of his and Emma's fraught final days. He'll be the bereaved boyfriend, nothing more.

If I can find him.

Owen and I don't have a single class together. Ravi has AP Chemistry with him, but not until the end of the day, and I don't want to wait that long to talk to him.

I don't see him at lunch, but it's possible we don't have the same lunch block. I notice Bryce sitting with a couple of the other wrestlers and consider asking him if he knows where his teammate is, but decide against it. The last thing I need is to drag Cassidy's maybe-boyfriend into a murder investigation.

"What do we think?" I ask Ravi. "Absent? Skipping lunch?"

"Don't know," he says. "Guess we'll find out last block?"

I groan. As much as I trust Ravi, I like to be the first to approach potential interviewees. For one thing, having Ravi do the pitch would feel like sending a *Do you like me?* note to a crush through a friend. More importantly, I would have to sacrifice seeing Owen's initial reaction to the interview request. Body language can reveal as much, if not more, than words, and I want to be there to see it.

"Maybe I can crash your chem class?"

"Or maybe you could meet us at the end of class and not look like a weirdo. I can wait to mention it to him until we're in the hall."

"What if he's hell-bent on getting out of here when the bell rings? We might not have time."

"Chance we'll have to take." Ravi shrugs. "I mean, we can try hunting him down now, but he could be anywhere. At least we know he'll be in chemistry."

I glance at the wall clock, automatically accounting for the fact that it's four minutes slow, and figure we have twelve minutes before Journalism starts. "We could look now, and if we don't find him, you can corner him in chemistry."

Ravi groans. "But the starvation is real."

"You're not gonna die. Besides, it's not like you're missing anything special. School pizza is basically pepperoni-flavored reconstituted cardboard. You're above that." I spin on my heel before he can protest.

He follows, as I knew he would. "So says the girl with a grocery store in her locker. You owe me sustenance for this mission."

"Fair enough." Half the reason I keep the stash of snacks in my locker is so he can raid it, but I'm not about to tell him that. "Where should we start? Gym?"

"Probably. At least that's somewhat logical. But really, he could be anywhere."

"Your optimism is inspiring." I fix him with a look.

He raises his hands in mock surrender. "We'll find him. I have the faith."

"You have the lies. Faith, you lack."

"But I'm willing to lie about it," he says. "Least that's something."

The gym is on the same floor as the cafeteria, and we can hear the dull thuds of basketballs bouncing off the floors, punctuated by the peal of whistles, before we even make it to the door. A peek through the window reveals a herd of freshmen doing a poor job of getting balls into nets.

"Freshman Gym," I say. "Shit."

"Oh, ye of little faith. Follow me."

He pulls open the heavy gym door, and the scent of sweat and worn rubber swamps me.

"He's not gonna be in freshman gym," I protest.

"No shit. But he might be in the weight room."

"Where the hell is the weight room?"

Ravi eyes me like he can't believe I'm serious.

I glare at him. "Oh, come on. Don't give me that look. It's not my fault my time is better spent writing stories than chasing after balls. It's not like you're Captain Athleticism either."

"But I am the one who knows where the weight room is."

We skirt the edge of the gym, and when one of the teachers gives us a *What do you need?* gesture—palms up, eyebrows drawn—Ravi points to a door near the boy's locker room, and the teacher nods. Apparently, Ravi does know what he was talking about, because when he pushes the door open, he reveals a room full of barbells and weight machines.

Several of the machines are in use, and luck is on our side, because one is occupied by Owen. He has a barbell balanced on his shoulders and is pushing it up from a squat position as we approach. He stops with it braced against the back of his neck and watches us.

"Hi," I say.

Owen shifts the barbell into a set of slots on the rack and steps out from beneath it. He reaches down to retrieve a small towel from the floor, then wipes his face.

"I hope we're not interrupting."

"Just finishing," he says. "Were you looking for me?"

"We were, actually. I don't know if you've heard, but we're going to be doing a feature on Emma for the *Monitor* print edition at the end of the year. We're talking to all of her friends and her teachers to get quotes, and we were wondering if you could sit down with us, maybe during Directed Study, for a short interview."

Owen grabs a water bottle from beside the barbell rack and takes a long swallow.

"What do you think?" I ask. "We can do it today if you want, or whenever is convenient."

"I don't know if I have anything that will help your story." His expression is wary. "You know we broke up, right?"

I didn't know that and try to keep any reaction from my face. "I'm so sorry. When was that exactly?"

"The day before she died." Owen speaks the words without emotion, like he's reciting a homework assignment, but his cheeks pale despite the recent exertion of exercise.

I make a split-second decision to gamble on his desire to talk. "I still want to talk to you," I say, as gently as possible. "The fact that you broke up doesn't negate the fact that you shared something special. If you don't have anything to do during Directed Study, we'll be up in room 331. It might help to talk about it. We don't have to publish everything you say. You can control what we share." That last bit isn't strictly true, but I thought he might be swayed by the promise of some anonymity.

He scrubs at his ashen cheeks with the towel and nods. "Yeah, sure. I can do that."

WHEN RAVI and I get to 331, I'm surprised to find two sophomore girls waiting there instead of Owen.

"Are you guys still doing the picture thing?" one of them asks.

"We are," Ravi says before I can chase them off. Which is fair. Even though Owen agreed to come, there's still a solid chance he won't show.

"Cool," the girl says. "I'm Maritza. And this is Claudia."

I give them the sign-in sheet while Ravi preps the camera. The girls know exactly what they want to say and quickly fill out their boards.

I show Maritza to the scuffed piece of tape, then stick my head into the hall, but there's no sign of Owen. I curse myself for not jumping straight to the interview during lunch. What did it matter if we were late to class when there was a murder to investigate?

Maritza has her sign flipped up when I turn around, and it reads *I Am Owning My Mental Health*. She's smiling, but it doesn't quite reach her dark eyes. I have to admit, I'm curious about what she means.

The other girl—tall and plain where her friend is short and dark—gets in position and holds up a sign reading *I Am Willing To*

Listen. To Anyone. Reach Out. This girl doesn't smile, but there's nothing hostile in her expression.

I weigh my options, wanting to interview these two, but not wanting to appear busy if Owen comes by. In the end, I let them go, knowing I can hunt them down later.

"Do we have a picture for Owen yet?"

"Nope," Ravi says. "We're only missing eleven seniors, but he's one of them. This probably won't be the right time to ask him for it, huh?"

"Probably not." I'm interested in what he would write though. *I am heartbroken? I am bereft? I am guilty?*

"We taking bets on if he shows?" Ravi asks when we're down to ten minutes before the final bell. "Because I'm going with a big no."

I sigh and sit next to him on the whiteboard table. "I knew I should've just cornered him at lunch."

"Wasn't enough time. Nothing you could do."

"Which is exactly what we're doing now—nothing. Does the wrestling team have practice today?"

"We don't," Owen says, stepping hesitantly into the room. "But Coach needed to see me. I didn't know if I should still come up or not."

"I'm glad you did." I hop down from the table. "Do you have time to talk? Can you stay after?"

"For a while, yeah." He shoves his hands into the back pockets of his jeans.

"Here, sit down." I gesture to a chair at the whiteboard station and pull out the other one, turning it so they face each other. Ravi shuts the door and settles himself back on the table.

I thank Owen for coming, rattle off the phony project opening, and ask, "What can you tell us about Emma?"

Owen ducks his head and runs a hand over his buzzed red hair. He drops his elbows to his widespread knees and speaks to the floor as much as to me. "We'd been dating a little over nine months. She was out of my league—I knew that—but we had something. God, I know how stupid that sounds; every guy batting above his average must say the same thing, but it was true. At first, anyway. We kept it a secret in the beginning. I didn't blame her. I was a nobody—the quiet new kid—and she was homecoming queen. We had anatomy together, and Mr. Laramie seats everyone alphabetically, so we shared a table. We dissected frogs and pig hearts together, and at first, I only thought she talked to me because she had to, but she was better than people gave her credit for. We started hanging out after school to work on projects and stuff, but then it started to be more about hanging out and less about homework, you know? I would've been fine with her keeping it a secret. I understood. But eventually, she brought me into her group. I think joining the wrestling team helped, because I might still be the weird new kid, but at least I became the weird new kid with a talent."

He's quiet for a minute, and I'm about to give him a prompt, something to direct his thoughts, when he continues on his own.

"She became my world. My reason for getting up. My life has kind of been shit, if I'm being honest, and she was my bright spot. I really thought she cared about me. I was so fucking stupid."

"What happened?"

He still hasn't moved his eyes from the scarred floor tiles, but the tendons in his hands bulge as he clutches at fistfuls of empty air. "She humiliated me. Used me. I shouldn't have been surprised, but I was. I really was. I let myself believe we had something—that it was okay that I didn't get to see her every day. I was okay letting her have a life as long as I got to be a tiny part of it. But she made a fool out of me. I don't even know why she bothered. Maybe just to prove she could, I guess."

Owen's jaw is tight, taut muscle rippling beneath the skin, and his eyes shine with unshed tears. I shoot a glance at Ravi that Owen doesn't see and press on.

"Tell me what happened, Owen." The bell rings to release us from the building, but no one reacts.

Owen doesn't look at us when he confesses. "She cheated on me. I shouldn't have been surprised, but I was." He shakes his head, cheeks red with shame. "I was."

"I'm sorry. That must've been awful." I mean it, because he looks absolutely shattered, but his head snaps up and his hands close into fists like I've insulted him.

"What would you know about it?" His eyes are hard and dangerous. "It's not like you care what people think of you."

Ravi keeps his perch on the table but shifts forward like he's ready to launch himself on Owen at the first sign of aggression.

I give a tiny shake of my head, stilling him, and keep my eyes on Owen. "Of course I care what people think. Everyone does. It's human nature."

"Well, Emma didn't. All she cared about was herself and what she wanted."

"And what was that?"

"Jacob Harris, apparently." He all but spits the name, his lips pulled back in a grimace, the disgust written plain as day across his face.

I try to keep the shock off my own face and don't know if I succeed. "Emma and Jacob? Are you sure?"

"Yes, I'm fucking sure. Do you think I'd have left her if I hadn't been?"

Okay, that's probably true. "How did you find out?"

"Kylie told me. I think she just wanted to stir shit up, but she wasn't wrong. When I checked Emma's phone, the evidence was right there. All these texts back and forth, deciding when to meet up, times and places, all right there for everyone to see."

I want to ask if Emma knew he had looked at her phone but wasn't sure how to without setting him off.

Ravi picks that moment to step in. "Shit, man. That's rubbish. What a nightmare."

"No shit. I just couldn't take it. A year ago, I might've stood for it—just let it go and forgotten about it—but the side effect of being with someone like Emma is you start to think you're as important as they are, so I told her to fuck off, said I was done. If she was willing to stoop as low as Jacob Harris, then I wanted nothing to do with her."

"How did she react to that?" I ask.

Owen's lips peel back farther, revealing his gums like a snarling dog. "Denied it, of course. Said I didn't understand and 'please don't leave,' but the evidence was right in my face. I saw the texts, and she couldn't deny them away. Maybe if she hadn't saved his number under his real name, she could've gotten away with it, but she couldn't even bother to be sneaky. She just took for granted that she wouldn't have any consequences. Well, she was wrong, wasn't she? You reap what you sow. There's no escaping it."

The Making of a Monster
Continued

The boy concocted fairy tales about life in high school, where there would be new faces for the monsters to go after, but high school was nothing like he had hoped.

On the first day, the gym teacher jokingly said there would be no stuffing freshmen in lockers, mostly because they wouldn't fit. The monsters took it as a challenge to prove that a ginger boy could indeed fit if they tried hard enough. They stuffed him in like a discarded jockstrap and left him locked in the dank darkness long after the bell rang. It was only when a janitor heard him crying that he was discovered at all.

It didn't help that his sister, now firmly separated from the boy, was making friends. A group of pretty girls, some who were friends with the monsters, had swept her into their coven. The boy would see them in the hall between classes, giggling and fawning over each other, and his chest would ache with longing.

The swarming chaos between bells was the hardest time for him because there was nowhere to hide, nowhere to duck away when someone locked on to him. With a backpack nearly as big as he was and that flaming hair, he was a magnet for casual cruelty. Any time he could make it to his next class without being shoved, knocked down, or taunted was a win.

He didn't get a lot of wins.

During one hallway gauntlet, his sister appeared just as a huge sophomore ran up, grabbed ahold of the boy's backpack, and used it to vault right over his head. The bag and the boy spilled to the tile floor as hoots of laughter echoed through the corridor.

The girl dropped her own bag and rocketed down the hall after the vaulter, not slowing as she barreled into him. They hit the lockers in a tangle of limbs and a clatter of metal. The girl got three good punches in before being pulled off by a teacher. She earned three days of suspension—one for each blow—and a reputation as a badass, while he became known as the kid who had to be saved by a girl.

But she hadn't saved him, not really. She had cursed him, and he began to hate her for it, just a little.

Chapter Fifteen

I **'M STILL** reeling from our talk with Owen when we get to The Donut Hole. Things are slow enough that Mr. B doesn't put us to work, so we make drinks and take a trio of donuts to the window counter.

This is definitely a three-pastry problem.

I peel the rainbow sprinkles off my chocolate-frosted and eat them one by one, lost in thought, when Ravi asks, "Do you really think he could've done it?"

I eat four more sprinkles before answering. "I do. I don't want to, but yeah, I think it's a possibility."

"Same." Ravi sighs. He wraps his hands around his mug and blows a breath into the rising steam as he stares out the window at the passing pedestrians.

"I'm not saying I think he did it for sure," I clarify. "I'm saying he could have. The rage is there, and he has no alibi." When we asked Owen where he was the day Emma was reported missing, he said he didn't remember. When pressed, he said he was home, alone, for the entire day.

"Owen isn't a bad guy." Ravi shakes his head. He hasn't even touched his maple blueberry donut yet. "I just can't picture it."

"That's always how it goes though, right? When they uncover freezers full of body parts and lampshades made of skin, the neighbors are always like, 'He was such a nice guy, so quiet. I never saw it coming.'"

Ravi eyes me. "I think there's a difference between a crime of passion and going full-blown Bundy."

"But it wasn't a crime of passion. It couldn't have been, not the way she was dressed. The last time she was seen, she was in running clothes. Where are they? Why is she wearing the dress? And again, the issue of her feet. Whoever killed her moved her there; they had to have. It's the only thing that explains her feet being clean."

"Maybe it started as a crime of passion: He was pissed, hauls off and grabs her. Maybe she hits her head. Then he panics, dumps her in the woods, tries to make it look like a suicide."

I go back to picking at sprinkles as I consider that. Owen is definitely strong enough to carry a girl through the woods, and that mark on her arm could easily have been from him squeezing her, but I'm not seeing the rest.

"But how did he kill her? What was the method? I can't help thinking that if it was him, it really would've been a crime of passion. She would've been beaten or stabbed or something equally violent. We don't even know how she was killed, just that whatever it was didn't leave enough evidence to pinpoint the cause. That indicates a high level of thought and planning, which don't strike me as Owen's strong suits."

Ravi shakes his head, worry darkening his brown eyes. "No, actually, you're wrong. He's smarter than you think. Not just smart-for-a-meathead smart, but scary-genius smart."

"Explain."

"He's in AP chem with me, and I've never seen someone breeze through science like this kid. The equations he can do in his head are like something out of a movie. It's seriously BBC Sherlock levels of brain power, just with science instead of crime."

"Huh, I had no idea." The next thought hits me like a meteor, and I whack Ravi's arm before I can stop myself, sending a tidal wave of tea sloshing into his saucer. "What if he killed her with science?"

Ravi mops up the spilled tea with a piece of donut. "I think you might be reaching a little there."

"No, I'm serious. There were no injuries and no obvious cause of death that led to a conclusive finding during the autopsy. What if he drugged her somehow? I read about a tree in Asia that can kill you just with a single seed, and it's hard to detect even with good toxicology labs."

"Owen lives in an apartment, surrounded by other apartments. I don't think he has anywhere to plant a magic murder tree."

"Maybe not that particular one, but something. Something poisonous that wouldn't leave a trace."

Ravi sips his tea, still not looking convinced. "Even if he had the capacity to find or make such a poison, Owen worshiped Emma. I don't think he could've killed her. If anything, I expect he'd maybe beat the piss out of Jacob, but he wouldn't hurt Emma—scientifically or otherwise."

I grab Ravi's arm, and he barely manages to avoid dumping tea all over his lap.

He shakes me off. "What do you have against my tea staying in its cup?"

"Jacob's face! Remember when he came in for his picture? How he was all beat to hell? What if Owen did that?"

Ravi sits up, brows drawn together and spilled tea forgotten. "I'll pull the file when I get home. Check the date marker. But wait, if Owen was busy beating Jacob into mashed potatoes, how would he have had time to kill Emma?"

"We'll have to work the timeline, but he could've done both. Of course he could've."

"Or he could've punched Jacob, and meanwhile, someone else killed Emma for completely unrelated reasons."

"Also possible. Look, Ravi, I don't like thinking about our classmates being capable of murder any more than you do, but the fact is, someone is capable of murder. And they might be capable of multiple murders. What if this guy strikes again? We can't afford to let this get away from us. So yes, if I seem a little obsessive over our suspects, it's because I am. Owen is at the top of the list for a reason."

"Fine, who's on the rest of the list?"

I reach over the back of my chair to get the notebook from my bag. I pull the pen out of the spiral and flip to the proper page, helpfully labeled *Suspects* across the top. Beneath the heading is a list of people who may be to blame for Emma's disappearance.

The first is Owen, obviously, because nine times out of ten, it's the lover. Jacob is next, because extra lovers usually make up that tenth instance.

But not always.

I tap the next name on the list with my pen. "Peter Vernon. Now, I admit, going from unsolicited dick pics to murder is a pretty huge leap, but we can't ignore him as a suspect. He does have a history of inappropriate interaction with teenage girls, he's physically capable of killing and moving her, and she wasn't found all that far from his house. It's not entirely inconceivable."

"You keep on using that word…" Ravi starts a quote from *The Princess Bride*, but I wave him off.

"We need to look into his movements the weekend Emma died. Maybe Lily or Vic know if they were texting or something. It's probably a long shot, but it needs to be on our radar."

Ravi pokes at the remaining chunk of donut on his plate and pushes it over to me. "Who else?"

"Random psychopath?" I write it down, even though it's probably unlikely. "I mean, it's a possibility. Statistically, most murders are committed by people the victims know, but there are exceptions. The more prolific—"

Ravi holds up a hand. "No, don't you dare. I see that look in your eye. Don't you dare get excited about a maybe serial killer. We knew Emma. Maybe we didn't like her, but we knew her. You can't be excited at the prospect of her murderer being the next Hannibal Lecter."

"But it'd be a great scoop, wouldn't it?" I pop the last of his donut into my mouth, appetite not the least bothered by our morbid topic of conversation. Not sure what that says about me.

"You're atrocious."

"I'm kidding. Mostly. But seriously, other than Owen, Jacob, and Peter, I don't know who else to look at."

Ravi's face gets serious. "Peter Vernon is a problem. Or rather, exactly how you're gonna deal with him. It's one thing to interview people at school, where we have a reasonable cover story and a certain amount of inherent safety, but that doesn't exist with Vernon. We can't just doorstep him and be all like 'G'day, mate. Would you like to talk about the girl you might've killed?'"

"Gimme some credit. I wouldn't be that obvious." I say it like I have it all figured out, even though I don't. Ravi's right—talking to Peter is different than talking to people at school, but I'm not about to back down.

"You're the last person who should be talking to him anyway," Ravi says, dark eyes flashing with an unsettling intensity. "Seriously. At best, he would just ignore you, but think for a minute if he actually is the killer."

Before he can continue, the bells at the door jangle, and a lady comes in with two kids. Ravi leans in and lowers his voice. "If he is the killer, there's every reason to believe he could kill you too. Hell, I'm inclined to call him not guilty based on the fact that you *weren't* the victim."

"Hey, I resent that."

"I'm being serious."

"You're being dramatic." I laugh, but he doesn't.

"No, I'm being serious. You remember when the story broke. It was your name on the byline, and he knew it. You were the catalyst. You exposed him."

"He exposed himself, actually."

Ravi grabs my arm, hard enough to hurt. "Kennedy, I'm not fucking kidding around."

The mother at the counter whirls and shoots us a dirty look, but neither of us acknowledge her.

"I don't want you talking to him alone," Ravi says, quieter now but no less intense. "You made sure everyone knew exactly what he did. As far as he's concerned, you're the reason his life in this town is ruined."

I drop my gaze from his face. His grip feels like a shackle on my arm, the intensity of his concern making the touch burn.

I gently pry his long fingers off with my free hand. "I'm not going to do anything stupid," I say, "but he is a suspect, and we do need to talk to him."

Ravi wraps his hands back around his mug like he's incapable of not clutching something. "Then I need to come with you."

"Notice my use of the word 'we.'" I meet his eyes and smile, waiting for him to relax even a fraction.

"Promise me."

I draw an X over my heart with one finger. "No crazy stunts."

He finally relents, offering a weary smile. "Good. Because if you get ax-murdered, I'm going to be very put out."

Chapter Sixteen

I WANT to talk to Kylie again before we zero in on Jacob, but the school's queen of gossip picks the one day I really need her to ignore my texts.

Jacob is a conundrum, because on the surface, there's no logical reason to interview him about Emma. They weren't friends—or they hadn't been publicly—and I'm not prepared to reveal Kylie as the source of their connection.

It's Cassidy, of all people, who solves it—albeit in a way that creates new problems. On the ride in, after we're both properly caffeinated, she says, "Bryce said there's a party at Jacob's this weekend. I think he's going to take me."

The party. Of course. That's the opening I need to talk to Jacob. His parties are legendary—weekend-long ragers that half the school attends any time his father is out of town. Emma definitely would've been at the last one. Of course, if Jacob is a plausible suspect, his party is the last place Cassidy should be going.

"Yeah, how 'bout no," I say.

"What? Why not? It's not like Mom and Dad have to know. We can say it's a movie or something."

"Or not. Jacob is a senior. You're a sophomore."

"And Bryce's a junior. It's not a big deal."

It is if Jacob killed someone, but I can't say that. "Cass, no. Seriously. Jacob's parties are all about drugs and embarrassing drunk videos."

"How would you know? It's not like you even go to parties," she says. "I thought you were on my side with this."

I sneak a glance at her before returning my eyes to the road. "I'm on your side with Bryce, totally. I'm down for the smoochies—as long as it's someone other than me doing the smooching—and I think Bryce is good people. Though if his idea of a date is a party at Jacob's, maybe I need to reconsider."

"That's not fair. Just because you're not into it doesn't mean I can't be allowed to have a normal high school experience. That means parties and poor decisions and yes, drunken videos. Of other people. I can be around stupid people without turning into one, you know."

I don't know how to explain that my concern with Jacob isn't the drugs or alcohol he'd be providing—though that's concern enough—but that he might've killed Emma Morgan. "I just don't think this is the best time to be getting wrapped up in all that. You have riding to think about too."

Cassidy sighs. "I know, but it's not like my entire life has to be about training, right? Like yes, the Paralympics are amazing and so is Mudd, but it's not guaranteed. I mean, what if I put all this work in and don't even qualify? Then I'll be missing out on the riding dream *and* the fun high school stuff. I lost a year and a half of my life after the fall. I'm sick of missing out."

This is more conversation than I'm remotely prepared for at quarter after seven in the morning, but it's obviously been heavy on Cassidy's mind. I wonder how long this has been stirring. "Of course you'll qualify," I say, and not just to be supportive. Cassidy could qualify in her sleep.

"But Mudd might get sold," she says, her voice suddenly rough.

I come to a halt at a stop sign and turn to face her. "What? He's for sale? Since when?" Mudd is owned by a boarder at the barn Cassidy trains at, but because the owner is busy with college, it's mutually beneficial that Cassidy keeps the horse in shape. The girl never goes out to see the horse, and even the barn staff think of him as Cassidy's.

"Since a few weeks ago. His owner's doing graduate school in France and wants to sell him before she goes."

The urge to punch the steering wheel—because Mudd's owner isn't handy—is real. Mudd is Cassidy's best friend, hands down. When she was in the hospital, he was the reason she got up.

I step on the gas and ask a question I'm not going to like the answer to. "How much does she want?"

Cassidy is silent, the only sound the screech of her straw as she stabs it in and out of her coffee.

I hit the blinker and turn in to the school lot. "How much, Cass?"

"Fifteen."

"Shit." Fifteen thousand dollars is a ridiculous amount of money, but I've been around horses long enough to know that it's not as astronomical as it sounds.

"He's totally worth it though," Cassidy says. "He's schooling fourth level, and he's still young enough to get someone a lot of years showing."

Someone like Cassidy.

"Do Mom and Dad know?"

"No. Don't tell them. It doesn't matter. We don't have that kind of money."

"What about GoFundMe? We have the video." As soon as the words leave my mouth, I regret them.

"I'm not a fucking charity case," Cassidy snaps. "I don't need a GoFundMe. There are families who are homeless, communities that don't have water. How would that even look—a middle-class white girl asking strangers to buy her a fancy pony?" She snorts. "I don't think so. That video was to get sponsors, like any other professional equestrian would, not pity payments."

I park in our usual space, kill the ignition, and hold up my hands in surrender. "I'm sorry. I was just thinking out loud."

"Look, I'm trying not to think about it at all." She takes a hard swallow of coffee. "Hence Bryce. Hence the party."

"Fair enough."

Cassidy's friends are converging on The Planet and continuing this conversation would be impossible with that audience.

"Go out with Bryce. Do something fun. But skip the party. Just trust me on this. Please."

Cassidy rolls her eyes. "Fine, whatever."

There's more to discuss, but the moment is lost as Cassidy's door is pulled open from the outside and cheerful squeals and giggles fill the morning air.

I spot Ravi pulling in and head his way instead of inside. I wave at Priya as she gets out of the car, but don't stop to chat. I march over to the driver's side and yank the door open. "Jacob is top priority today."

"Good morning to you too," Ravi says. He gets out and grabs his messenger bag from the back seat, along with a white paper bag, which he hands me. The contents are warm enough to steam in the cool morning air.

I fill him in on the morning's conversation as we walk toward the building.

"Okay, yeah," he says. "I'm not saying I think he is the murderer for sure, but we can't risk Cassidy going there if he is."

"I'm gonna talk to Bryce later. I'm assuming he's coming to the barn. I think I can convince him that they have better options than this party. In the meantime, Jacob."

"I think he spends mornings in the art suite."

"Really?"

"Yeah, he does art." Ravi says this like it's public knowledge, but I had no idea. Again.

When I hear the name Jacob Harris, all I can think of are the endless stories about parties being broken up by cops while his father was on long-haul truck runs. He was arrested once for possession when he was a sophomore, which would've been sealed information due to his age, but the network of sources at school had made sure that I knew. And besides, he didn't even try to deny the charge. If anything, he'd seemed disappointed when he was assigned probation instead of jail time.

"Then art room it is," I say. We don't have long before first period starts, but I've learned my lesson about waiting. It's better to get the information than be on time, consequences be damned.

The art room door is open, and Mrs. French bustles around the room, laying supplies out on each table. "Hello," she says, more to Ravi than me. "Here for the darkroom?"

I take a half-step back and let Ravi talk. I've learned it can be helpful to play into a subject's comfort zone when you need their help, and Mrs. French is obviously more comfortable with Ravi.

"Not today," he says. "We're looking for Jacob. Is he around?"

"Check the painting room. That's usually where he is."

Ravi thanks her, and we duck out of the room to the next corridor, where the studios are located. There's a pottery room, a silk-screening room, a darkroom with a red bulb above the door, and finally, a painting room. The painting room is long and narrow, with windows that face the courtyard, which allow in more natural light than probably any other room in the building.

When we step in, all I can see are black jeans and black sneakers beneath an easel.

"Jacob?" I ask.

The person that sticks his head around the edge of the easel reveals himself to be, as expected, Jacob. He wears a baseball hat twisted around backward and holds a brush in one hand.

"What do you want?"

"Just to talk a minute." I walk around the easel. "What are you working on?"

"None of your business," he says, but makes no effort to conceal the painting. It's a European cityscape—maybe Italian—and not at all what I expected.

The buildings look ancient and envelope the narrow, cobbled street like a hug. Silhouettes suggestive of children and shoppers give the scene movement, but it's the architecture that sells the scene. Golden sunlight makes everything feel warm, and the bricks of the buildings are textured in such a way that I itch to touch them to see if they feel as real as they look.

"This is amazing," I say, stunned into unabashed honesty.

Jacob shrugs and drops his paintbrush into a cup of dirty water. "What do you want?"

I find myself wanting to speak to the painting rather than the painter but force my eyes away from it. "We're doing a memorial piece about Emma Morgan for the *Monitor's* print edition and wondered if we could talk to you."

Jacob folds his arms across his chest and shrugs. "Don't think I can tell you much about her. Besides, bell's about to ring."

I mirror his shrug, confident he's not concerned with missing class. "Yeah, but I have somewhere to hide and a key to get in. Come with us."

Chapter Seventeen

IT'S THE prospect of missing class more than any sort of civic duty that persuades Jacob to accompany us to room 331.

By unspoken agreement, Ravi and I sit side by side on one of the tables while Jacob leans against the other. I don't speak, giving Jacob a chance to fill the silence on his own, but he seems content to wait us out.

It's Ravi who breaks first. "Can you tell us about the last time you saw Emma?"

Jacob adjusts the bill of his hat and shrugs. "I don't know. I just saw her around school, you know? It's not like we were having sleepovers and braiding each other's hair."

"Were you having sleepovers and doing other stuff?" I don't like asking yes-or-no questions, preferring ones that require the responder to elaborate at least a little bit, but the question has the desired effect.

Jacob straightens, folds his arms across his chest, and cocks his head back in a way that tempts me to punch him. He smirks. "So what if we were?"

"So what if you were the last one to see her alive?" I shoot back.

Jacob raises his chin even higher. "So what if I was? Suicide's a tragedy, but I couldn't have stopped her. I had no idea she was even planning that shit."

"Really? Because we heard you two were pretty close." I slide off the table.

"Heard from who?" The wariness on Jacob's face is as good as any verbal confirmation that there's some truth to it.

"Doesn't matter. It's true, isn't it?"

"Maybe. Maybe not."

"Humor me. When was the last time you saw her?"

He hesitates long enough that I know whatever his answer is, it's going to be a lie. "A week or so before she died. We ran into each other in the hall and hung out after school."

"Did you go out somewhere?"

"No. We dicked around after school for a while." His face changes at the memory, and he says, "Wait, is that what you're looking for? Like funny stories about hanging out with her? Because we were hanging out behind the stage in the auditorium and almost got caught. She freaked out, practically broke my arm trying to drag me out. It was like she'd never been in trouble before."

She probably hadn't been.

I shoot Ravi a look, recalling the day we scouted the auditorium for studio space. Had it been Jacob and Emma that we'd interrupted backstage? The more I think about it, the more plausible it seems. The girl had been small enough, and while Jacob wasn't the only guy who always wore a baseball hat, our mystery man had.

"Did you guys hang out a lot after school?"

Jacob shrugs. "Not really. Just sometimes."

"Did Owen hang out too?"

"What? No. It's not like we're tight or anything."

There's only so much relationship drama I can deal with while trying to solve a murder, and between Cassidy's fledgling romance and this trifecta, I'm at my limit. "Jacob, I'm gonna ask you this point-blank, and I want you to think before you answer. Were you having an affair with Emma?"

He bursts out laughing. "Seriously? Me and Emma? Romantic? Shit, you've got to be kidding."

The laughter appears genuine. Interesting. "You weren't dating?"

"No," Jacob says, still chuckling. "I can't even imagine the nightmare that would've been."

"You weren't interested in her at all?" Ravi asks.

"No, man. You've seen her. Do I look like the kind of guy with the time or skills for that brand of high-maintenance?" He shakes his head. "Hell no. If you thought that was the story you were getting today, I'm sorry to disappoint. There's no way in hell I would ever stick a toe in that particular puddle. And let's be real. Owen? Not a small dude. Manly though I may be, I'm not that stupid."

"Wait." I think he's being sincere, but how could that be true? "We heard the two of you were having an affair. That Owen broke up with Emma because she was seeing you. Is that not true?"

Jacob's face loses most of the previous amusement. "Not even a little bit."

"Why would people think that, then?"

"What people are we talking about?"

"Sources."

"Names. Or I have no way of guessing what they were thinking."

I hesitate, not wanting to reveal our source. I won't fall into the trap of thinking it doesn't matter because it's only high school journalism. Principles are principles.

"Was it Owen?"

I neither confirm nor deny.

Ravi leans forward and props his elbows on his dangling knees. "Hypothetically. If it were Owen, why might he think you were moving in on his girl?"

Jacob shrugs. "Beats me. Maybe he's insecure."

"Did you and Emma text each other?" I ask.

"Sometimes."

"About?"

"Stuff. And things."

I fix him with a glare. "Specifically."

"Not sure it's any of your business," Jacob says, sliding back into his natural douche mode.

"I have it on good authority, from multiple sources, that you and Emma were in a relationship and in frequent, regular contact," I say, working to keep my voice level. "If that's true, you might be able to provide us with some insight into her final days. We're not trying to out or embarrass anyone, and you can speak off the record."

"I got nothing to be embarrassed about. As you may know, I'm in contact with lots of people for lots of reasons. Emma was no different from anyone else. She wasn't special."

Something about the way he says that last line makes me think it's the first outright lie he's told us. I change tack. "Can you share your favorite memory of Emma? This part would be on the record."

"I don't know; there's nothing in particular. She was a cool chick to chill with sometimes. That's all."

"What'd you guys do together?"

Jacob looks at me from under lowered brows. "You seem pretty hung up on this whole me-and-Emma angle. This an interview or some kind of interrogation?"

"Little of both," I say, with a short laugh that turns the truth into a joke. "Did Owen know you and Emma sometimes hung out?"

Jacob smirks. "According to you, he did."

"What about according to you?"

"Don't know. What's the point of all this?"

"Like I said, we're trying to get some insight into Emma's last days. You claim you didn't see her that week, but we have two people who say you did. I'm just wondering why you'd hide that."

A storm of emotions crashes across Jacob's face, which he tries and fails to conceal. A more compassionate person would let him compose himself, but I use the moment to lean in harder.

"Did you have a fight with her? Did you ask her to leave Owen for you?" I'm reaching, but it doesn't matter if I get it right, only that I get a reaction. "Or did you tell you she was sick of you? That she didn't want to see you anymore? Did that piss you off? Make you do something you regret?"

Jacob shoves himself off the table hard enough to make the legs screech against the tile floor. He yanks his hat off, runs a hand over his head, and pulls the cap back down low over his eyes. "I don't need this shit."

Ravi hops down from his table, but Jacob makes no move to leave. Instead, he jams his hands in his pockets and starts pacing the room. "Look, I didn't know this was gonna happen, okay? I had no idea. If I did, I would've done something. I liked her, okay? She was a spoiled bitch, but she was all right. I knew she was under pressure, but I didn't know it was this bad. I had no idea." His voice is thick with emotion.

"What pressure was she under?" I ask gently, vaguely aware that I'm using the same tone Cassidy uses on spooked horses.

"Everything. School, grades, soccer, Owen, that stupid internship she was so excited about that her mother was turning into a nightmare. She didn't have enough hours in the day."

"But she spent some of them with you." I pitch it halfway between a statement and a question. "That must've made you feel good."

He meets my eyes and shakes his head with such scorn that I almost have to turn away.

"God, you're so clueless," he says.

"So enlighten me."

"Emma didn't hang out with me because she liked me. Emma barely hung out with me at all. Whatever Owen or whoever told you about the texts was making shit up. Yeah, there were texts. They were hellos and meeting arrangements. But they weren't dates. They weren't even social."

"What were they?" I have a hunch, and it's something I never even considered.

"They were her way of getting more hours in the day," Jacob says, all the fight gone out of his voice now.

"What does that mean?"

"It means she had too many things to fit into her day, and the only thing she could cut was sleep. Adderall helped with that. I helped with that."

I keep my expression neutral and resist the urge to ask any of a million follow-up questions. Behind Jacob, Ravi's eyes go wide with surprise. We got a story all right, just not the one we expected.

Jacob blows out a breath. "Happy now? That's the truth of things. It's off the record though. No one knew. She didn't want anyone knowing. Maybe that was the problem. Maybe if someone had known, she'd still be here."

The storm of emotions that had ravaged his face mere moments ago has calmed to a single one: guilt.

I take a second to gather my thoughts, knowing that the wrong question will send him out the door in an instant. "Was it just Adderall?"

He nods. "Not even pot. Not once."

"How long had she been getting it?" I make sure there's not a trace of judgment in the question.

Jacob drops into one of the chairs. "Middle of last year. Right after the first round of SATs. She wasn't happy with her score and was panicking about trying to cram for the next session."

"She approached you?"

He nods. "I mean, I'm pretty much the school's worst-kept secret. She threatened me at first." He smiles—a genuine one, one that crinkles the skin around his eyes—like maybe this is his favorite memory of Emma. "Said if I breathed a word about what she was about to ask me, she'd tell Larson I tried to roofie her and that Larson would believe her because she was Emma Morgan, fuck you very much."

"She probably wasn't wrong," Ravi says.

"Not even a little," he agrees, the smile fading. "At first, she was all nervous about it, but we got into a routine, and it got easier for her. It's not like I was judging her or making her feel like shit about it, you know? That was her big thing—always worrying that people would look down on her if they knew she was scoring. And the funny thing was, she wasn't even snorting them. She was taking them the same way you would if you had a prescription."

Which doesn't make it legal, but I see his point. As far as drug scandals go, this is pretty minor. "She wasn't taking more than usual this year? In the weeks before her death, maybe? She didn't seem extra stressed or anything?"

Jacob shakes his head. "It was normal. She was normal. I mean, she was still high-strung as all fuck, but it was her normal level of neurotic." He snorts, lips curling with disgust. "But that's a lie, right? She obviously wasn't normal. I just didn't fucking notice."

I realize his guilt isn't over an affair or the fact that he was dealing Emma drugs. It's for not noticing. For not saving Emma from herself. Before I can say anything, he continues.

"I know they don't know exactly how she died, but if she OD'd, I don't know what she took. I just know it didn't come from me."

The Making of a Monster
Continued

The boy spent his days wishing to disappear and his evenings praying for something to change. He researched other schools—Catholic schools, thinking the constant threat of nun-inflicted corporal punishment would keep the monsters at bay. He stayed up into the wee hours of the morning, a Bible open on his lap, bargaining with an unseen Holy Father to do more to protect him than his earthly father could. He tried to barter pages of the Bible in exchange for an intervention, no matter how slight. He'd read two pages if he could get through the next day without being touched. Five pages if his mom would let him stay home. Ten pages if his parents would at least consider sending him to a new school. By the end of sophomore year, he had made it to the end and back again without any heavenly intervention.

He knew his sister could hear him muttering his fervent prayers to an unresponsive God, because she offered to beat up the monsters for him, just to get him to go to sleep. He begged her not to. He couldn't take a repeat of the last time she'd come to his aid, and begged God to intervene instead.

Finally, He did.

His divine intervention came in the form of a massive growth spurt. Six and a half inches and thirty pounds in the span of a single summer, a voice that deepened and a chest that widened to accommodate it. The insides stayed the same, and the hair was still too bright and too bushy, but the body itself was a revelation. This new six-foot frame couldn't fit in a locker if you broke every bone in it.

Chapter Eighteen

AFTER THE talk with Jacob, I text Kylie for a meetup. I have a slew of follow-up questions for my favorite Irregular, but Kylie doesn't answer. I wish that surprised me. When Kylie wants an audience for her latest drama, there's no getting rid of her, but when the tables are turned, she's nowhere to be found.

I wonder if it's nice to have the world revolve around you like that.

After I drop Cassidy and Bryce at the barn—and extract a promise from the latter to take Cassidy somewhere classier than Jacob's party—I head to The Donut Hole. I greet Mr. B and duck behind the counter, grabbing a strawberry shortcake donut from the case and making an iced coffee before going back to the kitchen, where Ravi is up to his elbows in soapy water at the sink.

"Research date?" I ask.

"Oh god, yes." He shakes the suds off his hands. "You're a hero among mortals."

"I know." I eat the donut while he gathers his things and tells his father we're off to the library. Mr. B gives him the same raised eyebrow Ravi has perfected but lets him go. Teasing accusations of parental abandonment follow us out the door.

"I think the only reason he even had kids was to have ready access to child labor," Ravi gripes.

"You don't see Priya standing over a pile of dirty dishes," I point out. "Just you."

"Because I'm not the princess." He climbs into the passenger seat.

"Because you don't actually mind doing it. Dude, your dad's awesome. Seriously. You're lucky."

He doesn't argue because he knows I'm right.

At the library, we wave to the circulation librarian and go right upstairs. Silas gets us set up in the research room, and we get to work flicking through the old files. I can't believe the amount of nonsense that qualified as news back in the day. Weeks passed where the most exciting stories featured record-breaking pancake breakfasts and antique car shows. Sure, there was plenty of actual news—local politics, arrest records, and the like—but there was more filler than I would've expected for a print paper. It's one thing to devote an online gallery to the town's Halloween parade, but it seemed like a waste of actual print space. I guess it was different back then though, before sharing such pictures was as easy as opening Instagram.

Most of the sports section could double as the school newspaper since ninety percent of the articles in that section are Maplefield High stories. I skip as much of that and the classifieds as possible—I can't even imagine having to use classified ads now that we have the internet at our fingertips—but some of it still jumps out, like a group photo of Maplefield students lined up in neat rows, rifles slung across their chests.

"Holy shit." I freeze the page so Ravi can see. "Did you know Maplefield had a shooting team? Did you know shooting teams were even a thing?"

He looks up from his laptop to examine the image. "That's terrifying and fascinating in equal measure."

The photo, taken in 1956, shows thirteen white boys of varying ages, identically clad in button-down shirts tucked into belted pants. They're confident, poised, and completely at ease with the weapons they hold.

"Can you even imagine that today? Deliberately giving a bunch of teenagers guns to use at school-sanctioned events? That's crazy."

Ravi squints at the image, a single finger at his lips. "Okay, I don't know if I'm making this up because I'm looking at that picture, but I think I remember a rumor about a shooting range in the basement of Maplefield. I think it's under the original wing. I thought it was an urban legend. Like the curse. But maybe not."

I shudder. "I'm so glad this isn't a thing anymore." I make a mental note to look into it more if and when I need to fill space on the *Monitor*. It wouldn't be hard to do a contrast-of-cultures thing.

I page through three more issues and say, "I haven't seen a student death, disappearance, or alien abduction in almost a decade. I think it's gotta be James Blackwell or the crash kids that mark the start of our curse."

"Unless there were other quieter disappearances. Runaways and shit."

"I don't know. I've seen what they used to call news. I think a runaway would qualify, simply for the novelty."

"That's fair," Ravi says. "So, we have a start date. That's a lot of blanks to fill in."

"To *potentially* fill in. I figure we research backward, year by year, and see how far back we can go. We'll hit a wall at some point, probably way before James. Plus, we're not just looking for disappearances, but for mentions of the curse itself. When did people start calling it a curse?"

Ravi closes his laptop. "So we're on to the talking to people part of the research?"

"We are. I think we should start with Emma's parents. I'm on the fence as to whether we're calling her cursed or not, but either way, we need to know more."

"Same cover story we've been using?"

"Yup. No reason to mess with what works. Plus, that may actually be our story."

"Fair enough. You don't have Cassidy tomorrow, right? We can go after school."

"Sounds like a plan."

IN JOURNALISTIC lingo, *doorstepping* is the act of, well, showing up on someone's doorstep. Usually someone who doesn't want to talk to you. Doorstepping the Morgans so soon after their daughter's death makes me feel a little squirmy inside, but I acknowledge the unease and set it aside. I have a job to do. Or, if not precisely a job, an investigation to complete.

If most murders are committed by the people closest to the victim, the Morgans are as likely suspects as Owen is.

Ravi and I go side by side up the stone walkway, Ravi's camera banging his ribs with each step. He has it on a long strap, slung unobtrusively under his arm where it will be easy to access but not distractingly conspicuous.

I do the honors of ringing the bell, and the shrill tone pierces the air on our side of the door as much as inside the house.

Minutes tick by with no sound beyond the echo of the bell, despite the car sitting in the driveway. I lean on the bell again. Yes, someone may be sleeping; no, I don't care if I wake them.

I'm about to give the bell a third ring when the curtains on the window nearest the door part to reveal the pale face of Michael Morgan. I smile at him and seconds later hear the lock on the door snick open.

I start talking as soon as Michael opens the door, not giving him a chance to send us away. "Hi, I'm sorry to bother you. I'm Kennedy Carter, and this is Ravi Burman. We're from the *Maplefield Monitor*, which is the school's online newspaper. We're working on an end-of-the-year feature about Emma and were wondering if you would be willing to talk to us?"

"Yeah, I know who you are," Michael says. He doesn't invite us in. "Isn't it a little early for an end-of-the-year story?"

I plaster an anchor desk smile on my face—open and nonthreatening. "It's a print edition, so it takes longer to publish. We need to have all the stories done early so we can format it and get it printed."

"And you're doing a story about Emma?"

"We are. If we could come in and talk, I promise not to take up too much of your time."

Michael looks ready to shut the door in our faces when a voice from inside calls, "Sweetie, who is it?"

Michael rolls his eyes. "No one," he shouts. "Kids from Emma's school."

"Is that your mother?" I ask.

"I don't think you should be here," Michael says. "It's too soon."

"Mikey, don't stand there with the door open," Mrs. Morgan says, coming into view behind her son. She's so gaunt her skin seems a size too small for her skeleton. "Let them in. You're friends of Emma's?"

I can't bring myself to lie outright to this shattered-looking woman. "We go to Maplefield. We run the school's online newspaper and want to do a feature about Emma for our end-of-the-year print edition. Like a memorial."

"Oh, that's sweet." Mrs. Morgan shoos Michael aside and holds the door open. "Please, come in. I'm afraid I don't recognize you. What did you say your names are?"

I introduce us both, and we follow her inside. The house is dark, the blinds closed against the bright afternoon sun.

"Can I get you a soda? Juice?" Mrs. Morgan asks.

"That'd be great, thanks." I'm not thirsty, but a drink gives us an excuse to linger.

Michael follows us into the kitchen and leans against the doorway with his arms folded. I make a concerted effort to ignore him.

Mrs. Morgan pulls two cans of Coke from the refrigerator and hands them to Ravi and me. The three of us take seats at the granite-topped island that dominates most of the kitchen.

"It's so nice how supportive the school is being," Mrs. Morgan says. "That principal is just wonderful. She came over personally to express her condolences on behalf of the Maplefield community."

I didn't know that, but I'm not surprised. It's the kind of thing Ms. Larson would do.

"Is she the one behind this assignment?" Mrs. Morgan asks.

"No, ma'am. I run the school paper—well, me and Ravi both—and we thought it was the right thing to do. Her loss has affected the entire school."

Mrs. Morgan's eyes pool with tears, but they don't spill.

From the doorway, Michael snorts. "Yeah, I bet everyone misses her so much. All these people we never heard boo from before are suddenly crawling out of the woodwork like fucking tragedy vampires. It's disgusting."

"Mikey," Mrs. Morgan chastises. "That's not fair."

"But it's true. This is a perfect example." He shoves himself off the doorjamb and stalks out of the room.

"I'm so sorry," Mrs. Morgan says. "He's having a very hard time with this. We all are."

"Nothing to apologize for." Ravi pats the woman's hand.

I have a flash of envy at how natural that is for him, how the gesture isn't at all forced or awkward. Maybe I compartmentalize too much sometimes.

"What is it I can help you with?" Mrs. Morgan asks.

"We're mostly talking to people about their favorite memories of Emma," I say, a soft lead into the real questions.

Mrs. Morgan laughs, a choking sound that's perilously close to a sob. "Oh god, where to begin? Everything. Everything is precious. Her first word—it was *kitty*, not *mommy*—and her first steps; the first time she rode a bike without help; and the first time I had to ground her when I caught her ransacking the pantry in the middle of the night. She must've been about twelve and had chocolate chips everywhere. She tried to convince me she was sleepwalking."

I smile, as I'm expected to, but I'm not sure why a midnight snack was a groundable offense.

"She was always so driven," Mrs. Morgan continues. "There were so many dance recitals and soccer games and award banquets, and my god, I took it all for granted. I remember complaining about her schedule, telling her I didn't have kids for the sole purpose of becoming a chauffeur, but you know what? I'd give anything to drive her to one more activity."

She breaks then, in the way that pretty, controlled women do. The tears fall silently down sunken cheeks, and she holds a manicured hand up in apology, reaching for a napkin to blot her face with.

"I'm sorry," she says. "God, it just sneaks up on you—the reality of it. The fact that she's gone. I keep expecting her to come bursting through the front door, leaving a trail of shoes and school supplies for me to yell about, but she won't. Not ever."

"I'm so sorry," Ravi murmurs, but something Jacob said keeps nagging at me. He mentioned Emma's mother was making things difficult, but that wasn't the impression I'm getting from the woman.

"Did Emma seem to be under any extra pressure before she died?" I ask.

"No, that's why this is all so hard to believe." Mrs. Morgan dabs at fresh tears. "She was making plans for college and interning with my sister at BayStateNews. She was so excited and even added an extra gym session in the mornings so she could lose that extra ten pounds. She wanted to look her best for the evening news. She was going to guest-anchor."

Mrs. Morgan looks like she's envisioning her daughter's small-screen debut, but I'm stuck on the weight statement, unsure if it was Emma or Mrs. Morgan who thought Emma was carrying extra pounds when she couldn't have possibly been more than a size four on her heaviest day. Maybe this is what Jacob meant about her being difficult.

"I know this is going to be hard to answer," I say as gently as possible, "but did she give any indication, anything at all, that she was going to take her own life?"

Mrs. Morgan shakes her head, touching the sodden napkin to her nose. "No. She was the same old Emma."

"Do you know if she was taking drugs?" I keep my voice even and soft, as if I'm not asking something wildly inappropriate.

Mrs. Morgan's face falls, and she presses the napkin to her eyes. "Only after. The police said they found amphetamine in her system, and I searched her things. I found a pill—just one—in an empty ChapStick tube. It was Adderall." She looks at me like she's desperate to be believed. "Nothing like what the police said. I don't know where the marks came from, but it wasn't drugs. Bugbites, I bet. I'm just so glad the paper didn't mention it—and you can't either, please. I don't want my baby being remembered that way."

I want to ask more about the marks—does she mean track marks?—but before I can formulate the question, Ravi interjects.

"No, of course not," he says. "We're doing our best to honor Emma's memory. In fact, do you have any childhood pictures of Emma you could share? We don't need to take them; I can photograph them here. We were thinking about having some photos to accompany the article."

"Of course I do. Here, come see what we have on the mantle. That would be a nice picture."

The mantle has been turned into an Emma shrine, with photos documenting her life from infancy right up until the junior year soccer finals and prom.

Ravi moves around the living room, framing the mantle from different angles while my mind churns over the mystery of the alleged marks. He asks Mrs. Morgan to step into the frame for a few of them, and she looks at the photos rather than Ravi. Her sad gaze will be what makes the image tug at the heartstrings.

I have an even better idea.

"Would it be possible to see Emma's room?" I ask it knowing there's at least a fifty percent chance of being told no. Mrs. Morgan doesn't answer right away, but I push forward in full on-air mode. "Emma and I had different friends. I didn't get to know her as well as I would've liked." I hope the lie doesn't sound as obvious as it feels. "But a person's room can tell you so much about them, and it might give me a better sense of who she really was before I write the profile."

"Oh, I guess don't see the harm," Mrs. Morgan finally says. "It's just hard. Being in there. It still smells like her."

"We won't disturb anything," I promise, following her up the carpeted staircase.

Emma's door is closed, and Mrs. Morgan opens it slowly, as if she might be intruding.

The room hasn't been cleaned since Emma's death; that's clear at once. The bed is a tangle of purple sheets and fluffy pillows, but when Mrs. Morgan sits down on the edge of it, I can't help wondering if she's been sleeping there, trying to crawl into the hole her daughter left behind. I firmly set aside the feelings this realization evokes. That's a road I don't need to tread.

I catch the faint click of Ravi's camera but don't react. From the corner of my eye, I see he still has the DSLR at his hip, to all appearances merely holding it. The shot is a gamble, but if the angle is wide enough, he would've captured Mrs. Morgan on the bed along with the rest of the room. I could hug him for being so intuitive.

Emma's desk is cluttered with notebooks, gel pens, and a rose gold laptop. A rose gold laptop that perfectly matches the phone Emma was never seen without.

Mrs. Morgan must notice me looking, because she gives a little laugh. "I know. It's crazy. She had straight As but lived like a complete slob."

"Did they give you her phone back?" I ask before I can stop myself.

"It was never found. Why do you ask?"

"Just curious." Talk about an understatement. "Don't you wonder what she was looking at in her final days? Who she was talking to?"

Mrs. Morgan shakes her head, and her face pinches with an effort to keep her composure. "I don't know. I just know it wasn't me." She dissolves then, looking impossibly stranded on Emma's rumpled bed. "The last thing we did was fight."

Chapter Nineteen

I SPEND the weekend sending increasingly exasperated messages to Kylie with no response. I don't even get the courtesy of the bouncing dots to show she's even considering replying.

I don't have time to dwell on it though, because Cassidy is in the midst of a meltdown about what to wear for her date with Bryce. I forgive her for acting like it's more important than a murder investigation, because I've made damn sure she doesn't know anything about it. Far as I'm concerned, she can read about it on the *Monitor* once it's solved. She has other things to focus on.

Like whether the navy sweater with the shoulder cutouts is a better choice than a cute tee and cardigan.

"I vote cardigan," I say.

"Yeah, but you don't have a sexy bone in your body. I have many sexy bones. Like literally all of them." She chucks the cardigan on the bed. "I think the sweater."

"Then go with the sweater. But there will be no sexy bones or boning of any kind. This is only the first proper date, remember?"

"Barn dates totally count."

I hang the cardigan back in her closet. "No, barn dates are supervised by way too many middle-aged women to count."

"You're a fun-stealer." She pulls the sweater over her head and angles herself in front of the mirror.

"It's my sacred right as older sister."

"We've talked about it, you know." Her cheeks flush in a way that makes makeup completely unnecessary.

"Already?" This is so not my division. "Do we need to have the talk?"

"You don't even want to have *the sex*," she says with a wicked grin. "I don't think you want to be responsible for the talk either."

"Yeah, not really, but I also don't want a pregnant sister."

"I'm not stupid. Plus, all I have to do is email my doctor, and she'll write me a prescription for the pill. You'll just have to take me to pick it up, not Mom."

"Yeah, how 'bout no? Getting pregnant isn't the only thing that can happen, you know."

She rolls her eyes. "He'd use a condom too."

I cover my ears with both hands in mock horror. "La, la, la. I don't want to hear this. Shit, Cass. Look. It's the first real date. No sexy times yet. Promise me."

"Define sexy times."

"Times where sex takes place."

"Fine." She sifts through her lipstick drawer and settles on a berry shade that claims to be kiss-proof. "No promises on kissy times though."

"Deal." I don't begrudge her and her raging hormones, but I don't want her jumping into anything too serious too soon. Even though I'm not driven by such urges, I'm careful to remember that most other people are different. That doesn't mean I get it though. Wanting sex is like wanting a scallop-and-peanut butter sandwich—utterly incomprehensible, but maybe something certain people are into. And if it's my sister craving scallops and peanut butter, I want to make sure she's fully prepared for it.

Cassidy smacks her lips at her reflection and spins around. "Good?"

"Good," I confirm. "So, what's the plan?"

"Dinner. Movie. Zero drugs and rock and roll."

"Perfect. Rock and roll can be allowed though."

"How gracious of you."

"I'm a benevolent god."

"You're a benevolent pain in my ass."

The doorbell chimes, and Mom yells up that Bryce is here.

Cassidy squeals. "Wish me luck!"

"Have fun. Don't get pregnant."

Cassidy snaps a salute and wheels herself to the front door. Our father is already there interrogating Bryce, who's looking dapper in his plaid button-down and dark jeans, strawberry curls tamed with some sort of pomade.

I leave them to it, hoping to find a reply from Kylie when I get back to my room. No such luck. I finish up some sports articles for the *Monitor* and write a short promotion piece for the upcoming art show. Once those are uploaded, I open the suggestion folder and scroll through the submissions. A lot of the tips are things I'm covering anyway: a student council fundraiser for suicide prevention, upcoming games that are deemed extra important, the arrival of an Italian exchange student. There's also a handful of the usual nonsense to sift through, including overly romantic couples wanting to place relationship announcements and rumors about who was caught doing what in which bathroom. The bathroom submissions occasionally yield something newsworthy, which makes reading them a necessity, but mostly, they make me feel sorry for the janitors, who probably have no idea what stories those stalls could tell.

An anonymous submission with the subject line *Emma wasn't at a sleepover* catches my eye. I click it, heart racing, and find exactly nothing in the body of the message. Shit.

I text Ravi—*Gonna call you, pause your game*—and give him two minutes before FaceTiming him.

"Check this out." I flip the camera so he can see the message.

"That's interesting. And random enough that it might even be true. Any way we can trace it?"

"Yeah, if you're the police." I switch the camera back to front-facing. "But if it's true, that means Emma's whereabouts would've been unaccounted for from Friday afternoon on. They had a game, right, so we know she was seen at the school. But after that, if she wasn't at Victoria's, she could've been anywhere."

"Why would Vic and Lily lie about the sleepover though?"

"No clue. They must've been covering for her, helping her hide something."

Ravi's dark brows come together. "Or—and don't freak out, I'm just playing devil's advocate—maybe Emma lied to them too so that no one would know where she was while she killed herself. Maybe to avoid interruption." He cuts me off before I can protest. "Objectivity means considering all the options, even the ones you don't like. We can't force facts to fit the theory; the theory has to fit the facts."

"Thank you, Sherlock." Sometimes I really want to stab him. "Putting motive aside for a second, who would know Emma wasn't at Vic's?"

"Vic, obviously. And Lily, presumably."

"And whoever she was with."

"Assuming she was with someone."

"And whoever killed her."

"Assuming they killed her Friday night."

"Which they didn't."

"What? How do you know that?"

"Her feet. Again. Always the damn feet. She was…fresh when we found her. If she had been lying in the woods for almost two days, I think she would've looked a little more…decomposey."

"Decomposey," Ravi repeats. "That's what we're going with?"

I glare at him, then put on my snootiest on-air anchor voice. "I believe there would have been more evidence of advanced decomposition, particularly in the extremities. Better?"

He laughs. "Nah, I like decomposey."

"You're gonna be decomposey. But seriously, I'll need to research it to be sure, but I don't think she would've looked so intact if it had happened Friday night, regardless of whether it was her own work or someone else's."

"So, the question becomes where was she between the time she left the soccer game and the time we found her in the woods."

"Precisely. It completely changes the timeline."

"Do we go to the cops with this?" He doesn't sound excited by the prospect.

I consider this for a moment. "Not yet. We need to confirm it first. I wish we could get the autopsy report. I want to know more about the marks Mrs. Morgan mentioned. If they're needle marks, I could be right about Owen being a poisoner. Although, statistically speaking, women are more likely than men to use poison as a weapon." I wonder if we've inadvertently missed a whole pool of suspects based on gender.

Ravi chuckles, more than a little ruefully. "Ah, Saturday night conversations with your best mate. Normal teenagers are out getting drunk or getting laid, and we're discussing the finer points of murder."

"You love it."

"I don't hate it," he concedes. "Normal is vastly overrated."

"You got that right."

"So, plan?"

"Talk to Vic and Lily. Vic especially. I'm debating whether I message her on Instagram now or wait until Monday and do it in person."

"Hold on," Ravi says as his image freezes on the screen. "Let's see… Okay, third option: if you want to do it in person, I know where to find her."

"Do I look remotely prepared to leave the house?" I pan the camera down to my outfit, which consists of an oversized T-shirt and my very favorite flannel hedgehog pants.

"I'd be seen with you. Anyway, just saying it's an option. She's posting pictures from Jacob's as we speak."

I make a snap decision and lay the phone on my desk so Ravi has a view of the ceiling while I yank my shirt off. "You know what? That actually might be worthwhile. Let's do it."

"Seriously?"

"Seriously. Get dressed. Round-robin and meet behind The Donut Hole. Fifteen minutes?"

Ravi agrees and hangs up.

Round-robin is code for telling each set of parents we'll be at the other's house. The key to its success is the fact that it's built upon years of friendship filled with completely legitimate unscheduled visits and the fact that we rarely deploy it. It's mostly for emergency-only use. The last time was when Ravi snuck out on a date with an older girl he didn't want to introduce to his parents, and I had to rescue their drunk asses. It's not a scenario I care to repeat.

I don't waste time picking clothes and throw on my version of the outfit Cassidy passed on. Skinny jeans, a long-sleeve shirt, and a cardigan will do fine. I tousle my hair into something that looks halfway deliberate, stuff my phone in my pocket, and announce that I'm going to Ravi's when I'm already halfway out the door.

At The Donut Hole, I lock The Planet and climb into Ravi's passenger seat. He looks like he just threw his battered old leather jacket over what he already had on, but somehow it works. Boys have it so easy.

"I'm not sure Jacob's gonna be psyched that we're crashing his party," I say as we drive through the quiet streets.

"We're not crashing. It's open invite." He turns onto a road with no streetlights, and the high beams struggle to push back the dark. "We just usually skip this sort of thing."

"I'm not planning to make a night of it. We find Vic—and hopefully Kylie while we're at it—ask our questions, and go."

Jacob lives on the outskirts of town, in a double-wide trailer situated in a clearing at the end of a long dirt driveway. Haphazardly parked cars line one side of it, and I say a quick prayer to the patron saint of stupidity that I won't be reporting on any drunk driving accidents in the morning.

Ravi keeps the speed low as we roll up the rutted driveway to avoid bottoming out or running over any inebriated classmates. The thump of bass grows louder as the glow of the bonfire comes into view. Shrieks and peals of drunken laughter punctuate the music.

"Maybe this wasn't the best idea," I say.

Ravi pulls up alongside a Jeep and parks. "It beats stewing in impotent frustration until Monday."

"Fair enough." I grip the door handle and take a moment to steel myself. "Once more into the breach?"

"Let's do this thing."

We pile out of the car, and I pull the cardigan tighter around me. Ravi notices, shrugs out of his jacket, and wraps it around me. I burrow in. It's warm from his body and smells surprisingly good—something spicy and complex that's worlds away from Axe body spray. It's not a scent I've noticed on him before.

As we make our way around to the back of the trailer, dodging two couples making out and a boy providing an unpleasantly barfy soundtrack for them, Ravi exchanges greetings and fist bumps with various classmates.

I try to scrutinize his face in the dark. I'm positive the cologne on the jacket is new. "Are we here for research, or did you just dupe me into going on a date?"

"Column A, column B," he says, nudging my shoulder with his own.

"You're the devil."

"You love it."

I put a finger to my lips in a parody of thought. "What's the saying? You always hurt the ones you love?" I lunge at him, pinching the back of his arm hard enough to make him yelp, and giggle. Victory is mine.

He stops to rub his arm. "I don't know why I take you anywhere."

I hook my arm through his wounded one and tug him along. "So we can find a murderer and be hero reporters."

"Okay, yeah, that." He adjusts his arm so we're linked comfortably at the elbow, like we're off to see the wizard.

I want to make a joke about it, start skipping, but I don't.

It's an experiment, the arm thing. Just to see what it's like to walk this way in the dark, snuggled in his good-smelling coat, like a proper couple on a maybe-date. It's nice. Nicer than I want to admit, maybe. I know it can't be real, for so many reasons. It's not worth risking a literal lifetime of friendship over something destined to fail. But just for a minute, it's nice to pretend.

A monstrous bonfire lights up the field behind the trailer. Groups of students sit in clusters around the roaring inferno, and others are reduced to mere smudges of shapes in the darkness beyond the blaze. It's a miracle they don't burn the woods down.

"Keep your eyes peeled for Vic," I say.

We pass Jacob on the way to the fire. He's got two open bottles of beer in each hand and a sway in his step that makes me wonder if he drank all four himself. Any thoughts I had of reinterviewing him vanish. This is definitely not the time.

Jacob smiles at us. "Oh, you're here too. Cool, cool." He waves a hand at us and foam spills over the top of one of the bottles. "Have a drink?"

I shake my head. "No th—"

"Sure, thanks," Ravi says, his voice louder than mine, dropping my arm to relieve Jacob of two of the bottles. He hands one to me, mouthing, *"When in Rome."* I set mine on a flat spot near my feet as Ravi raises his bottle to Jacob in a toast. "Good turnout, man."

Jacob shrugs. "'S okay. Nothing better to do."

"Hey, have you seen Victoria around?"

Jacob nods and starts to gesture with the hand still holding a pair of bottles but catches himself. "Yeah, yeah. Over there. Somewhere. Cornhole maybe?"

Ravi claps him on the shoulder. "Thanks, man."

We slip past our host in the direction he pointed, but he follows along, asking, "Have you found the truth?"

I curse his drunkenness, not wanting the entire party to know we're here to inquire about Emma. Ravi nudges me ahead. "Go. I'll deal with him."

Thank god. "You're my very favorite human."

"I know."

Jacob grabs my arm before I can make my escape. "You have to find out why. It's not right. It's not right. She was better than that. Better than us. You have to find out what really happened."

"That's what we're doing." Ravi hooks an arm around Jacob's shoulders. "We're working on it. Did you remember something? Maybe about someone giving her a hard time?"

Jacob shakes his head, the movement rippling down the rest of his body. "She shouldn't be dead. I don't want her to be dead."

"Yeah, I know, man. None of us do." Ravi gives me a *What can you do?* look. I'm going to owe him big-time for taking this one for the team.

I melt back into the darkness, Jacob's plaintive voice trailing after me, and go in search of Victoria. My eyes adjust enough that I can see the silhouettes beyond the bonfire do appear to be pitching beanbags at targets, which they can't possibly see, but judging by their laughter, they don't much care.

I pick my way around the edge of the fire, noting who's gathered where, and make my way to the cornhole game beyond. As I get closer, the glow sticks looped around the holes on the boards come into view, and there's a decent crowd surrounding the game. I try to make out which player could be Victoria, but it's impossible to tell.

What I can make out, even from a distance, is that one player, a girl, is playing from a wheelchair.

Chapter Twenty

"**WHAT THE** hell are you doing here?" I ask my sister, not caring that I'm causing a scene.

"What are *you* doing here?" Cassidy giggles in the flickering light of the fire, but her face goes quickly serious. "Wait. Are you checking up on me? Seriously? I'm allowed to have a life, you know."

"This is your version of a life? Drunken parties with people older and stupider than you?"

"You're here. Guess you fit both categories." Cassidy folds her arms across her chest.

"You told me you were going to dinner and a movie."

"And I changed my mind during dinner." Her voice has an edge I usually only hear her use to address misbehaving horses.

A figure approaches from the other end of the game—a guy. Bryce. He has his hands jammed in his pockets and his shoulders drawn up.

"Don't you even start," I tell him. "I trusted you to take care of her."

"I can take care of myself," Cassidy protests. "I really can. I'm the one who convinced Bryce to come, not the other way around."

Bryce looks like he wants the ground to swallow him whole, and I can absolutely picture Cassidy badgering him into doing what she wanted.

"Look," Cassidy says, softer, almost pleading, "I'm still planning to make curfew. This is okay. It is. I'm not shooting up heroin. I'm not even doing shots."

"I'm stone-sober," Bryce says. "I swear. I know I'm driving her home."

I look between them, regretting this excursion with every ounce of my being. A bottle glints on the ground near Cassidy's chair, and I pick it up. A hard lemonade, nearly empty. "Are you drunk?"

"Maybe." Cassidy giggles again. "But only from that. It's all I've had, cross my heart. I think I'm a lightweight."

I want to laugh at the profound disappointment in that final declaration, but I don't. "You realize Mom and Dad—especially Dad—will never let you leave the house again if they find out about this? If you come home drunk, I'm not covering for you."

"But you *are* covering for me?"

I sigh. "I never saw you. I wasn't here. You weren't here. No one was here."

Cassidy squeals. "Thank you, thank you! Now go away, fun-stealer. No, wait. Why *are* you here?"

"I'm looking for Victoria. Have you seen her?"

"Yeah, she played the last game with us. Took off with Abel when they lost though. I fucking rock at this game, by the way."

"Well, if riding falls through, you can always be a cornholer. Any idea where they went?"

"House, I think. She had to pee and refused to go in the woods. Said she didn't want poison ivy all up her ass."

"Yeah, no one wants that." I pin Bryce and my sister with separate glares. "Be home on time."

Cassidy salutes, and Bryce nods earnestly. I leave them to their game, hoping I won't regret it.

I find Victoria sitting atop the thin metal railing that rings the trailer's tiny porch. She's staring at the sky and swinging her feet in a way that makes me think of Humpty Dumpty. I approach carefully, afraid of startling her into falling from her narrow perch. "Hey, Vic."

Victoria's eyes find my face, and there's a pause while she struggles to focus. "Oh, Kennedy. Hi. Cool party, right?"

"Yeah, it's great. You got a sec? I was wondering if I could talk to you."

"I'm just waiting for Abel." She waves a breezy hand, and the motion almost sends her toppling. She laughs, catching herself just in time, and slides off the railing onto unstable feet. "Screw him though, right? Boys. Fuck 'em."

Before I can respond to that burst of vehemence, we're forced to squeeze to the side as the trailer door slams open and disgorges a pack of laughing boys.

"See," Victoria says, slurring the word into a *shh* sound. She crinkles her nose. "Boys."

"That they are." I have exactly zero interest in whatever boy drama Victoria has brewing and wonder if she's in any state to answer serious questions. The best I can hope is that she's a chatty drunk and that the booze will loosen her up enough to tell the secrets she kept during our interview. "Want to take a walk?"

Victoria hooks an overly friendly arm through mine and leans heavily on me. "Yes. Let's go away from the boys."

I lead her down the steps and away from the crowd, letting her prattle about how she thinks Abel's cheating on her and how he's definitely getting high right now even though he promised not to. For someone who doesn't want to talk about boys, she sure has a lot to say on the subject.

I wait until we're at the edge of the forest, well away from the ears of the others, and ask, "Vic, can I ask you a couple questions about Emma?"

She staggers a bit and tightens her hold on my arm. "Oh god, Emma. I just wanted to forget Emma for a few minutes. Just a few minutes. Is that awful of me? I thought a few drinks would quiet her down a little, right? But she's still there, still in my head."

I keep walking, knowing motion can sometimes make it easier to talk. I also hope it has a sobering effect on drunk girls. "When was the last time you saw Emma?"

"The game. It was so bad. We got our asses handed to us."

I don't want a rehash of the entire game and forestall the possibility by asking, "What happened after the game? Did you guys go out? Get food or something?"

"Emma was supposed to come back to my house. We were gonna have a spa night—do masks and manicures and have ice cream."

"But you didn't, did you?" I ask it gently, without judgment, but Victoria moans like she's been punched in the stomach. I really hope she's not about to barf.

Victoria lurches to a stop, drops my arm, and sinks to the ground in a heap.

I swallow a sigh and crouch beside the weeping girl. "It's okay. Just breathe. You can talk to me."

"I lied." Victoria draws in a hitching breath and sniffles hard. "I lied. There was no sleepover. There was supposed to be, but Emma canceled at the last minute, told me to cover for her. I was a little pissed—I'd bought all sorts of stuff for our spa night—but I did it anyway. I always covered for her, right? I figured she was meeting Owen like she usually did."

"But she didn't?"

"She told me not to mention anything to him and was real serious about it. I should've told though. I should've told someone how weird she was being. The texts didn't sound like her at all." She curls in on herself, almost disappearing in the dark. "I let my best friend kill herself. I gave her the chance to sneak off instead of helping her."

I groan inwardly. I have no desire to do what I'm about to, but it might be the only thing that jolts any sense into the person who may have been the last one to talk to Emma before she died. On the plus side, Victoria is drunk enough that she might not remember this conversation anyway. It's a risk I'll have to take. "Vic, I'm not so sure Emma killed herself."

The result is instantaneous. Victoria flies up from her fetal position and grabs at me in the dark. "What do you mean? It was an accident? Or did someone else kill her? Did I let my friend get murdered?"

Oh shit. That's not the road I meant to send her down. "You didn't do anything," I assure her. "None of this is your fault."

"Then why do I feel so awful?" She's close to dissolving again.

"Because brains are stupid." I vow never to do a drunk interview again. "Do you still have the texts?"

"Yeah, of course. And screenshots of all our DMs and like two voice mails from when she called. I can't delete it."

"No, of course not. Can I see the texts? It might be helpful."

"You think? Really?" The hope in her voice is heartbreaking.

"It's possible."

Victoria fumbles around and manages to free her phone from her back pocket. She hits the home button, and the glow of the screen is blinding in so much blackness. She adjusts the brightness, squinting against the glare, and opens her texts. She finds the correct ones and hands the device over. "See? It's weird. It doesn't sound like her at all."

I scroll to the start of the day of Emma's disappearance and read a string of hyperbolic messages about how she was on her period and wanted to kill her mother for not letting her have chocolate in the house and how she might literally die before she could get an ice cream bar at lunch. Next is a detailed list of self-care plans for the evening's sleepover and messages about leaving class early to get changed for the game because she was *sooooo bored* in Directed Study.

The time stamps show a jump of several hours between that text and the next, and Victoria's right. There's a shift, however slight. Emma's earlier texts were run-on sentences, punctuated only with strings of emojis, but the two texts that come after are clipped to the point of being taciturn.

The first reads: *Can't make it. Sorry. Pretend I'm there.*

Victoria had responded by asking: *But spa night!!! [crying face] Is it Owen? Again?*

Emma's response was delayed by nearly ten minutes. *No. Do not mention this to him. If anyone asks, I was with you. Will explain later.*

Victoria had responded: *fine, whatev.*

I know the period meant she was pissed. There are six more outgoing texts from Victoria, inquiring about her friend's whereabouts the following day and asking her to check in with varying degrees of concern.

But nothing else from Emma.

I hand the phone back, ready to bet my arm that the final texts from Emma had been sent under duress or from another person entirely. The killer. What I wouldn't give to lay my hands on Emma's phone.

"See?" Victoria asks, still sniffling. "It's like she was possessed."

"It is weird," I agree. "Vic, is there anything else you haven't told me about Emma? Anything at all?"

"Like what?" Victoria, in her drunkenness, might be eager to help, but she's not very good at it.

"Do you know if she was into drugs at all? Hanging out with anyone new? Or anyone that was bothering her?"

"I don't think so. She wasn't like that. She was perfect. She went out with Owen and hung out with me and Lil. She had her internship. I mean, maybe something happened there—her aunt would know—but I think Em would've told us about any creepers. She was really happy there. She was dying to be on TV."

I hear her clap her hand over her mouth at the turn of phrase, but I pretend not to notice. "That's what I heard."

"You wanted it too," Victoria says in a way that most definitely is not a question. "That's what Emma said. She was glad she beat you. I know she's—she *was*—my best friend, but she could be like that sometimes, right? Everything was a competition for her."

I do an acknowledge-and-set-aside with the flashes of jealousy threatening to crop up, reminding myself that I have plenty of mentors, run my own news site, and don't have to be confined by corporate standards. On good days, I can convince myself I dodged a bullet, but sitting in Jacob's field with a tearful Victoria, I can't help but wonder if that bullet had been more literal than I thought.

The Making of a Monster
Continued

The boy decided junior year would be different. God had come through on His end of the bargain, and the boy had read all the promised pages and more. He sought out the Old Testament, just to have new pages to read, to prove how grateful he was. Without consulting anyone, he took the clippers they used on the dog and buzzed his head down to the scalp. He had an okay-shaped head under all that hair, and his eyes looked wider than ever. Almost nice, even. He told his mother he wanted contact lenses instead of the plastic glasses he hid behind and let his sister choose new back-to-school clothes since he had outgrown everything he owned.

He didn't just look like a new person; he felt like one. For the first time ever, he was optimistic about the start of school.

At first, no one noticed, or if they did, they didn't say so. It wasn't until first period when they were waiting for the teacher to get started that he heard someone whisper, 'Hey, who's the new kid?' and his heart soared. He felt reborn. He turned around to see who had been wondering and locked eyes with the actual new kid. A girl. A pretty girl.

One of the monsters caught him looking and sneered, then told him to fuck off. His face flushed, straight to the top of his freshly shorn head. His overgrown body suddenly felt too big for the desk, crammed in tight like the boy in the locker. He was barely aware of the teacher talking as he silently asked God why. Why did this feel so much like it used to?

Chapter Twenty-one

WHEN I pull in to school on Monday, I know something is very wrong.

For one thing, the buses driving away from the school are still full of students, but that's not what sets the hair on my neck on end.

It's the row of police cars, along with an ambulance and a fire truck, that are parked outside the school's entrance. Teachers stand in small huddles near cars and along the walkways, and I could almost believe it's a fire drill if not for the early hour, the fleeing buses, and the fact that the ambulance has its lights flashing.

"What the hell?" I park in our usual spot and turn to Cassidy. "Stay here. Check social media, see if you can find out—"

"Text from Mom," Cassidy says. "School's canceled. Unspecified emergency, details will be released at a later time."

I open the door and hop out. "Start texting. See what rumors are out there. Someone knows what's happening." I hope whatever drama is unfolding is enough to get Kylie to ping the *Monitor's* inbox. "I'm going to see what I can find out."

I debate walking straight into the building, but the police officer at the door sees me coming and shouts, "No school today. You can head home."

"What's going on?" I ask in my best on-air voice, still striding purposefully toward the entrance.

He holds up a hand, halting me with a palm. "Afraid I can't tell you that. Also, can't let you in the building, miss. I'm sure the principal will be in touch later today. For now, head home. Try to enjoy your day off."

I don't push it. Not yet, anyway. I scan the pods of teachers, realizing how distraught they look. Several dab at their eyes as if they're crying.

My chest constricts. Teachers in tears before their classes have even started can't possibly bode well. I spot Mr. Monroe near the tennis courts and jog over, the hammering of my heart having nothing to do with the burst of exercise. "What's going on?"

Mr. Monroe looks slightly taken aback. "Kennedy, dear, we're canceled today. There's been an accident. You shouldn't still be here. A call went out."

The softness of his voice, the fact that he calls me "dear" instead of "Ms. Carter," turns my knees to rubber. "Yeah, my mom texted just as we got here. What's going on?"

Visions of school shootings whiz through my head like bullets, but surely we would've heard about that. The cancellation call would've said if there was an armed intruder; there would've been barricades and more cops. Maplefield doesn't have a large police department, but surely the state cops would send cars if there had been a shooting.

My phone buzzes with a text alert. It's Ravi. *The fuck is going on? We got sent home!*

I don't reply.

"Mr. Monroe, please. What's going on?" He smiles that sad smile adults think is sympathetic but is mostly just patronizing. Anger at being kept in the dark, at being treated like a child, is overriding the lizard-brain fear about who the ambulance is for. "I have a right to know what's going on. As a student and as a reporter. The *Monitor's* readers will expect a story."

He meets my eyes. "And you'll get it to them. Just not yet." He shakes his head, breaking our gaze. "You're not gonna want this one, Carter."

The rubber band feeling in my knees intensifies, but I keep the on-air mask on. "Why not?"

"We can't discuss it yet."

"Off the record?"

He gives me a look. "At all. Look around. You see any other press here? No." He holds an arm out as if to guide me back to the parking lot. "Let it rest, Carter. Take your sister home. There will be plenty of time for stories later."

"This is obstruction," I say, but Mr. Monroe only chuckles.

"Get used to it. Uncooperative witnesses and tight-lipped police forces are facts of investigative life."

"Can you at least tell me if we're having school tomorrow?"

"To my knowledge, yes, but at this point, I know little more than you do."

"Which is still more."

When he doesn't offer anything else, I turn to go. I know when I'm being stonewalled and hope Cassidy has learned something through the rumor mill.

I consider ducking around the back of the building to sneak in that way, but Mr. Monroe is still watching me. I wave at him, more to show I know he's thwarting me than in farewell, and pick a route that goes by the school entrance instead of straight to the car.

And luck is finally on my side. The officer who had been manning the door is gone.

I'm about to go in when I see the EMTs coming down the hall, a stretcher between them and the cop who'd banished me walking alongside it. The EMTs move a lot slower than the ones on TV, and I wonder if maybe they hadn't been needed after all.

I step out of the door and into the bushes to make room for the trio—and to avoid being caught—and watch as the cop holds the door open and the first EMT backs out, guiding her end of the stretcher through the opening. The stretcher is draped in black.

No, not draped.

Something black rests on the stretcher, atop the white sheet. Something big.

The second EMT emerges, and the cop lets the door whoosh shut.

I don't realize how far I've backed into the bushes until a branch scratches my cheek. I brush it away, barely noticing. All I can focus on is the stretcher being loaded into the back of the ambulance and the body bag that's securely strapped to it.

I DRIVE home in a fog as Cassidy runs through the rumors she's dug up: a gas leak; a shooting; an electrical fire; Henry bit someone; someone died; Ms. Larson died. I don't confirm that she's right—someone did die.

I texted Ravi to meet me at home, and he's waiting when we arrive. "Any news?" he asks.

I give a tight shake of my head as I wait for Cassidy to transfer herself out the car. The conversation I need to have with Ravi is not for her ears.

As she wheels herself up the ramp—she always insists on going first, even though she never has the key—she says, "Savannah and Janice are coming over. Can Bryce come too?"

"Negative, Ghost Rider." I unlock the front door and let her go through. "Savannah and Janice fine, but I'm not being responsible for you having boys over without the parentals' permission."

Cassidy pouts. "You get to have Ravi over. How is that even fair?"

"Because there's exactly zero chance that I'm gonna make out with Ravi. Or worse."

"Hey," Ravi says. "I resent that. I'm very make-out-with-able."

"You kind of are," Cassidy says, and he winks at her.

"Cass, that's gross. He's like family."

"Again with the resentment," he says.

My patience for the whole conversation is fraying rapidly. "Look, Savannah and Janice only. I'll give you takeout money. Get it delivered. I'll let Mom know you're here and with who. Have Bryce over for dinner if you want."

"Can we have takeout for dinner too?"

"Not my division. That's Mom's call. If Bryce's coming over, let's hope so, for his sake."

"Where are you going?"

"Out. With Ravi. Call me if you need me. Just don't burn the house down or anything."

Cass salutes. "Captain Fun-Stealer till the end."

"House fires—not as fun as you'd think," Ravi says while I go raid my cash stash. "The mess alone, plus the paperwork. You want small fires. Like dumpsters. Or trash cans."

"Not helping!" I shout from the hall.

"Trash fires only—got it," Cassidy says.

I return and hand her a pile of fives that she takes with a wicked smile.

"Oooh, maybe I'll buy drugs with this."

I glare at her. "You are the literal worst."

"I know. Go. I'll be good, promise. No drugs, no fires, no fun."

"And no boys."

"That fell under the 'fun' category."

I manage to wait until I'm in Ravi's car and at the end of the street before breaking. I drop my head back against the seat, scrub my face with my hands, and blow out a hard breath that's shakier than I'd have liked. With eyes closed, I press steepled fingers to my lips, not praying, but thinking. Organizing. Setting aside feelings in favor of facts.

First fact: "There's another body."

The car swerves slightly, and I know without opening my eyes that Ravi turned to look at me. "At the school? Who?"

"Don't know. Don't like not knowing." I recount the events of the morning, keeping my eyes closed to visualize every detail, trying to find a clue I overlooked.

"Shit."

We drive in silence for a few minutes, both lost in thought, until Ravi says, "We can't jump to conclusions. It could be something innocuous like a janitor slipping on a wet floor and hitting his head or Mr. Allard having another heart attack."

I drop my hands in my lap and open my eyes. "Or it could be another murder."

"Or a suicide. There's that correlation between highly publicized suicides and increased attempts."

"Or a suicide." None of these options are good. Even if Emma's death wasn't a suicide, almost everyone seems to think it was thanks to the note, and that alone might be enough to push someone else into ending their own life. If that's what happened, then it's all the more reason we have to prove Emma was murdered. I don't want impressionable underclassmen making stupid decisions just because they thought it worked for the popular senior.

When we arrive at The Donut Hole, the place is packed. Almost as packed as the day of Emma's search party. Some of the crowd are students in search of sugar to fuel their bonus day off, but many of the customers are adults, who take up the front counters and the few tables with coffees and laptops. They're too late to be part of the morning commuter rush, and besides, they definitely don't look like they're rushing to be anywhere. Press, perhaps, waiting on news from the school?

"So much for a quiet hangout," Ravi says.

Mr. Burman spots us and grins. "Ah, my two favorite people. Tell me you're here to help. We have an unexpected boon happening."

We retreat to the kitchen, leaving the counter girl to deal with the line.

"We have another death at Maplefield," Ravi tells him quietly.

His father's eyes widen. "Oh heavens, not another child?"

"We don't know," I say. "You haven't overheard anything from the crowd?"

"I wasn't listening for anything like that. How do you know?" He turns to Ravi. "When your mother called, she said there were no details—just that it was a day off and not to be surprised if I saw you."

"Kennedy was at the school. She got in before they blocked off the driveway."

"And where were you?"

Ravi waves the question off like it isn't worth considering given everything else. "Late. Priya had a hair crisis. Kennedy saw the stretcher with a body bag on it. None of the teachers would say who it was."

Mr. B steps forward and crushes me in a shocking hug. "That must've been awful. I'm sorry you had to see that. Shame on that school for letting students witness such a thing."

I wiggle free, not wanting to admit that I'm fully responsible for seeing what I saw. "It's okay. I didn't see much, really. Just a black bag."

Just a black bag draped around a body that was far too small to be Mr. Allard, who had to weigh three hundred pounds.

I curse myself.

I'd seen, but I hadn't observed.

Chapter Twenty-two

"I T'S A student," I say. "I'm sure of it. Maybe a small teacher, like Mrs. Garrison, but I'll bet money it's not."

Ravi looks skeptical. "A body bag isn't going to give you an accurate depiction of what's inside."

"No, but they come in sizes." Like Sherlock, I am an omnivorous reader with a strangely retentive memory for trifles. I hoard random knowledge for occasions like this when it proves useful. "This one wasn't large. It's definitely not a grown man."

We're sitting on overturned milk crates behind the bakery with steaming mugs of cocoa to ward off the day's chill. We pass a grease-stained paper bag of donut holes between us, sugar being vital to quality deductions.

"And the amount of police present makes me think it wasn't an accident. If someone fell down the stairs and broke their neck, they wouldn't need that many cops. Maybe one, because it's a death on school grounds. But the whole force wouldn't show up."

"What about the fire truck?"

I pop a donut in my mouth and chew thoughtfully. "Not sure. It might be part of a protocol we don't know about."

"There were no signs of fire?"

"Not that I noticed."

My phone dings, signaling another message landing in the *Monitor's* inbox. Almost all of them have suggested we investigate at the school, as if that hadn't occurred to us. Some had offered the "real story" about why we have the day off, but all the stories conflicted. I open the latest, and the donut turns to rock in my stomach. I turn the phone so Ravi can see.

"A girl died in the auditorium. My mom's friend is a teacher, and she told her," he reads. "Shit."

It's an anonymous tip, of course, and never in my life have I regretted providing that option as much as I do now. I'd give anything to be able to track the sender and have someone specific to question.

"It fits," I say. "The body bag was the right size for a girl."

The grim reality of another lost student makes us both quiet. I open my texts and send a message to Kylie: *Any insight into the situation at school?* It feels too crass to reference the death in a text, but if anyone can identify who it was before the press, it'll be Kylie. If she bothers replying.

I scroll through social media, but so far, there's no indication that anyone knows who died. In fact, based on the nonsense that's posted, it appears no one even knows anyone died at all.

Which is suspicious in and of itself. Maplefield isn't a huge school. Several students have family members who work there or in the elementary and middle schools that feed to it. Surely someone knows something. The question is: why aren't they talking?

If we want answers, we're going to have to get them ourselves. I stand and push the milk crate against the building with my foot. "Let's swing by the school. I want to see if it's still blocked off."

Ravi shrugs. "Sure. Why wouldn't we want to go to school after we've already been sent home for the day?"

"Like you have anything better to do." I grab his mug and dash the cocoa dregs onto the pavement. I sneak both mugs back in the kitchen, drop them in the sink, and scoot out before Mr. B can put us to work.

The school's driveway is clear of barricades and police cars, and the parking lot is all but deserted. Ms. Larson's Subaru sits in the principal's spot, and only four other cars, none of which I recognize, keep it company. An empty police car is parked in the fire lane.

Ravi parks. "If we get suspended or arrested or anything, my parents are gonna flip."

"We're not going to get in trouble for being at school. I just want to talk to Ms. Larson."

"We might when we were expressly told not to be here," he says but follows me anyway.

There isn't a police guard at the front door anymore, but the doors themselves are shut and locked. I press the buzzer, but nothing happens. I try again—a longer buzz that's sure to irritate anyone within earshot.

I look up at the camera mounted above the door and wave, knowing it's probably futile. It's common knowledge that the few cameras the building has are only for show, a fact famously confirmed by a ninth-grade boy who systematically mooned each one and was only reprimanded when the video his friend took of the experiment hit YouTube.

"Oh, come on. I know someone can hear me." I cup my hands against the glass in the door and peer in, trying to spot someone who can open the door, but the hall is empty.

"We can try the back."

I clap him on the shoulder, grinning. "That's the spirit."

We set off around the building, looking into windows of darkened classrooms as we go. The place is a ghost town.

The rear parking lot holds only a single car, and whoever it is has gone in the back entrance and—a miracle of miracles—pegged the door with the edge of a pockmarked wooden doorstop.

"Jackpot."

Ravi hesitates. "This feels like sneaking in."

"Because it is. Come on. Don't wimp out now. You're the one who said try the back."

"I'm full of bad ideas."

"It's part of your charm. C'mon."

We leave the doorstop wedged where we found it and set off down the hall. The only sound is the soft squeak of our sneakers on the tiled floor. The hallway lights are off, and the high windows offer only dim illumination thanks to the cloudy skies.

"This is weird," Ravi whispers. "It's so quiet."

"Because you're whispering," I say, but my voice is barely audible either. It seems wrong, somehow, to break the silence of the abandoned building.

By unspoken agreement, we head in the direction of the main office. If anyone has answers, it'll be Ms. Larson. Of course, if she were in the office, she should've heard us ringing the buzzer, but I don't know where else to start.

"This feels like a horror movie," Ravi says. "I keep expecting zombies."

"That'd be a story." But I get it. The rows of lockers loom like silent sentries, wardens watching our progress. Even in the days following Emma's death, when it seemed like the entire school was subdued, the building was still full of life and movement. It was nothing like the utter stillness that surrounds us now.

Ravi turns the corner just ahead of me and slams to a halt, thrusting an arm out like a mother trying to restrain her kid after hitting the brakes too hard.

Light spills from beneath the auditorium doors, leaving bright puddles on the shadowed floor, but that isn't what caused Ravi's sharp intake of breath.

The auditorium's entrance is marked with an X of yellow crime scene tape.

Ravi, for want of his camera, pulls his phone out and snaps a photo. It's as automatic as breathing for him; the barrier of the camera matters, even if it's only on a cell phone. I leave him standing there and creep up to the closed door.

"No, Kennedy, get back here," Ravi whispers, rooted to his spot.

Keeping to the side of the door, I peek through the glass. The stage and seating lights are turned up as high as they go, bathing the room in a brightness that's shocking after the dim corridors and shuttered classrooms. I see no one. I crane my neck, trying to get a better view, and feel Ravi hovering at my elbow. I don't get it. There's nothing here that indicates a crime scene. There's nothing that indicates any kind of scene at all.

Emboldened by this lack of, well, anything, I try the door handle. Ravi's hand closes on my arm, pulling me back, but the handle turns easily, and I shake him off. As I ease the door open, a single bark echoes from somewhere beyond, startling me so completely that I nearly knock Ravi over as I jump.

Henry. It has to be Henry, but I don't see him, don't see anyone, and my heart is galloping like a spooked horse at the sheer unexpectedness of another's presence.

"This is a bad idea." Ravi drags me away from the closing door. "Let's go."

"No, we're here for information," I protest, but he's already propelling me down the hall.

There comes a soft whoosh of the door opening behind us and a rustle of plastic. "Who's there?"

Claws click on the floor tiles as Henry trots up, tail wagging. I stop and Ravi stifles a groan as he does too.

Ms. Larson looks as startled as I was just moments ago. "Kennedy? Ravi? What are you doing?"

I try to act calmer than I am. "Looking for you, actually."

"You shouldn't be here. School is closed for the day." She sounds tired and irritated and nothing like her usual self.

"I know, and I'm sorry to intrude. We were just concerned." I need to stay on Ms. Larson's good side. "We've been hearing rumors all day about what happened, and I thought you'd be able to tell us something." I gesture at the crime scene tape on the auditorium doors, one half now dangling in the open space. "Was there a crime?"

Ms. Larson sighs. "There wasn't a crime. The tape is just to stop people from entering. There was…an incident."

"Another death?"

Ms. Larson regards us for what feels like forever in the silence of the hall. "Where did you hear that?"

"Around. Like I said, rumors have been flying. And because of the *Monitor*, I'm hearing them all. I just want to know the truth."

Ms. Larson nods once, sharp and decisive. "Let's go to my office."

I shoot Ravi a surprised glance, but we follow her down the hall. Once inside, at Ms. Larson's insistence, we take seats at the small conference table, which Henry settles himself under.

"Tell me what you've heard," she says.

"Rumors. Everything from fires to school shootings to suicide."

Ms. Larson purses her lips, igniting a starburst of wrinkles around her mouth. She glances at the clock on the wall. "I've been sitting in the back of the auditorium for over an hour trying to decide what to say in the all-call."

The air crackles with unspoken truths, but I hold the silence, wait for Ms. Larson to fill it.

She takes a strawberry candy from the bowl on her desk and unwraps it slowly, like it's a delicate but important task. Then she laughs, sudden and harsh, and there's nothing funny in it. It's a bitter, broken sound and completely unnerving. Ravi presses his knee into mine, and I press back hard, keeping my face neutral. My fingers itch to hold his, to hold on against whatever horror is unhinging Ms. Larson.

She pops the red candy in her mouth. "You'd think the third time would be the charm, right? That there'd be a script. But there isn't. There never is for these things." She pauses, inhales a breath that flares her nostrils wide. When she exhales, it's like she becomes a new person. It's almost eerie. Maybe Ms. Larson has her own version of acknowledge-and-set-aside. "The call will go out as soon as I finish with you both, so I see no harm in being the one to break it to you."

I steel myself, for although I already know someone is dead, a tiny irrational part of me hopes for a different explanation.

"There has been another death." Ms. Larson sounds almost robotic. "And another note."

I don't flinch at the confirmation, but it takes effort. I'm aware of Ravi's leg against mine and the blood in my ears, but I don't waver. "Who was it?"

Ms. Larson takes a long time answering. Long enough for my stomach to tie itself into a noose of fear.

"Who was it, Ms. Larson?"

"Kylie Auger."

Chapter Twenty-three

IT'S WORSE with Kylie.

It shouldn't be—it's not like we were close, not really—but I find myself opening our text history and staring at all the unanswered messages I sent, torturing myself with scenarios of Kylie's final hours.

The rumor mill at school is in a frenzy, and the *Monitor's* inbox is flooded with stories of suicide pacts and internet death games and ritual sacrifice. The halls are just as bad, and it seems like everyone has a theory about how and why it happened.

Ms. Larson gathers everyone for an assembly, but it's held in the gym this time, not the auditorium. We're crammed shoulder to shoulder on the bleachers like this is some kind of morbid pep rally.

The local media are relegated to the side of the bleachers where they can record Ms. Larson's speech. It's evident by the hard set of her features that Ms. Larson was expecting the press and is aware of the controversy they're already stirring up.

A podium is situated on the centerline of the basketball court before the bleachers, and Ms. Larson spends a long time surveying her audience before adjusting the microphone's height.

"I won't say good morning," she begins, "because there is nothing good about this morning."

Murmurs of agreement ripple through the crowd.

"What I will say is that this has to stop. We cannot continue to do this, to have these same meetings and cry these same tears. Maplefield is stronger than this. We need to learn from our mistakes, and we need to come together. This school has lost too many students. Seniors, who had their entire lives ahead of them. I know you joke about a senior curse, but this is no joke. This is not some urban legend. This is real, and this is a problem.

"I call on you, students and faculty of Maplefield, to help me solve it. I have brought in counselors, I have brought in Henry, I have done my best to foster an open and inviting school community where the staff genuinely care about the students in front of them. When I found Kylie, I also found her note. One line: *Now you know what it was like.* But we don't, do we? No one saw it coming any more than we saw Emma or Liam. So I'm calling on you to help me stop it. Help me understand what it is we need to do to stop this from happening again."

I lean into Ravi and whisper, "A murder investigation would be a good start."

Ms. Larson goes on. "I will be leaving suggestion boxes in various places. One will be with the nurse, one in the library, and one outside the main office. I am open to all suggestions. My door is always open. Once again, I implore you to talk *to* each other, not about each other. Talk to your teachers. Talk to the counselors. We are already looking into hiring another full-time adjustment counselor. Your advisory groups will be discussing suicide prevention and sharing some resources in the coming weeks. This is not something we can shy away from, but something we must face head-on. We are Maplefield, and we are stronger than this."

Applause thunders through the gym, and Henry rises from his spot at Ms. Larson's feet to bark twice. The reporters watch it all, and when the assembly is dismissed, they converge on Ms. Larson like a swarm of fire ants.

I DON'T even bother checking in with my Directed Study teacher. I go straight to room 331 when the bell rings.

Ravi is already letting himself in when I get there, and I tell him to lock it behind us. I doubt anyone is planning to sit for photos today anyway.

We leave the lights off and sit with our backs against the cold cinder block wall where we'll be hidden from anyone looking in, much like Ms. Larson had been yesterday in the auditorium.

Ravi slings his bag into his lap and fishes around, extracting a pack of peanut butter cups. He tosses them to me and closes his bag. I open them, take one out, and hand the pack back to him. I finish the candy in three bites, but it doesn't make me feel better.

Ravi nibbles at his, the way he always does, biting the ridged edge off first and saving the middle for last. When the rim is gone, he breaks the remaining part—the best part—in two and holds half out. I open my mouth like a baby bird, and he sets it on my tongue. This bite makes me feel a fraction better.

I close my eyes and lean into Ravi's shoulder, heaving a frustrated sigh at my inability to set aside the emotions clogging up my thought process. He drops an arm around my shoulder, and I allow myself a full minute of self-indulgent burrowing, enjoying the warmth and solidity of his body next to mine. It's a feeling I could wallow in for days, comfortable and comforting all at once, satisfying in a way I imagine sex must be to other people. But thoughts of Kylie crowd my brain like buzzing bees, and I shrug out from under him.

"I fucking hate this," I say. "Just to get that out of the way."

"I know. Me too."

"I hate all of it. I hate that she's fucking dead for no fucking reason. I hate that we didn't stop this in time."

"Whoa. No. Don't even." He spins to face me, dark eyes serious. "Don't. Even. This is not our fault. At all. There is literally nothing we could've done to prevent this."

"We could've caught whoever killed Emma before he got to Kylie." My voice cracks, but I grit my teeth. "I could've caught him. I could've done that. I could've saved her. I could've figured it out."

Ravi grabs my hands and folds them into both of his, shaking his head. Frown lines bracket his full lips like parentheses. "No. God, no. Ken, you couldn't have. Please, love, don't do this to yourself. None of this was your fault."

His eyes are heavy with sadness, and for a disconcerting moment, I can't tell whether it's for me or Kylie. Either way, I close my eyes against the weight of it. That much sympathy, if there's even a chance it was for me, is more than I can acknowledge.

I refuse to break down.

I have a job to do—now, more than ever.

Ravi's hands are warm around mine, his grip tight enough to be an anchor. I focus on that and set aside everything else.

When I open my eyes, I'm steady. I slip my hands free and squeeze his in the quickest of thank-yous before pulling the red notebook from my bag. I flip to a blank page, write Kylie's name at the top and underline it. I feel Ravi watching me but soldier on. I have to do this. "Okay, our biggest problem right now is lack of data. Can't make bricks without clay and all that. With Emma, we had as much information as everyone else. We knew more, even. We had photographs; we had an organized missing person search. With Kylie, we have none of that."

"Which is information in itself, right?" he asks. "Why wasn't she reported missing?"

"Exactly. I've been trying to get ahold of her for days. Where was she? We need to find out. We also need to find out how she died." I write *Last seen when?* then *Manner/cause of death?* a few lines below. "Ms. Larson is calling it suicide, but is that a fact? Was there an obvious method, or was it like Emma? That's important to know." I tap my pen against paper. "We need to get back into the auditorium, see if there are stains. That could be why the auditorium is still closed."

"Or just the general creep factor."

"Or that, but still, we need to check."

"Plan for getting in?"

"To be determined." I make a note, not wanting to get bogged down with details just yet. "We need to establish a timeline like we did for Emma. Social media will help, especially since Kylie posted every minute of her existence, including when she had to poop. We need to figure out when she stopped posting and see if anyone heard from her after that. And determine where she was physically seen last."

"I wonder if there's a way we can check the cameras, see if any were working. If she was found in the school, maybe they picked something up."

I snort. "Yeah, like they were working." But I write *Cameras?* down anyway. "Seems unlikely, but we can try."

Ravi opens his mouth to say something, stops, then says, "Not to sing the same old song, but are we going to entertain that it might actually have been a suicide?"

"No." I'm not even considering it. "Kylie wasn't depressed. Kylie was a dramatic drama queen, but she had to be alive to enjoy the drama. Death would be too dull for her."

"I'm inclined to agree," Ravi admits. "Just felt we had to put it out there."

"And we have. Moving on." I flip back a few pages until I find the one labeled *Suspects*. "If we're going off the assumption that it was the same guy who killed Emma, and I think we should, because even I can't come up with a plausible scenario involving two separate killers targeting Maplefield students within weeks of each other, then we need to find the overlap between who might've wanted them both dead."

I dog-ear the page for easy locating, turn back to Kylie's section, and write *Suspects* atop a fresh page. "Okay. Suspects for Kylie."

I write *Owen* at the top of the list. "She meddled in their relationship."

"Plus, she turned down his promposal last year before he got with Emma. But I don't think that's a murderous offense."

"But stacked on the meddling, maybe. Relationships make people stupid."

Ravi laughs. "You're not wrong. But in that case, we better add Jacob too, since he was part of said relationship meddling."

I do, then tap the paper with the pen, thinking. "This list could get really long if we include everyone who's been pissed off by her gossiping."

"Again with the not being wrong."

I'm tempted to list everyone who might be on that list anyway, just for the sake of thoroughness, but hold off. "I think starting with the people who overlap with Emma makes the most sense. If we don't get anything there, we can add to the list. There might be a connection somewhere we aren't aware of, but we might as well start with the obvious."

Ravi looks at the list, then flips back to Emma's *Suspects* page and back again. "Which leaves us with Owen and Jacob, who we pretty much cleared the first time around."

"Then we missed something. It's Occam's razor. Hoofbeats mean horses, not centaurs. It's got to be one of them."

"Or a genuine psycho. Someone who gets his kicks killing girls. It's not like those don't exist."

"Like Peter Vernon? Kylie's seen him at her church, and I think Emma went there too. It's loose, but it's a connection. If we're considering the possibility of a psycho, we might as well start with the one we know about."

Ravi shakes his head, worry creasing his forehead. "If it's him—and I'm not saying I think it is—that means you'd be on his list. You'd have to be. If there was a girl in this school he'd want dead, it's you."

"Not his type," I counter. "Emma and Kylie are both blond—*were* both blond—and had long hair. They were both thin. They were both the same kind of pretty. I don't fit that profile. Plus, I'm too stubborn to die."

"And Emma was too bitchy to die, and Kylie was too dramatic to die. Yet here we are." He shoves his hair off his forehead. He starts to speak, then stops, the muscles along his jaw flexing. When he meets my gaze, his eyes are dark with imagined horror. He shakes his head, but it does nothing to dislodge the haunted look. "I couldn't bear it. Not if it were you."

My first instinct is to make a joke, but I can't find one, not when the tightness in my chest is back. In fact, I can't speak at all under the realization that the look he's giving me isn't just fear. It's love. And as much as I know love is a problem—an interference, a weakness among those for whom objectivity is of the highest importance—I want to fall into it. I want to tangle myself in it the way Sherlock and Moriarty tangled on the Reichenbach and throw myself over the edge in the same way, locked in its embrace.

Instead, I hold a pinkie out and wait for him to hook it with his own. The place where our fingers meet is charged with everything I'm not ready to give into, but I keep my composure. I have to, if I'm going to solve this. I give him what I hope is a wry smile and pretend he's not seeing straight through it. "I solemnly swear not to get ax-murdered."

In my head, I add a vow to stop anyone else from getting murdered too. Then, and only then, can I deal with the emotions swirling through me like rapids.

Chapter Twenty-four

BREAKING INTO the auditorium is harder than either of us anticipated.

The doors are locked, as we knew they would be, but I figured the key for 331 probably opened more than just that door, and indeed, it slipped into the lock like it had been made for it.

But when I turned it, nothing happened.

"You knew that would be too easy," Ravi says.

"Just once, I could stand for something to be too easy."

We have a limited window of time to get inside before any evidence gets erased by the janitors, and a quick perusal of YouTube convinces me lock-picking is a skill I desperately need to have in my arsenal, but not one that can be learned in a day.

I consider and quickly dismiss the idea of simply asking Ms. Larson to let us in. She's too unlikely to agree, and drawing that attention would only complicate the break-in.

So we stalk the janitors.

The school employs three people—two men and a woman who oversees them—to clean and maintain the building. Miss Caroline, the head, works regular school hours and hands things over to the men at the end of the day. They share a suite of rooms consisting of a cluttered office-break room—the door is always open so no one feels like they're bothering Miss Caroline during the day—and storage areas for various pieces of maintenance equipment.

Miss Caroline always says hi when she sees me in the halls, having been a subject of the *Unsung Heroes* series I ran in ninth grade about the custodians, cafeteria workers, and bus drivers that served

Maplefield. Ravi had taken black-and-white portraits to go with each profile, and it ended up being a surprisingly popular piece.

That doesn't mean we have the kind of relationship that would convince the woman to let us into an unauthorized area, but I spent enough time with the head custodian during the shadowing portion of the interview to know where the spare keys live.

Getting them will just be a matter of timing.

The custodial suite is on the first floor, tucked in an alcove near the gym. Since we have no plausible reason to be in the gym, we park ourselves at the top of the stairs, which doesn't give us a direct line of sight to the break room, but lets us watch the hallway leading up to it.

If I remember correctly, the shift change happens at 3:30, and our best chance will be right when the second-shift guys leave to begin their rounds. We'll be able to watch their progress in the hall and make our move.

As expected, we hear Miss Caroline say hello and deliver instructions to her replacements at 3:25, then catch a glimpse of her walking down the hall shortly thereafter. Moments later, the rattle of laden carts indicates the night men are starting their rounds. One gets in the elevator near the base of the stairs, while the other disappears into the Health room. I'm ready to shoot down the stairs the instant his cart clears the door, but Ravi's hand on my arm stays me.

"Let him get a few down," he says.

It proves to be good advice, as the custodian is quicker than I expected he'd be, though I guess the sooner they finish, the sooner they can slack off for the rest of their shift in the break room. We wait until he finishes all the rooms we can see, which means he's around the corner when I dart down the stairs. Ravi follows more slowly, prepared to be a distraction should the need arise.

I slip into the office without issue and find the tall filing cabinet unlocked. Perfect. I search for the black cash box and find it in the second drawer. There's still no lock on it, just as I remembered. I pop it open to reveal a ring of keys labeled *M1*, *M2*, *M3*, and I slide *M1* off the ring. Master key, first floor. That's what we need. I return the remaining keys to the box and the box to the drawer. I wave the key at Ravi, and we race to the auditorium, needing to beat the custodians there.

The key fits into the lock as easily as the 331 key had, but this one turns easily. We duck inside and push the door shut behind us. I pocket the key and pull out my phone.

"We don't know where she was found," I say, "so look everywhere."

Using our phones as flashlights, we scan the dim rows of seats and the aisles for any sign of violence, but I'm drawn to the stage. If someone died in the auditorium, whether by their own hand or that of a madman, chances are it happened there.

We each take a side, searching the scarred floorboards for signs of violence, but find no bloodstains or anything out of the ordinary. When we meet in the center of the stage, we both look up to where the heavy velvet curtain is suspended from metal tracks as if the answers might be hiding in the rafters.

I sigh. "So far, there's nothing to indicate she died…messy."

"At least there's that," Ravi says grimly.

"At least there's that."

I head down the stairs, frustrated at the lack of clear evidence, then freeze when I spot a figure silhouetted against the door. "Shit." I push Ravi back up the steps. "Go, go, go."

I shoot past him and pull him toward the velvet drapes along the rear of the stage. We find a gap and duck behind the curtains, stopping to peer out through a tiny slit to see who nearly caught us. If it's one of our suspects, that could mean something.

But it's only Ms. Larson, striding down the center aisle with Henry at her heels.

I let the curtain fall closed and lay a hand on Ravi's arm, easing him back into the darkness. We move carefully, not wanting to knock into something that would inadvertently reveal our presence. I have a sudden flash of watching Emma and Jacob in a similar retreat, but I set the memory aside. After pushing through the second layer of curtains, thinner than the velvet ones that line the stage, I see a strip of light that can only be the edge of a door. Ravi gets there first, pushes the bar, and dumps us into the blinding light of the hall.

"That was close," he says.

"Thank you, Captain States-the-Obvious." It's not him I'm frustrated with though; it's myself. I know in my bones that we missed something important before Ms. Larson rushed us out, and if I were a better investigator—more observant, more astute—I would've seen it.

KYLIE'S FUNERAL is set for Thursday, and although the school doesn't officially shut down, Ms. Larson makes it clear that anyone wishing to attend will receive an excused absence. Judging by the number of people filing into the church, most of the school has taken advantage of that.

I linger with Ravi on the church lawn as mourners arrive, surveying who's there, who isn't, and who might be acting strangely. That last factor is the hardest to judge, as even I'm acting strange. Or at least feeling strange.

There's a dreamlike surrealism as we stand here—Ravi clad in a black suit that pulls across his shoulders, and me in a similarly somber black-on-black outfit of pin-striped pants and cowl-neck sweater. The air is crisp enough to make me wish I'd brought a jacket, but my bright red peacoat had seemed too festive.

Cassidy, looking like she should be going to some kind of award ceremony in her sleek black cocktail dress, is here, along with Bryce and her morning crew. My brain renames them the *Mourning Crew*, but I don't share that thought. I'm glad they have absorbed Priya into their pod, because the girl is abandoned by Mrs. B the moment the hearse arrives. Mrs. B's face is swollen from crying, and she embraces Kylie's mother as soon as she's out of the limo. Mrs. B knows everyone in town, that's true, but unlike Emma's dad, whom she had been friends with only in high school, she and Kylie's mom are one of those sets of lifelong friends that are so common in Maplefield. Sort of like me and Ravi would be if we didn't have bigger goals than this small town.

The pallbearers assemble at the rear of the hearse as the latecomers make their way inside. The funeral director opens the hatch of the black car and slides a gleaming white casket out onto a wheeled cart while I struggle to acknowledge and set aside a wave of sadness. The men and boys, including two I recognize from school, take hold of the gold handles and lift the casket as easily as if it were empty.

Ravi and I slip into the church before the family procession, opting to stand along the back wall rather than search for seats. The air outside might be cold, but the church itself is stifling with the heat of too many bodies packed in one place.

As the preacher begins the service, I scan the pews, searching for Owen's unmistakable auburn buzz cut, but I don't see it. Odd. I'd have thought he'd be there.

Locating Jacob by the back of his head proves to be impossible. There are too many dark-haired males of similar build to pinpoint which one is him.

As I search the room, the baby hairs on the back of my neck stand up, and when I scan the back rows, I see why. Peter Vernon is watching me as intently as I'm watching the pews.

I stiffen but meet his gaze and hold it. I'm furious that he would dare show his face at a teenage girl's memorial service. His lip curls in the slightest of sneers, then he turns away like I'm not worth his attention.

Ravi is focused on the preacher and misses the entire interaction—if I can even call it that—and I'm grateful for that small mercy at least. The last thing I need is for Ravi to go all knight-in-shining-armor at our friend's funeral.

I find myself wishing for another task, another person to search for, anything that could take my attention away from the sound of crying and the reality of the situation. The choking odor of incense has made its way to the rear of the church, and it feels like it's infecting my lungs.

When Kylie's best friend, Anna Torres, steps up to the pulpit to read a poem, Ravi's fingers twine into mine, and something hard and crinkly presses between our palms. I accept the mystery object—a green apple Jolly Rancher—and unwrap it gratefully. The pungent apple-shampoo scent of it helps to chase away the stink of incense. I pocket the wrapper and find Ravi's hand again. Our fingers lace together and stay that way until the end.

Chapter Twenty-five

T HE NUMBER of mourners swells between the church and the re-
ception, and the function room at Giovanni's, where a buffet is
being set up along one wall, is overflowing. Mourners spill into the
restaurant itself, especially the men. Groups of middle-aged dads hug
the bar, looking simultaneously horrified at the Augers' loss and grateful that it isn't their own daughters being buried.

Ravi removes his tie, stuffs it in his pocket, and undoes the top
button of his starched shirt. "So, who are we looking for?" The hair at
his temples is damp with sweat. "It's bloody hot in here."

"You'll survive." I pat his arm. "We still need to talk to Owen and
Jacob and the person who saw her last."

"Oh, hey." Ravi waves to someone behind me. "Sorry, it's Ms.
Larson. There was eye contact; I couldn't ignore her. Okay, so Jacob,
Owen, last known sighting. Got it."

"And anything we can pick up about manner of death. This might
not be the best venue for this, but people will be talking. We just need
to listen."

We split up, circulating through the room. I absorb snippets of
conversations as I walk, slowing when something sounds important,
but it isn't until I reach the table where Kylie's grandmother sits that
I actually stop.

The old lady has a small, puckered mouth and the same sharp
blue eyes as Kylie. "Don't you dare talk to me about sin," she says, jab-
bing a finger at the two women sitting with her. A near-empty tum-
bler of amber liquid is on the table before her. "My granddaughter was
not suicidal. Not for an instant."

"It's teens these days." One of the other women clucks her tongue. "Such horrible decisions they make, putting Lord knows what poisons into their bodies with no regard for their families or their own immortal souls. It's just so sad. I blame society, I really do."

"My granddaughter's death was an accident. Her immortal soul has nothing to worry about. I don't need you old biddies acting like you know more about my family than I do. My daughter's doing enough of that for everyone."

I don't even pretend I'm not eavesdropping. When silence falls on the trio's conversation, I square my shoulders and introduce myself. "I couldn't help overhearing what you said about Kylie's death being an accident."

Kylie's grandmother shoots a smug look at her tablemates. "It's just awful, isn't it, dear? How everyone's spreading such terrible rumors?"

I nod sympathetically.

"And so few real answers," the grandmother continues as the other two women excuse themselves. "I blame that school. What were they thinking, letting her muck about in that auditorium by herself with no supervision at all?" Her voice thickens with tears, but she doesn't cry.

"I'm so sorry for your loss, Mrs. Auger—"

"Oh, dear, Maggie is fine."

"Maggie, I'm so sorry to ask you this, but it might help me move on. It's so hard to have closure when we don't even know how she died. I keep imagining such horrible things." The lump that rises in my throat on that last sentence betrays the truth of it, and I have to swallow hard to keep from choking. *Set it aside. Get the story.*

Kylie's grandmother lays a wrinkled hand on top of mine. "The police don't know," she says. "They're calling it an accidental overdose because of the needle marks, but they can't tell us what the drug was yet, so it's technically still pending. They're doing some sort of specialized testing at the state lab, and the waiting is just dreadful." She shakes her head, the bitterness—or denial—twisting her mouth into a hard frown. "It's maddening her poor mother."

The words hit like a kick in the gut. More needle marks? So the killer is consistent, then, which makes sense. Once a murderer finds a method they like, they don't usually switch it up.

Over Maggie's shoulder, I see Kylie's mother marching toward us and try to work out a tactful way to ask when the last time she saw her daughter was, but the younger Mrs. Auger doesn't give me a chance.

"You," she snarls. Her hands clench into knobby fists at her sides. "How dare you show your face here?"

Kylie's grandmother clucks her tongue and raises a hand, palm out. "Maura, leave the girl alone. She's been through enough."

Mrs. Auger is mere feet away, and I rise, taking a step away from the table. I have no idea what I've done to upset her, but Kylie's mother looks dangerously unhinged. "Mrs. Auger, I'm so—"

"Don't you 'Mrs. Auger' me." Her breath is sharp with wine fumes. "You think I don't know who you are? This is your fault, you know."

"What? No. I–I'm sorry," I stammer, my brain whirring ahead of my tongue as I try to get a fix on what's going on.

"You're the reason my girl is dead!" Mrs. Auger's wrath draws stares from surrounding tables, and silence spreads like a sickness through the crowd.

The accusation roots me to the floor. I'm stunned into silence.

"Her death was an accident, Maura," Kylie's grandmother says, but no one acknowledges her.

"There was a note, Mother! You don't accidentally leave a note!" She jabs a finger at me. "It's you and that goddamn *Monitor*. You think my daughter didn't tell me what was going on in her life? Well, she did. I know all about how bitter you were about missing out on your little internship and how you need some big story to win a prize. But nothing ever happens in this Podunk town, so you had to make your own news. Like you haven't done that before. Kylie told me all about your little 'senior curse'"—she hooks exaggerated air quotes around the phrase—"but there is no curse, and you know it. And when poor Emma Morgan died, you saw a golden opportunity, didn't you? You could make your own curse."

Blood roars in my ears.

Mrs. Auger sways, unsteady on her feet, but manages to stab a finger into my chest. The force of her rage rocks me back a step. "You published all those stories about Emma and how tragic her loss was, like she was the only one in the world who mattered, knowing that that kind of attention would encourage others to follow in her footsteps. You wanted them to. And my Kylie, who only wanted to be friends with you, who was only worth your time when she was giving you stories, paid the ultimate price. Is she worth your time now? Is my girl worth a story yet?"

I have no comeback, no words at all, because I can barely comprehend the onslaught of anger and accusations being hurled at me. Had I treated Kylie the way Mrs. Auger claimed? I'd thought it was the other way around, but maybe I'd misread things.

"Did you encourage her? What did you say to her that led her down this path?" Spittle flies from Mrs. Auger's mouth as tears rain down her cheeks. "Did you tell her what drugs Emma used? Because the police can't even figure that out. But they will. My little girl has never touched a drug in her life, and now she's covered in needle marks? It's not right. If you have a shred of human decency in you, you'll tell the police what the drug was and where it came from. You owe us that. Your story wasn't worth the price of my daughter's life, you selfish little shit."

Footsteps pound behind me, and Ravi's voice cuts through the air, demanding to know what's going on. I stumble as someone pushes past me, not realizing it's Mrs. B until she wraps Mrs. Auger in a hug that forcibly turns the furious woman away from me. "Maura, Maura. Shh now," she soothes. Mrs. B meets my eyes over her friend's shoulder and tilts her chin toward the exit, a signal to leave that I can't obey because my feet are still frozen to the floor.

I jolt at a hand on my back, but it's only Ravi saying, "Let's go."

I allow him to lead me away, aware of all the eyes that follow our retreat and unable to set the scrutiny aside. I soak up the stares like a sponge, and they water the seed of doubt that has planted itself in my belly.

❖   ❖   ❖

RAVI DRIVES in silence, and I love him for it. He goes through the Dunkin' drive-thru and orders a tooth-rottingly sweet iced coffee that I don't have to ask for. He lets me finish half of it before asking, "What the hell was that about?"

I shake my head. I have nothing resembling an answer.

"I mean, I heard what it was about. Everyone heard, but holy shit. Now we know where Kylie got her dramatic streak."

I let miles go by without answering. Doubt blossoms into a writhing thing inside me. I don't want to give voice to it, but I can't help it. I have to know. "Was she right?"

"What?" Ravi's head snaps around, along with the wheel of the car. He rights the car and returns his eyes to the road before saying, "You're kidding, right?"

"I don't know. She could've been right."

"About which bit?"

"Any of it." I use the straw to stab at the ice in my cup. My cheeks scorch with shame at the possibility of how badly I might've fucked up. "All of it."

"Talk," Ravi orders when I lapse back into silence.

"Okay, so if you'd asked me a year ago, or even last week, what I thought of Kylie Auger, I'd have called us…casual friends. More than acquaintances, but less than you and me."

"That's fair."

"But what if she really did think we were proper friends, like you and me. But I didn't. What if she really did tell her mom how awful I was? What if, in her mind, I really was just using her? I think every conversation we've had has been story related." The next admission is hard to say, even to Ravi. "I sent her eight texts before her body was found and not even one was asking if she was all right."

"Don't do that. Don't torture yourself with this. You can't know or control what was going on in her head." He pulls in to my driveway and turns the engine off. "If you had asked me, I would've called us acquaintances too. And I think Kylie would've as well. Her mom was probably just looking for someone to blame, and you were who she latched on to."

"But if she's right—"

"Which she's not."

"But if she is, and I really did make Kylie feel like shit... What if she really did kill herself?"

Chapter Twenty-six

THE DOUBT grows like ivy until it's twined around my every thought. If I was wrong about Kylie, what else have I been wrong about?

The day after the funeral, I'm the topic on everyone's lips, and the *Monitor's* inbox overflows with requests for the whole scoop on the funeral fight. The gossip mill has turned it from the horror show it was into a physical confrontation with blows exchanged and police involvement.

I almost write the story just to set the record straight and stop the speculation, but I don't. I tell stories; I don't star in them. In the days I lose to doubt, I wonder if I even belong in journalism at all.

But stories are in my blood, and they're what keeps me going. Even as I back off from the murder investigation, I pour myself into the *I Am Maplefield* project. I corral the missing students, personally march them to 331, and conduct detailed interviews with the ones sharing the most interesting statements. And then doubt worms its way into that too, because who am I to decide what's interesting? Isn't the kid who wrote *I Am Lactose Intolerant* every bit as story-worthy as the one who said *I Am Hiding Every Day*?

"I think we should merge projects," I announce after our very last holdout—a junior who held her *I Am Camera Shy* confession so that it completely blocked her face—is gone. "I want to do write-ups of everyone we shot and tell their stories."

"Bullshit you do," Ravi says. "And we still have to do our shots, by the way. Then we'll literally have the entire school."

I allow myself a moment to revel in the awesomeness of that fact. It's hard enough to get the entire school to do something required, like show up for ID pictures, never mind something that was one hundred percent optional. But once people started hearing about the project, they wanted to add their voices to the collective. Even the rebels and the apathetics had turned up, offering gems like *I Am A Potato* and *I Am Trying Not To Fart*.

With Mrs. Auger's accusations still ringing in my ears, I'm overcome with a rush of affection for the people who stood before Ravi's camera and bared pieces of their souls. I want the world to know who they are. They deserve that. Kylie deserved that.

Ravi checks the time on his phone. "We'll have to do ours later. We gotta get to the shop before Dad has an aneurysm."

We agreed to help Mr. B with four hundred specialty donuts for a wedding, and if I'm honest, I'm craving the distraction.

The four hundred donuts turn into five hundred by the time we don our aprons. They're all cake donuts, five flavors total, baked and ready for decoration. Mr. B leaves the sketch he did with the bride, barely explaining the scribbled image, before disappearing out front to deal with customers, cursing his regular afternoon counter girl for calling out as he goes.

I gather bowls of white icing for dipping while Ravi arranges the various sprinkles, rock sugars, and edible bling we'll need. The sketch leaves a lot to the imagination, but after a few false starts, we fall into a rhythm. We work in companionable silence, and I'm finally able to set aside the feelings that have plagued me since the funeral.

At least until Ravi ruins it.

He's focused on swirling his donut through the icing, letting the excess drip off in tendrils, when he says, "You're not hijacking my project because Kylie's mom fucked with your head."

My hand freezes above a donut, grip tightening on the paintbrush I've got loaded with edible glitter. "I'm not hijacking your project." I tap the brush harder than I mean to, and a massive clump of glitter lands in a blob on the icing. "Shit," I mutter, blowing on it to try to spread it out.

"You are." Ravi sets the iced donut on a tray for me to decorate. "And I get it."

I give up on the glitter blob and add a few extra sprinkles to cover it up. No one will notice. "I am not. I just think I was shortsighted in dismissing the idea of human-interest profiles being important."

"More important than a murder investigation?"

Heat floods up my neck, but my hands don't slow. "Possible murder investigation, you mean." I add a swirl of sanding sugar to the icing with more care than is required.

"Bullshit. What about Emma's feet?"

"I don't know." I try to acknowledge and set aside my rising anxiety.

"You do know. If you want to give up this investigation because the facts tell you you're off course, fine—admit defeat and move on. But don't you dare quit because someone tried to make you her whipping girl. The Kennedy I know is better than that."

The heat spreads from my neck to my temples, and my hand shakes when I pick the glitter brush back up. "The cops don't think there's anything to investigate."

"Because they're morons." Ravi slams the donut he has onto the tray. "You saw something. You convinced me that what you saw mattered. I don't think you're wrong about this, and if you give up now, you're not only letting someone get away with murder, you're pissing all over Emma and Kylie's memory. And you're better than that."

"That's not fair."

"Life's not fair. I'm not going to watch you throw all your work away over one stupid conversation."

I finish the donut I'm working on, stalling because I'm embarrassed to admit what I'm feeling even to Ravi. Finally, I just blurt it out: "She might've been right. I might be responsible for what happened to Kylie—at least a little bit."

"And I might be the sexiest man on the planet. Fuck 'might.' What you do know is that your gut is telling you that Emma was murdered. Then Kylie dies and you, Miss Morally-Opposed-to-Coincidence, are just going to back off? Bull. Shit."

"What do you want me to do?" I'm dangerously close to tears and grab another donut, desperate for something to occupy my hands.

Ravi slaps the edge of the stainless steel tabletop. "Investigate, dammit. Tell the story. That's what you do," he says. "It's who you are."

We decorate the next two dozen donuts in blistering silence. The doubt might be a cancer infecting my brain, but Ravi's words are radiation, shrinking it enough to focus.

"How do we know Emma was murdered?" Ravi asks, voice low and even, as conversational as if he were inquiring about the weather.

"Her feet," I answer. "They were clean, and she was in a forest. They should've been dirty."

"What else?"

"She wasn't suicidal. She was planning for the future. She was actively engaging in life."

"What else?"

"The texts she sent to Vic were off, and the note. They didn't sound like her."

"What about Kylie?"

"She wasn't suicidal either, and her note was too vague, like Emma's was. She would have left a manifesto if she'd done it herself."

"What else?"

Something in me starts to thaw. My hands move faster over the donuts, sugar and glitter flying. "Kylie's grandma swore she wasn't suicidal. And even if she were, she went to church. She'd have thought it was a sin."

"So she didn't kill herself either."

I meet Ravi's eyes over the workspace. "I don't see how. And she drank, but she wasn't into recreational drugs. So not an accidental overdose either."

He grins. "Then it's murder."

"Try not to look so happy about it."

"That's not what I'm happy about." For a split second, his face softens into something impossibly tender. Love isn't a recognized micro-expression, but if it were, it would look like this.

I don't acknowledge what that look does to my heart. "You're such a cornball."

"But I'm your cornball."

"You think there's an ointment for that?"

He throws a scrap of donut at me. "Focus, woman. We have a murder to solve. Give me suspects."

"Owen. Dated Emma and thought she was cheating thanks to Kylie. That's motive for both murders."

"Check."

"Jacob. Implicated in said affair, but was actually just supplying drugs to Emma. No known connection to Kylie beyond crossing paths in school and at parties. Will need to look into that more. Could definitely have access to the drug that killed them."

"Great. Who else?"

I sprinkle a donut with sanding sugar and consider. "Peter Vernon. We can't discount a known offender."

"On a scale of one to ten, how likely is it that he's our guy?"

"Seven," I say. "No, wait. Five. Kylie was found in the school. I'm not sure a grown man, even looking as young as he does, could sneak into the building and not be noticed."

"Fair enough. So worth looking at, but below those with regular access to the building."

I'm decorating faster than Ravi can dip now, hands keeping pace with my thoughts. "We can't rule out that we're dealing with a serial killer. Two victims and he's a murdering scumbag, three and he's a serial killer. I think we need to talk to the police again. I'm all for uncovering this on my own, but I don't want anyone else to die before I can do it."

"You think that's wise?"

"I think we should at least try. Maybe an anonymous tip this time. That way, they won't know it's coming from us, and they might actually pay attention."

"Okay, sure. I'm all for not walking back in there again."

"I'll do it tonight. In the meantime, I think we need to consider the next victim. If we can figure out who she is, we can protect her."

"If it's Vernon, I'm still keeping you on that list," he says. "And just to be clear, I don't like thinking about that."

"Dually noted." A new warmth has been suffusing my body as we've talked—nothing like the shame and doubt of before. Ravi has fixed my brain in a way that only he can, and I realize that's what love is. My heart flutters like a trapped bat against my sternum, but I don't fight it. I can't, not when it feels as vital as breath. "Okay. So the real Watson—Sherlock tells him he has a grand gift for silence that makes him an invaluable companion. You're the opposite. It's not your silence that matters; it's your not shutting up."

"Gee, thanks," he says, but he's gone still, his body belying his light tone.

The air in the kitchen is different now, charged in a way I'm not used to. The electricity gives my next words power. "I know I'm not an easy person to deal with. I'm so worried about being the perfectly objective investigative reporter that most days, I'm bad at being an actual human. But somehow, against all odds and logic, you still like me. You are better than me in every way, kinder especially, and I would be utterly adrift without you. You always know exactly what to say to save me from myself." I go to his side of the table, where he's rooted, eyes boring into mine. My heart and brain are at war, but it's time for objectivity to rest. I touch his cheek—a gesture more intimate than I normally would've done. My voice is raw under the weight of it. "You are my invaluable companion."

It is the highest compliment I can give him. And when I kiss him, it's not because I want to devour him or because I want anything more than that singular action. It's because I need him to know that he is loved as wholly and as completely as I am capable of.

The donut he drops drowns in the bowl of icing as his hand comes up to my neck, pulling me in. It's a strange thing to be kissing my best friend, but perhaps most strange is how nice it is. His lips are warm and soft, insistent without making demands. It's a kiss that doesn't ask to be more than it is, which makes it safe to get lost in. His hands cup my face, and there's a swallowed-up feeling, like going over the falls at Reichenbach, only with the knowledge that the landing will be soft.

The Making of a Monster
Continued

He was adrift, as alone and isolated as ever, until Coach Miller appeared, like an angel. Miller was the new gym teacher and wrestling coach, and when he announced tryouts were coming up, he specifically invited the boy. Coach said that he had the right body for it and that he could get him on a program to build more muscle before the season started. The boy instantly forgave God, realizing everything else had merely been a test. He learned everything he could about high school wrestling so that he would be ready, and when tryouts came, he was. The workouts were grueling, but the boy was good at suffering. He'd had plenty of practice.

Seeing his name at the top of the list of chosen athletes was the happiest day of his life. The monsters made the team too, but he didn't care, because the curse had lifted and everything would change.

But the monsters didn't change; they just let the boy think they had. They lulled him into a false sense of security and ambushed him in the shower, one with a video camera and the other in a ski mask. They didn't jump him, because he was too strong for that, but they took his clothes and filmed him as he ran naked through the locker room in pursuit. They passed the video off to one of the monsters' girlfriends—a drama student with full access to the auditorium—who rigged it to play on the projector during a school-wide assembly. By the time the principal turned it off, the whole student body had seen the boy's entire body, and even if some of the hoots and whistles were appreciative, he only heard the taunts as he fled.

Chapter Twenty-seven

"**THERE'S NO** way this isn't going to be complicated," I say. Ravi laughs. "It's you. Naturally it's going to be complicated."

"Bite me."

It's the day after the kiss, and while I don't regret it, I don't want to examine it. Not now. Not when it's still so new. But here we are, sitting side by side on my bed, as if that doesn't make having *the talk* even more awkward.

We decided against meeting at The Donut Hole, because the last thing we need is Mr. B lending his opinion to anything. Privacy is now important in a way it never was before yesterday. And how many times have we sat on this bed over the years? Just because we kissed shouldn't make it weird. And yet I know Ravi. I know what he likes, and it's not something I can give him, and that makes it weird.

"This doesn't make me any less asexual," I tell him.

"I know."

"It's not going to magically change. You're not going to cure me. I'm not going to wake up one day and ravage you."

He grins. "I know."

I heave a frustrated sigh. "But that smile says you like being ravaged." I hold up a hand to stop his interruption. "It's an important thing for you, and that matters. I know right now you think you want to give that up, but you don't. Not any more than I want to give up *not* having sex."

And god, what does this mean for sleepovers? We've always been allowed to have them because there's never been a question of our relationship being anything other than platonic, and even though I still have no intention of sleeping with Ravi, I can already see my father outlawing sleepovers on the mere principle.

This is exactly why I've always kept my brain in charge. Hearts are stupid and only lead to poor decisions and complication.

"Just because I like something doesn't mean I have to have it. I'd like a Hasselblad camera and car that isn't running on luck and duct tape, but that doesn't mean I'm not happy with what I have."

"But you have a sex drive. I don't. Period."

"And I also have a right hand for when it becomes an issue." He waggles his fingers at me. "Give me some credit here."

"I am. I'm just trying to be realistic, and the reality is, this is the one area where we're just not compatible."

"You're the one who kissed me," he says, as if there is any way, on any planet, that I could've forgotten. "I'm not pressuring you to do anything you don't want to do, but I don't want to pretend it didn't mean anything when I know it did. I've left this ball in your court for a long time, and now it's in play. We'll figure it out. There are ways to make it work. I've looked into it. And you have too. I know you have, because you're the one who showed me the websites."

He's right, of course. Because he always is. The "ways" include everything from voluntary celibacy to open relationships to agreeing to sex on very specific terms. Hell, I think these relationships are a perfect market for sex robots, but who knows. What I do know is for each success story about an ace dating an allo, there are dozens more where it all ends in abject failure. I don't want to risk that with Ravi, because what if we can't come back from it? The thought of throwing away everything we are for something we might never be is enough to tie my stomach into knots.

"It's just us," he says gently, as if reading my thoughts. "We've been halfway to this for a long time now. We make sense. We make too much sense not to at least give it a try."

I tuck my legs up to my chest and lean against the cool wall. "This is the literal opposite of sense."

"You know it's not."

And I do. It's the chill of the wall against my back that brings forward the memory of the day after Kylie was killed, when we sat snuggled together in 331 and I understood, in an abstract sense that was entirely inappropriate for the circumstances, the appeal of having a romantic partner. No, not just a romantic partner, not just anyone, but Ravi specifically.

Only...

Maybe we really have always been halfway here.

There's only one way to be sure, and as Sherlock said, any truth is better than indefinite doubt. "It's better to know than to wonder," I say, more to myself than Ravi. I look at him, and his dark eyes are as familiar as my own. If I make sense with anyone, it's him.

I stretch my legs out so they're draped across his. He rests a hand on my calf but doesn't say anything. The weight of his hand is comforting, cozy like a favorite blanket.

"I have no idea what this is going to look like," I say. "And you know I hate—"

"Not knowing things," he finishes, squeezing my leg. "I do know who you are."

"Better than anyone."

"I also know that we'll make this work, however it has to look, even if it means returning to just friends."

"I hate that phrase. *Just friends*. It's like the *just* barges in and tries to make it seem like friendship is somehow less valuable than a romantic relationship. It's so stupid. There are more friendships that last forever than marriages."

"Exactly. So there's no lose here. Either we defy the odds—"

"The *many* odds."

"—and make this work, or we be friends until we're a couple of old geezers getting in trouble at a nursing home for having wheelchair races and sword fights with our canes. I'm down for any and all of those eventualities."

I laugh in spite of myself, because I can totally see us ending up like that, and it really isn't a bad outcome. "I just don't want to implode and miss out on our elderly shenanigans."

"I'm morally opposed to imploding. Promise." He raises three fingers like a Boy Scout, then grows serious. "Look, however I get to have you in my life, I'm happy with. Even if we decide going out doesn't work, it's not the end of us. There's no such thing as the end of us."

WE DECIDE to put this new venture to the test right away, on the idea that if it's going to fail, I'd rather fail quickly so we can move on.

The plan is simple to the point of cliché: dinner and movie. But it's the first time I've ever worried about what to wear on an outing with Ravi.

After swearing Cassidy to secrecy, I endure a barrage of whoops and I-told-you-sos while she tears through my closet.

"Do you even own anything other than hoodies and T-shirts?" She groans. "This is hopeless."

"He already knows how I dress, and it hasn't put him off yet," I say, wondering if telling her was a mistake.

"Because he's been smitten with you since before he understood what the word meant. I'll be right back."

She disappears down the hall, and I consider my wardrobe. My clothes aren't exciting, but they're mine. I'm comfortable in them.

Cassidy returns with a bundle of gray fabric over her shoulder and a pair of shoeboxes in her lap. She throws the shirt at me. "This and your black skinny jeans. Trust me."

She spins around while I change. The shirt is long and flowy with a scooped neck and a lighter gray ruffle peeking out from the bottom hem. The fabric is soft, and even though I'm not thrilled with the ruffle, I admit it's a step up from the *Stranger Things* shirt I just took off.

I step around so she can see. "Yes?"

She claps her hands together with delight. "Yes! Okay, now shoes." She opens the first box, revealing a pair of silver heels that would guarantee me a trip to the emergency room. I shake my head. She rolls her eyes and tosses them on my bed. She offers me the second box. "Ankle boots it is then."

The second box holds a pair of black suede booties with a chunky heel. "I'm not sure this is a high heel kind of outing."

"They're boots, not high heels."

"So says the girl who doesn't have to walk in them."

"That was low," Cassidy says, but she's grinning. Her postaccident affinity for ankle-breaking shoes hasn't been a secret. "Just try them on."

I sit on my bed and undo the little zipper on the inside of the boots. What's even the point of a two-inch zipper? "I feel like I'm cheating on my Chucks." I slide the boots on.

"Life is more than sneakers."

"Thank you, Gandhi." I stand and take a slightly wobbly step to the mirror.

Cassidy squeals. "Ahhh, you're adorable. I love it."

"I feel like a baby giraffe."

"Which are adorable," she insists. A wicked gleam lights up her eyes. "Can I do your makeup?"

"Negative, Ghost Rider." She pouts, but I have to draw the line somewhere. "I already feel like I'm playing dress-up as it is. Maybe next time."

"Oooh, so you're already planning a next time? This is so exciting! We should totally go on a double date. Ravi would like Bryce. We could do that escape room at the mall! Yes? Please?"

I laugh. "We'll see. This is all weird and new. Let me get through tonight first."

"Fine," she says. "But I want details when you get home."

"My details are going to be much more PG than you're looking for," I remind her.

"So what? Romance is way more than just the sexy bits. It's the little looks he gives you and whether he opens doors for you and if he says nice things to you."

"Ravi already holds doors and says nice things. It's who he is."

"A romantic." Cassidy nods.

"Perfect for the asexual."

She misses the joke. "Exactly what I've been saying for literally ever!" There are practically cartoon cupids in her eyes, and I'm worried she's going to burst into song like a Disney princess at any second.

My phone chirps, saving me from having to throttle her. A text from Ravi asking, *Still on for 6?*

I text back a yes and banish my sister to finish getting ready.

"I better get to be maid of honor," she calls as she leaves.

I meet Ravi in the driveway to spare him—and myself—from another wave of sisterly enthusiasm. He jumps out of the car and runs to open the passenger door.

"You're such a dork," I say, but it's cute.

He bows. "At your service. You look amazing, by the way."

I feel my cheeks flush. "Style by Cassidy."

He looks good too, clad in his dark jeans and burgundy shirt. His hair is still a bit damp from the shower, so the curls are contained, but by the end of the night, they'll be wild. The spicy-citrus scent of cologne hangs in the car, and I decide it's a scent I could get used to.

In the objective journalist part of my brain I can never shut off, I'm aware that it's self-indulgent to be doing this—going out and having fun while a murderer is still on the loose—but my heart, which has gotten obnoxiously loud these past few days, insists it's as necessary as any investigating. What good is uncovering the lives of others if you're not living one of your own?

I let Ravi pay for dinner and the movie because I understand chivalry is important to him. We find seats at the back of the mostly deserted theater for a superhero movie that's almost finished its run. We have an impressive array of smuggled-in candy, and Ravi managed to con us extra bags to go with our supersized popcorn from the kid at the concession counter. We spend the opening credits topping our popcorn in a way that would make Mr. B proud: M&M's and Reese's Pieces into one bag, Hot Tamales into another, and Raisinets into the last. Raisinets are the unsung hero of the candy world, because even though they're nobody's first choice, there's something about the chewy texture with crunchy popcorn that just works.

For the first half of the movie, it's exactly like every other time we've been out together. We prop our feet on the seats in front of us, fight for the gooiest popcorn pieces, and whisper predictions about what's coming.

Then the popcorn runs out and something shifts.

It's not that my head is on his shoulder, because that's not odd. It's not even the way his arm snakes around my shoulders.

It's the crackle beneath each of these touches, the electricity at the points of contact. It's new, despite being normal.

I'm the one who changes it, because I have to be.

I drop my feet down from the seat and sit up. Ravi shoots me a questioning look that intensifies when I nudge his arm into his own space.

I fumble in the dark for the button on the armrest and depress it. The barrier swings up and slots between the seats, and I move over, settling myself against Ravi's side. His arm closes back over my shoulder, and I burrow in.

I don't see his smile as the screen flashes black, but I feel it, because his entire body radiates with it.

Chapter Twenty-eight

MR. MONROE is absent, and the substitute—a crotchety old man—greets the class by saying, "You may use the period to work on your final projects, missing assignments, or anything that doesn't involve noise."

Between the murder investigation and subsequent post-funeral funk, I've been neglecting the curse research, so this is just what I need.

So far, the earliest confirmed mention of the curse we can find was ten years ago, which was verified by the year's class advisor as well as Carlos Garcia, Claribel's oldest brother. According to Carlos, they were the class that started calling it that, because they had watched seniors disappear since their freshman year. As juniors, when the third senior went missing—a mountain of a bully no one was sad to see the back of—they joked that the senior curse had claimed another victim. When Carlos's own senior year rolled around and Willa Butler—universally hated by girls and beloved by boys—vanished, he found it less funny. Apparently, Ms. Larson had tried to squash the curse rumors those first few years, but she was still new to school and let it go pretty easily.

I raise my hand and ask the sub if I can go to the office. Ravi looks up from his laptop, where he has the *I Am Maplefield* photos open in Lightroom, a question on his face.

"Gonna try to interview Larson about the curse," I whisper, not wanting to anger the cranky sub.

"Want me to come?"

"Nah, you're busy. Keep doing your pictures."

There's a solid chance Ms. Larson will be too busy to talk anyway, but when I get to the office, the principal's door is open and Henry is curled up on his bed.

"Knock, knock." I stick my head in.

Ms. Larson is on her computer, but she smiles and waves me in. "What can I do for you?"

"I was hoping you had a couple minutes to talk for a project I'm doing in Journalism."

She spins her chair away from her monitor and offers me her full attention. "Ah, yes. How have the photos been coming?"

"Really good, actually, but this is for a different part." I take a seat in one of the cushy chairs in front of Ms. Larson's wide desk and set my notebook on my lap. "You're aware of the senior curse?"

"Of course," she says, a smile tugging at the edge of her mouth. "Yes, there were a couple, shall we say, impressive disappearances from senior classes. One girl, a gymnast, literally joined the circus. Her parents were furious because she used school computers to make the arrangements. Though, for the record, I have to tell you the curse is nonsense."

"Yes, I know. That's what I'm researching. The origin of the *idea* of the curse."

"I see. There are perfectly boring explanations for several of the supposed victims, but it was more fun to blame a curse, I suppose."

"Do you remember when people first started talking about the curse?"

"Oh, it was years ago. Probably a year or two after I started here, I think."

"Do you think there's any truth to it?"

"No, like I said, many of the so-called disappearances were completely mundane, but privacy laws prevent the school from sharing the details, which is how rumors start."

"Do you think students believing in the curse is a problem?"

"I think it's impossible to stop teenagers from believing in anything they want to be true," she says. "I tried to put an end to it at first, but the more I tried to take it away, the more they clung to it. Soon, it was conspiracy this, curse that. It was the lure of forbidden fruit. I fig-ured it would fade away on its own."

"But it hasn't."

"But it hasn't," Ms. Larson echoes.

"But you think it's harmless?"

"I do. It's no worse than my generation locking ourselves in bath-rooms and trying to summon the ghost of Bloody Mary." She laughs, sounding almost embarrassed for her younger self.

"Even now, in light of Emma and Kylie? And Liam, for that matter. I've seen what the papers have said about the school not doing enough to prevent student suicide."

Ms. Larson's face darkens. "They are two separate issues. On the first, I say if students find comfort in this curse, I'm not going to stop them. We use stories to make sense of the world around us, and for many, it may be easier to process these deaths through the lens of an urban legend than it is to confront their own mortality. One thing the media has right is that suicide *is* an epidemic. But they're looking for someone to blame, and it isn't me. Suicide plagued this school long before I became principal."

"What? Really?" I don't know why I'm surprised. It's not like my generation invented depression. "The only other student deaths I've uncovered were from a car crash forever ago and then a kid name James Blackwell, but the obituary only said he died at home, not how."

"I think that's enough, Kennedy," Ms. Larson says. "Dig up the curse, discuss the urban legend, but let the dead lie. You don't need to drag every tragedy the school has seen into it. We have enough to deal with right in front of us."

TED BUNDY was caught on a routine traffic stop. The Son of Sam was brought down by a parking ticket. Sometimes, all the investigating in the world can't make up for the dumb luck of being in the right place at the right time.

The yellow caution tape is gone from the auditorium doors, but even so, no one makes much use of the space anymore. That's why catching Owen opening the door makes me think the universe is finally aligning in my favor for once.

Ms. Larson was right; I have plenty of tragedy to keep me busy right now.

Owen doesn't see me approaching and ducks inside without hesitation, like he has every right to be there.

I stop and glance up and down the hall. Content that no one's watching, I creep to the door and peer in. Owen sits in the front row, dead center, like he's watching a performance only he can see.

My heart races with the anticipated thrill of victory. I have him. Killers are known to return to the scene of their crimes. It's one of the things that get them caught.

I'm tempted to run back to Mr. Monroe's room and get Ravi, but I can't risk Owen leaving. I quickly run through my options. If Owen killed Emma and Kylie—and he's certainly strong enough to—I could be marching straight into physical danger by interrupting his reverie. On the other hand, I doubt he would attack me in the middle of a school day, in a building teeming with potential witnesses. Plus, I'm prepared. There's no element of surprise working to his advantage, and I'm certainly not above screaming for my life.

I ease open the door and step inside.

The air is cooler than in the hallway, and the only light filters in from the skylights. Owen keeps his eyes on the stage and doesn't acknowledge me. I consider walking across the stage and sitting on the edge of it, but it feels too dramatic. Instead, I take a seat beside him, leaving one empty chair between us as a buffer.

It's like he's been waiting for an audience, because the words tumble out as soon as I sit down.

"I wanted to kill her," he says. "Kylie. When she told me about Emma's affair, I wanted to choke her and shake her for corrupting the one good thing I had in my life. That's how it felt—like she ruined it. Not Emma, but Kylie. If Kylie had just minded her own business for once in her nosy life, we might've been okay."

He keeps his eyes on the stage as he talks, and I don't think it matters that it's me he's speaking to. He would say the words to the air if he had to.

"Even when I saw the texts on Emma's phone, I thought about ignoring it. I thought if we didn't talk about it, maybe it wouldn't have to be real. But I couldn't keep it in. I have anger issues. I've done the classes, but it's hard. Especially when it's with people I care about. I know that doesn't make sense, but strangers can piss me off and it's fine—I can do the breathing and let it go—but when it's people close to me, people who should know better... It's harder with them."

I bite back a lecture on victim-blaming and instead shrug into my on-air persona like it's an old coat. I'm relieved the days I lost to self-doubt haven't destroyed it. "That sounds hard."

His head whips around like he's only just realized I'm here.

"I didn't do it though," he says. "I wanted to, but I didn't do it. Then Emma died, and I blamed Kylie even more. The feeling didn't go away. I blamed her for Emma's death—still do—but I think all the wishing made it real."

"Are you saying you made it real? You made Kylie die?"

He runs a hand over his shorn head. "Yeah. I think I did. In anger management, we talk about how the energy you project matters and has consequences. I think I spent so much time wishing Kylie dead that the universe made it so."

I mull this over, wary of coming at it wrong and scaring him away. I keep my tone gentle and free of blame. "Are you saying you killed her with your brain? By thinking it?"

He pulls his lips in until they disappear and nods. In the dim light, his eyes are huge with horror. He's guilt-ridden all right, but my sureness of his crime slips away. "Owen, did you see Kylie the day she died?"

He shakes his head.

"Then how can you be responsible?"

"Because I wanted it to happen," he whispers.

"But did you actually do it?"

"No."

I believe him. He could be lying to my face, but dammit, I don't think he is. A disturbing wave of disappointment floods over me at this conclusion, and I shake it off, set it aside. I should be happy my classmate isn't a murderer. I should be sympathetic to his grief over a dead girlfriend and a dead ex-crush, but more than anything, I'm frustrated.

Owen had made so much sense. He was intimately involved with both victims, physically capable of committing the act, and has a history of unstable behavior. But he's so contrite, so earnest in his shame, that I just can't see it.

Chapter Twenty-nine

WHEN I step through the front door, I almost turn right back around. A barn has exploded in our living room. Riding boots, a tangle of leather straps I can't identify, and two helmets—one sparkly, one plain black—are piled in front of the door. A saddle is draped over the back of the couch like a sleeping cat. I step over the debris, nearly breaking my shin on Cassidy's wooden tack trunk, and am greeted by my weary-faced mother.

"Oh, good. You can help pack," she says instead of hello.

"I literally just walked in."

"Just when I needed you." She kisses my cheek. "Please. Your father is picking Cass up from the barn, and I would like to have one family dinner before we leave."

I sigh and return to the bulky wooden trunk, hefting it up by the metal handles on either side. "God, does she have a body in here?"

"Probably. It's going in the SUV." She holds the door open for me. "You're a peach. You can still join us, you know."

"Yeah, no. You guys go be horse show parents; that's your jam. I'm all for being the cheering squad when it's local, but four days sitting around a barn? No thanks."

Cassidy and the parentals are making the four-hour drive up to Pineland Farm, a world-class training facility in Maine that's hosting a winter qualifier for the Paralympics. They leave first thing in the morning and won't be back until late Sunday. Four whole days of having the house and car to myself.

Mom retreats to the kitchen to put the bread in the oven while I rid the living room of everything horse-related. When I'm done, I join her and start assembling a salad.

"How is your school project coming?" she asks.

"Really good." I fill her in on the details of Ravi's photos and the curse research. I don't mention the murder investigation, or that Ravi and I are turning into something undefinable but exciting.

"You know, we had a senior die when I was in school," she says. "A suicide. It was awful."

"Seriously? I didn't know that." I try to do the math, wondering if this is one of the historical suicides Ms. Larson had alluded to.

Mom nods as she slices a cucumber into half-moons. "It was so sad. In those days, you didn't really talk about depression and death though, so it was very hush-hush. I was friendly with his sister. She was the one who found him. He'd overdosed on their diabetes medicine. I think she blamed herself. She stopped coming to school after it happened. Awful, awful thing."

"Whoa." I can't help picturing Emma's lifeless body in the woods and how hard it had been to look at. I can't even fathom finding Cassidy like that. The thought alone takes my breath away.

But then Cassidy comes in, reeking of horse and trailing bits of hay in her wake, and I realize there's too much life in her for me to have to worry about such things. Still, I have to fight an uncharacteristically strong urge to hug her and profess uncomfortable feelings.

Rather than embarrass us both, I get the salad on the table while Mom dishes out lasagna and let Cassidy go over her entire schedule, in excruciating detail, for her upcoming weekend.

"And guess what?" She's vibrating with excitement. "Guess who's driving up to watch my freestyle?"

"Charlotte Dujardin," I say, naming the only famous rider I know.

"Nope. Bryce." She practically sings his name.

"Cool. Have him video it for me."

"It's the same one you've seen like three times." She waves me off. "Nothing special. But it'll be the first time for him, and it's a long drive, so yeah. Pretty psyched."

I sneak a glance at Dad, who looks anything but psyched. I hope he doesn't scare the poor kid away.

"Sounds awesome."

"Aren't you gonna be bored without us?" Cassidy asks, eyes twinkling. "What are you gonna do, have raging parties? Go on dates?"

Dad clears his throat. "Yes, what are your plans for while we're gone?"

"Wild parties," I deadpan. "All the orgies."

Cassidy giggles, and Dad glares.

I sigh. "School. Donut Hole. Dinner at Ravi's." And solving a double murder. "You know, the usual."

"I expect you to check in with us every day," Dad says. "Staying alone is a big responsibility."

"I'm eighteen. Pretty sure I can handle it."

"We'll see."

"I'll be good," I promise. "I'll check in. Make sure the plants are watered. Nothing to worry about."

"I'M WORRIED about Jacob," I announce at lunch the next day.

"In what way?" Ravi asks.

"Where the hell is he? I've been looking for him all week, and I haven't seen him once."

"Suspended?"

That hadn't occurred to me. "Okay, yeah, maybe. But I think he's actively avoiding me."

Ravi studies me. "Like you thought Kylie was?"

That's not something I want to think about. "No, like he's hiding. That night at the party, he seemed so distraught, but what if that was actually guilt? What if we misread him and he did a runner?"

"I didn't misread him," Ravi says. "Trust me. After you took off with Vic, all he did was wax poetic about Emma's grace and beauty and world-changing awesomeness before he turned into a snoring, drooling mess. I'm inclined to believe it was genuine."

"And I'm inclined to believe Owen was genuine."

"Then one of us is a poor judge of character." Ravi breaks off the end of his ice cream bar and offers it to me.

"Or we're looking at the wrong people," I say around the bite of ice cream. "We need to talk to Peter Vernon. He was acting shifty at Kylie's funeral, and if Owen and Jacob are both besotted fools, then maybe he really is our guy."

"Okay, but we need a plan. We can't just ambush him. I have an eye doctor appointment after school, but we can talk later, figure out how to approach it. Maybe we should try to catch him at the church."

I nod, but the idea of ambushing him and catching him off guard was a solid enough plan for me. Having the conversation we need to have with an entire church congregation milling around will be all but impossible.

Thoughts of Peter plague me for the rest of the day. If it was him, there's every reason to expect him to strike again. Same if it was someone else or a random psychopath. But if Owen or Jacob is the killer, and the link between victims is only the affair-that-wasn't, it's logical to assume the murders are done. I have to find out which it was before the next body turns up.

After school, I go to The Donut Hole in hopes of being put to work, but it's a slow day, and Mr. B doesn't need me. I make a coffee and take a donut to go, wishing Ravi didn't have his stupid appointment. I need to be doing something, anything, to move the investigation forward.

I opt for a bit of recon. Just a drive by Peter's house to see if he's home. If he is, I'll pick up Ravi after his appointment, and we'll get this over with—no waiting three days for Sunday church service, no risking more lives.

Peter's street is quiet, lined with small, older houses with neat lawns and trimmed hedges. His house is at the end of the road, right at the entrance to the reservoir trails. I'll drive through to the reservoir's parking lot—a route that will allow me to check Peter's driveway for a car—then be on my merry way.

I repeat this plan in my head, but when I coast by the gray cottage, not only is Peter's car in the driveway, he is too.

His eyes meet mine through the windshield, and he goes rigid with recognition.

"Fuck it," I mutter, swinging into the driveway and missing the mailbox by a hair's breadth.

I set my phone to record, shove it in my pocket, and leave the keys in the ignition in case I need to make a quick getaway. "Look, I know I'm probably the last person you want to talk to—"

"Then why are you here?" He folds his arms across his chest, and angry lines crease the space between his eyes.

"Just to talk." I hold up my hands, trying to appear as nonconfrontational as possible.

"I got nothing to say to you, and you got no business being here." He turns and climbs the steps to his front porch.

I follow him up. "Can we sit here a minute? I only have a few questions."

He pauses at the door but doesn't turn to face me. "What are you accusing me of this time?"

I want to remind him that my previous accusations were not baseless, that they hadn't even come from me, but that wouldn't be helpful at the moment. I need to get him on my side. "I'm just trying to find the truth." I let my voice go hoarse, as if fighting back tears. "About my friends. I know you have no reason to talk to me, but your house is right here. Did you see Emma before she died? Did she come through here?"

"I didn't see nothing," he snaps. "And even if I did, it's no business of yours. You ain't the cops."

"Were they here? The cops?"

"Told 'em the same thing I told you. I didn't see a thing. A girl wants to take herself up into the woods and die, that's her business, not mine. Learned a lot about minding my own business this past year." He opens the door and steps inside. "You'd do well to learn that too."

I wedge my foot between the door and the jamb before he gets it closed. Through the gap, I get a glimpse of his living room, and what I see there has me shoving my shoulder into the door, forcing it wider even as a cocktail of fear and adrenaline floods my veins. Beside the couch is a tall metal stand. Draped over its hook is a long coil of clear tubing attached to a nearly empty bag of clear fluid. "What is that?"

"Not your business." He plants a hand against the door before I can open it farther, his broad body blocking my view of the room.

"Why do you have an IV in your house? Have the police seen it?"

"The police don't give a fuck about my cat's kidney failure." The muscles in his jaw jump. "They might care about you trying to force your way into my house though."

"I'm supposed to believe you have an IV for your cat?" Even if I saw the supposed cat, I don't think I could ever picture this man giving it an IV.

"What you're supposed to be doing is getting off my damn property."

I can't go yet though—not without answers. "Why were you at Kylie's funeral?"

He sighs. "Because it's my uncle's church and she was a member. Her parents were regulars. I was showing support."

"Showing support or admiring your handiwork?" The accusation leaves my mouth before I can stop it.

He lunges at me then, whipping the door wide and forcing me back across the porch. A vein pulses dangerously in his forehead. "I am not some monster, no matter what you put on your little website. I could've had a life here, you know, if it wasn't for you digging up things that were no concern of yours. It was a three-year age difference. It was mutual. If it happened now, it'd be perfectly legal. You're the one who turned it into something perverted."

He's in my face, close enough for me to smell the stale mix of coffee and cigarettes on his breath, and I realize just how easy it would be for him to hurt me. To kill me. My bravery suddenly feels like stupidity in disguise, but I hold my ground. "You were in a position of power. They were underage. That's like the literal definition of perverted. But that's not why I'm here now, and you know it."

"Get off my property." Fists twitch at his side, his rage a living thing. "I never want to see you here again."

"Did you kill them?" I demand. "Did you kill Emma and Kylie?"

"Get. Off. My. Property."

My knees are like water, but I refuse to flee. "I don't hear you de-nying it."

"I don't answer to you." He closes in until I have no choice but to back down the creaking porch steps. "You show up here again, you're going to regret it. I promise you that."

"If you killed them, I'm going to find out. Then we can talk about regret."

I don't turn my back on him as I go down the driveway. I yank The Planet's door open and collapse into the driver's seat before my legs give out. The adrenaline has me shaking so hard, I have to pull over at the end of the street just to get my bearings. When I'm steady, I take out my phone and stop the recording. I skip back and let it play, listening as his anger fills the vehicle, confirming that I was right. He didn't deny it. Not once.

Chapter Thirty

RAVI IS apoplectic with rage.

I knew he'd be pissed. What I did *was* stupid and impulsive, but I didn't think he'd be the scary, quiet kind of pissed.

I'm used to Dad's temper, where anger gets expressed through shouting and the occasional throwing of things, but with Ravi, it's a coiled stillness, like a jaguar ready to pounce or a serpent waiting to strike. It's stony and complete, and I haven't been on the receiving end of it since third grade when I ripped the arms off his Spider-Man action figure.

As a writer, I know there's a pox on the phrase *a long moment*, but the moment between telling Ravi what I did and waiting for his response is one of the longest of my life. I think he might let it stretch all night, and I totally get now why the silent treatment works on interview subjects. The need to fill the vacuum with words is overwhelming.

"I think he's our guy," I say after the silence has dragged on for an excruciating interval. "I know I should've waited, but if he's our guy, then he's due to strike again. Maybe he won't now that he knows we're onto him."

Ravi sits on the ottoman in front of my living room sofa and spends a long time cleaning his glasses. His jaw works like he's chewing something tough, and when he puts his glasses back on and speaks, the condemnation in his voice makes me want the silence back.

"You had no right," he says, fury making his words tremble. "No right to put yourself in that kind of danger. This might be all fun and games to you, but if you're right, if it is him, then he's killed two girls already. You're not Sherlock Holmes, no matter how much you want to be. You're a girl, just like they were. He could've killed you. Don't you get that? Your life isn't worth some fucking story."

"But he didn't."

"We talked about this. We sat on the floor and fucking talked about this exact thing, and you didn't give a shit about anything I said."

"That's not true—"

"I get that you don't care about yourself," he cuts me off, his voice low and dangerous. "That's your own business. But if you cared about me at all, even a fraction of a tiny bit, you wouldn't have put yourself in that kind of danger. But all you cared about was the story."

"That's not fair."

He shakes his head. "No, it's not. I'm sorry if I expected better from you, but I thought we were partners. I thought our history meant something. I thought *I* meant something. Especially after the past few days. But I ask you for a simple thing—don't talk to him alone—and you couldn't even do that for me."

"It's okay though. I'm okay. Nothing happened."

Another horrible stretch of silence fills the room while my heart races like a spooked horse, erratic and terrified. I've been so worried about us imploding over a failed romance that I never stopped to consider that there were other ways to destroy us.

I want to undo the entire day. I want to have waited, not until Sunday, but until Ravi was out of his appointment like I'd originally planned. I should've done that. I know that. But I can't deny that the visit had been worthwhile. I don't regret the information I got, just that the method has upset Ravi so much.

"Remember finding Emma, what that was like?" He closes his eyes, lids twitching like he's in the throes of a dream. Or a nightmare. "What do you think I would do if I found you like that, and it was because you were too stupid to wait three days for me to go with you? You didn't even tell anyone where you were going."

"Yes, I fucked up. I get that. But I also handled it. Can we focus on that for a minute? Please? We had a potential suspect who needed interviewing, and I interviewed him. He didn't deny the crimes. I think we need to be discussing next steps, not dwelling in a perpetual state of pissed-offness. You're angry. Great, that's fair. But set it aside so we can deal with what's important."

"I *am* trying to deal with what's important." He enunciates each word pointedly.

I tuck my feet up under me on the couch. "No, you're badgering me and being dramatic." He doesn't deny it, and I take that as acquiescence. "I recorded it. If you listen, you'll see what I mean. He doesn't admit that he did it, but he definitely doesn't state that he didn't."

"No," he says, ignoring what I just said. "What I'm doing is seeing you murdered every time I blink."

I groan. "Ravi, please. I'm sorry. I'm sorry I worried you. I'm sorry I acted without thinking. But we need to move forward with this, and I need your help to do it. I don't think we have enough for the cops to take us seriously yet, so we need to figure out how to get more evidence."

The stony silence settles over us again, and I'm about to give up on a reply when he says, "Tomorrow. We'll figure it out tomorrow. I'm too pissed at you to be rational right now."

"That sounded pretty rational to me," I say, wanting more than anything to be at a point where we can look at this and laugh.

His glare says we're definitely not there yet. "Sleep at my house tonight. Please. Ma won't care if you take the guest room."

"I'm fine here."

"You pissed off a maybe-murderer today. Who probably knows where you live." He slaps the side of the ottoman, sucking in a deep breath through his nose that he exhales sharply. "Just sleep at my damn house so I don't have to spend the entire fucking night wondering if you're alive or not."

"It's okay, really."

"Then I'm sleeping here," he says. "But I'm done talking about this for tonight."

I see no point in continuing to argue, so I leave him sitting there and take a long shower, trying to wash the fight off with a slick of honey-vanilla bodywash. It doesn't work. When I turn the water off, I hear the low drone of the TV and know he's probably not even watching it, just stewing in his thoughts.

I pull on my flannel hedgehog pants and a baggy shirt, then make a decision while I brush my teeth. I gather up the spare blankets and one of my pillows and go to the living room.

Ravi flicks the TV off when I come in, and for a second, I'm worried we're about to pick up the fight again.

I hold the blankets out as a peace offering. "If you're still mad at me, you can stay out here." I take a deep breath. "But you're welcome to my bed too."

"I'm not taking your bed."

My body feels light, giddy, like gravity is out of whack. I hug the blankets tighter, in case they float away too. "That's not what I meant." His forehead crinkles up in confusion, and I laugh. "Wait, I don't mean that either. Just sleep. But it's up to you."

He's quiet long enough that I start to regret the offer. It was poor timing. I should've known that. I set the blankets on the ottoman. "I am sorry, you know. I never meant to worry you."

Alone in bed, I stare at the ceiling for a long time, wondering if Ravi is doing the same in the living room. I don't know how things got so complicated. Would we be fighting like this if we hadn't kissed, hadn't gone out?

I think we would, and I can't tell if that makes it better or worse.

The house is eerily silent without the static hum of Dad's white noise machine and the muffled sounds of Cassidy mumbling in her sleep. Every heartbeat sounds like a bomb, and the creak of the floorboard is like a gunshot.

I hold my breath and go very still. It's probably just Ravi going to the bathroom. But no, his shadow falls into my open doorway. I exhale.

"That offer still good?"

I scoot over and raise the covers in response.

He settles in, facing away from me, and I curl myself around him. He relaxes into me with a sigh, and I wonder if this is a mistake, if asking him to share a bed with a girl he can't actually sleep with is cruel, but I like the feel of him here too much to risk him leaving by discussing it. He knew the boundaries when he came in.

I pull him closer, and incrementally, the tension eases out of him. I know he's still upset with me and that he has a right to be, but it's enough to know we haven't imploded. I snuggle against his back, and when I kiss his shoulder, he pulls my arm tighter around his chest and kisses the top of my hand.

In the morning, we're probably going to have to finish hashing out the fight, but for right now, I'm content.

And far less content when I wake the next morning to find him gone.

I tell myself it's because he had to go home to get fresh clothes and pick up Priya, but his absence stings.

Still, the morning brings with it a clarity that the adrenaline-fueled afternoon and evening had lacked, and I send Ravi a long text while I eat breakfast: *I'm so sorry for being rash. You were right. I wasn't thinking. I understand why you're upset, and I really am sorry. Really, really. Thank you for staying over and scaring off the monsters. You're my very favorite human. My invaluable companion.*

I immediately follow it up with *And an ace snuggler* just to be cheeky.

He doesn't reply right away, but the little check that indicates the text was opened appears, and that's something. At least he didn't delete it unread. We'll talk at school, and everything will be okay.

ONLY I can't find him at school. His car is in the lot, but he apparently didn't wait for me and is nowhere to be seen. Even 331 is empty, the door locked and lights off.

I don't see him until lunch, when I find him at our usual table devouring a tray of nachos like nothing's wrong.

I drop down across from him. "Do you still hate me?"

"I never hate you." He lifts a white paper bag from the seat beside him and slides it across the table. "Not warm but made this morning. By me. Peace offering."

"You can't placate me with donuts."

He snorts. "Even white chocolate mocha ones?"

I open the bag and am hit with an intoxicating wave of coffee-scented sugar. "I didn't say I'm not going to eat them. But it doesn't make up for you sneaking out and avoiding me all morning."

"I wasn't ignoring you," he says. "Larson caught me when I walked in and wanted to talk about the *I Am Maplefield* pictures. For ages. Then roped me into helping Miss Caroline move a bookshelf."

"Fun times."

"The funnest."

"So, Captain Over-Reacty Pants. We cool?"

He sighs. "I'm still pissed at you. Probably gonna be until we get whoever we need to behind bars. But you're my favorite human, and I'm mostly just glad you weren't ax-murdered."

"Yeah, me too." I bump his leg with my foot under the table. He doesn't move away, and it's nice, that secret connection.

"And the plan is to keep you that way. I know you don't think you fit the profile if it's Vernon, but I'm not willing to risk it. Also, Ma will be pissed if you skip out on dinner tonight, so you better still be coming, and you might as well bring shit with you to stay over, because you're not staying alone at your house." He raises a hand to forestall any protest. "Nope. Not up for discussion. You come willingly, or I kidnap. Priya's going home with Sabrina today, so we can hash out everything we need to without her interrupting every two seconds."

Priya does have a tendency to think I sleep over to hang out with her as much as Ravi, which is usually fine, but Ravi's right. The last thing we need is a fourteen year old overhearing the finer points of our murder investigation.

"Deal. I'll swing home after school to get clothes, then head to your place." I'm not about to say it out loud, but I don't hate the idea of not being alone. Peter made it perfectly clear that he'd be more than capable of hurting me if he chose to.

"Oh, by the way"—Ravi crunches into his last nacho—"Jacob texted me back yesterday. He was with his father on a run down to Virginia. He got back last night."

"Wait, like a drug run or a legit truck haul?"

"Uh, he made it sound like just a regular work trip, but I guess maybe both?" He shrugs. "Who knows."

"Family bonding at its finest."

"You know it." He tosses his napkin onto his tray of nacho crumbs. "So, my place, dinner and murder. Maybe me getting to be big spoon." He flashes me a grin that says we're definitely okay again. "Try not to do anything horrifically stupid before you get there, yeah?"

"Cross my heart."

The Making of a Monster
Continued

In the wake of his public shaming, the only thing that saved him was the girl. Not his sister, but the pretty new girl he noticed on the first day of school, who'd started passing him notes in class. She became his new guardian angel, and even though she was out of his league by a long shot, she was nice, and he convinced himself she hadn't seen the video, even though it was all anyone mentioned when they saw him.

It was through a note—a prayer on paper folded into the shape of a heart—that he asked her to homecoming. It was the bravest thing he'd ever done, and she stunned him by saying yes. She even invited him to the bonfire after-party at Stone Reservoir.

His sister wasn't happy for him, even though she already had a date, but he didn't care. He floated through the weeks leading up to the big night, arranging a limo and flowers to match the girl's purple dress.

He wanted it to be a night to remember.

Chapter Thirty-one

I GET to Ravi's before he does and figure he probably got hung up at The Donut Hole, hopefully making donuts for the night's deductions. I don't mind. I'm as comfortable sitting at the kitchen island watching Mrs. B knead the dough for samosas as I am at my own house.

"These," Mrs. B says, "are the sole reason I gained fifteen pounds when I married Ravi's dad."

I laugh but don't doubt it. The little dough-wrapped potato pockets are usually a snack or appetizer, but Mrs. B makes oversized ones that are hands down my favorite thing to have when I'm here for dinner. I wouldn't put it past Ravi to have requested them specifically as yet another edible peace offering.

Maybe I really can be bought by food.

"Had you ever had them before meeting him?" I ask.

"Honey, I grew up a white girl in Maplefield. If you think restaurant pickings are slim now, you should've seen it back when your mom and I were in school. We had the drive-in during the summer and Gio's for pizza. That's it." She sprinkles more flour on the dough and drives the heels of her hands into it. "No, I fell in love with food about the same time I fell in love with Ravi's dad, in Boston. We did a culinary world tour without ever leaving the city. Every semester, we'd pick a continent, and we'd find as many restaurants that represented the countries as we could and try them all. Even then, I think Ravi's dad wanted to be a chef, but he also wanted to please his family."

"Who wouldn't be pleased to have an epic donut shop in the family?" But I know the answer. People like my father. People who think worth is tied to how much money you make.

"Oh, they're on board now. It's just that Ravi's dad came from a family of corporate types, and back then, business and banking was where it was at."

"According to my dad, that's still how it is."

Mrs. B gathers the dough into a ball. "Pass me that bowl, would you, dear? Don't you worry about your dad. You just stay true to who you are and what you want to do. He'll come around."

"I hope you're right. Hey, what was he like in high school?"

Mrs. B laughs. "He was a few years older than your mom and me—they didn't start dating until after graduation, which I'm sure you know—so I didn't know him that well, but he was on the debate team and president of TAR —Teen Age Republicans—club. He was very into politics, always trying to rally people for different issues."

"That was actually a thing?" I can't imagine such a club existing in a Massachusetts school. "Wait, did you guys have a shooting team too?"

Mrs. B cocks her head like she's trying to remember.

"I saw a picture," I explain. "I found it when I was doing research on the senior curse, and apparently, there was an actual gun club at the school."

"That rings a bell." Mrs. B checks the pot of potatoes boiling on the stove. "But I'm not sure if it was a team or just a club. If it wasn't basketball or cheerleading, it wasn't really on my radar."

Even though I've seen pictures, I have a hard time picturing soft, motherly Mrs. B as a cheerleader.

"Ravi said your research is going well?"

"It is. It took some looking, but I think we found the origin of the curse. We were searching too far back for a while." As I talk, I check my phone, looking for a message from Ravi, but there's only a text from my mother. He probably stopped by The Donut Hole on his way home and got put to work. "I actually thought it might've started with your graduating class."

"Really?" She turns off the stove and puts a colander in the sink.

"Yeah, we found a kid who died, James Blackwell, and Mom sa—"

An unholy crash startles me as Mrs. B drops the pot of boiling potatoes and sends a cascade of foamy water pouring off the counter. I jump up, grabbing a dish towel. "Oh, shit. Are you okay?"

Mrs. B's rosy complexion has gone ghostly, and her shirt is dotted with droplets of potato water. She laughs—a thin, high sound that's more animal than anything. "Oh, how clumsy! Don't worry. It looks like most of them landed in the strainer anyway."

I drape the dish towel over the biggest puddle and tear off a length of paper towels to swipe at the counter. "Did you get burned?"

"No, no, I'm fine," Mrs. B says, but she sinks onto my empty stool and stares at something only she can see.

I keep mopping up, and by the time the counter is dry, the color has returned to Mrs. B's face. "All set. Potato catastrophe averted."

"I haven't thought of James Blackwell in years."

"You knew him?"

Mrs. B nods, a tight spasm of motion that looks almost painful.

"You were friends?"

"No. Your mom was friends with Jennifer, his sister—they were twins—but the rest of us, well, we thought they were weird. And they were. Weird. Him especially. But that doesn't make what we did okay."

Mrs. B is being more than a little weird herself, but I don't say so. Ravi needs to get home.

"What do you mean, what you did? My mom didn't say anything like that."

Mrs. B shakes her head. "Not your mom. The rest of us though…" She trails off into a silence that lasts long enough for me to imagine all sorts of scenarios, none of them good. The thought of my best friend's mother being involved in her classmate's death is enough to make me wonder how much I really want the truth. I won't be able to unhear anything she's about to say. But no. Sherlock Holmes wouldn't shy away from the pursuit of truth and neither will I. My inner journalist has to know.

"You can tell me," I say gently.

"We were awful to him. We really were. At the time, it seemed harmless, the kind of jokes you do for laughs, but when I think about

Ravi or Priya acting like that—or worse, being treated like that—it makes me sick."

"What happened?"

Mrs. B's gaze loses its eerie unfocused quality, and she meets my eyes. "We were bullies," she says bluntly. "All of us. Not your mom, but the rest of us. The boys were the worst. They would push him and steal his stuff, but what I did was awful. I let Chad talk me into it. It was one prank, but I could've said no. Your mother tried to stop me, but I liked Chad and wanted to be cool, so I agreed." She pauses, and a complicated mix of emotions flashes across her face before settling on one: shame. "Everyone knew James had a crush on me, so I hinted that he should ask me to homecoming, and when he did, I said yes, like Chad instructed. Then, on the night of the dance, I dumped him— right in front of everyone, during photos." Mrs. B shakes her head, her remorse real and palpable. "It's the worst thing I've ever done to another person. He killed himself shortly after."

Mrs. B excuses herself to the bathroom, and I'm grateful to be saved from having to reply. I have no idea what to do with this new information. Having a hard time seeing middle-aged Mrs. B as a cheerleader is one thing, but reconciling huggable, home-cooking, practically-a-second-mother Mrs. B with the image of a high school bully is impossible.

I check my phone again for messages from Ravi, but still nothing. There's a check-in from Mom though, and I tell her I'm at the Burmans' for the night, then text Ravi: *Did you get lost??*

I wait for the bouncing dots that would herald a reply but get nothing. Not even a little check mark to show it's been opened.

When Mrs. B returns, her face is damp, but her eyes are clear. "Okay, let's see what we can do about this filling," she says. "Be a dear and start mashing the potatoes while I get everything else."

I do as I'm told while Mrs. B slides a pile of diced onions into a sauté pan. Neither of us mentions James Blackwell again, even though I'm sure he's on her mind as much as mine. We work in companionable silence, making the filling and rolling out dough, until Mr. B walks in and she goes to greet him.

"Ravi's not with you?" I ask.

"No. Was I supposed to get him?" Mr. B shoots a nervous look at his wife like he might've screwed up.

"Oh, no." Mrs. B pats him on the arm. "He told me he was staying after school to finish the pictures he needed for his project. He should be back soon."

The hair on my neck stands up. "He told you that?"

"He texted earlier, right after school. He didn't tell you?"

I shake my head slowly, wary of dislodging the thing picking at the edge of my brain. "But we have all the photos," I say, more to myself than Ravi's parents. "Except our own. There's no reason…"

I drop the spoon I've been using to scoop the spiced potato mixture onto the squares of dough and open my texts, not caring that I smear potato on the screen. My last message still hasn't been read. I reach for Mrs. B's phone. "Can I see it? The text?"

Mrs. B looks confused but hands her phone over. Her background is an old photo of Ravi and Priya at the beach, taken two or three summers ago. She doesn't have a passcode, and I pull up the message I need: *Hi Mom. Staying after 2 take pictures. Will b late.* And check the time stamp: *3:34.* Blood drains from my face and pools at my feet, making me sway.

It's wrong. The texts are wrong. I put a hand on the island to steady myself, check it again. It says *Mom*, just like I thought, and the confirmation makes the world tilt. He never calls Mrs. B Mom, only Ma, purely because it drives her nuts. And he never uses abbreviations.

"Wait." Synapses fire faster than my conscious mind can keep up with. The phone shakes in my hand, and I set it down before I drop it. The Burmans look at me like I'm losing it. I might be.

"What's the matter?" Mrs. B asks.

I grab my own phone, open the gallery, and scroll until I find it— the photo from the library. "No. No, no, no." The words come out like a moan. I look up at Mrs. B. "Your friends. Your high school friends. Who were they?"

"What are you talking about?"

"The boy! James. You and your friends, the ones who tormented him." I don't care that I sound unhinged. My mind is racing faster than logic, faster than it ever has in my life, and I'm not wrong. The hair on my arms and the vise on my heart tell me I'm not wrong, even though I want to be. "It was you. It was Emma's dad. Who else?"

"Maura Bannon." Mrs. B's wide eyes mimic my own. "And Billy Mackenzie. Why?"

"Maura Bannon, she's Maura Auger now, right?"

"Well, yes. Why?" Mrs. B asks, bewildered.

"And Billy Mackenzie, he was Liam's father?"

"Yes. Kennedy, what's the matter?"

"That's it. That's the connection." The ground tilts beneath me, and I'm utterly unable to acknowledge or set aside the truth. "We were wrong. We were so, so wrong. It did start with your class."

The world tips again, shuffling the pieces in and out of place. The link is clear, but something is missing—a final connection not quite made.

The photo I snapped of the obituary is fuzzy but readable. *James Henry Blackwell, 17, passed away at home on December 9th.* Today is the ninth.

Every gut instinct screams that this is how Peter is choosing his victims. Not by looks, not because of his own scandal, but somehow because of this long-dead boy. My mind whirls in a frantic search for the connection. Could they be related? Could Peter have been bullied to the brink of suicide too? Is it a vigilante thing?

It doesn't matter. Not now. All that matters is stopping him.

I snatch my keys from the counter as the bag of clear fluid hanging from the IV stand in Peter's living room flashes across my brain, along with the fact that James died from an insulin overdose. "Call the police. Tell them Ravi's missing, that he's in danger. Tell them to look for Peter Vernon. They won't believe me; you have to do it. Make them listen. I need to go. I need to find him."

Ravi's parents try to stop me, try to make me explain, but there isn't time. "Just call the police," I shout and dart for The Planet.

Chapter Thirty-two

I CALL Ravi as I drive, but it dumps me straight to voice mail each time. I knew it would. That after-school text to Mrs. B was probably the last message to go out before whoever sent it powered down the phone.

I open the Find My Friends app, something I installed for a story about cyberstalking but haven't used since. I only have two people that I follow: Cassidy, who's listed as being 187 miles away in New Gloucester, Maine, and Ravi, whose status says *Location Unavailable.* Shit.

I call Priya, who answers on the third ring sounding wary. "Hello?"

I do my best to set aside the panic coursing through my veins. Scaring the girl won't help. "Pri, sorry to be weird, but have you talked to Ravi since school got out?"

"Oh god, are you guys still fighting?" I can practically hear her roll her eyes. "He was wicked pissed at you this morning, but he'll get over it."

"No, it's not that. I was just wondering if you'd seen him is all. He's late to dinner, and you know how rare that is."

"Ha, no shit. Did you try calling him?"

I fight the urge to scream that I wouldn't be calling his sister if he were answering his phone. "Yeah," I say tightly. "But it's off."

"Oh, weird," Priya says in the verbal equivalent of a shrug. "Don't know. His car was still at school when Sabrina's mom picked us up, but I haven't seen him since this morning."

"Okay, thanks anyway." I hang up before Priya can say goodbye. "Don't panic, don't panic. You just have to think."

Even though it's barely past seven, the sky is dark as midnight, and I barely slow at the stop sign when I see there's no glow of headlights to signal any approaching cars.

I need to be logical. I have to start with what I know, and what I know is that the last place anyone saw Ravi was at the school and that Kylie was killed there too, but I don't let myself dwell on that second part. I can't.

I make it there in record time and almost cry when I see his car still sitting in its usual spot, looking lost and alone in the otherwise empty parking lot. I park next to it and nearly fall out of The Planet in my rush to look inside. I cup my hands to the window, hoping against hope that he's inside, sleeping for some reason, or even injured and unconscious because at least he would be found and alive. But the car is empty, without even his messenger bag to show that he'd been in it at all since the morning.

I whip around, searching the darkness like he might be lurking there, just out of sight. The headlights of The Planet illuminate the side of the building and cast spindly shadows up from the bushes that make me think of monsters.

"Set. It. Aside," I tell myself, needing the words to cut through the clutter of my panicked brain. And it works. I scramble back into The Planet, searching the passenger seat for my phone. This time, I open Find My iPhone, cursing myself for not trying it earlier, and click *Sign Out*. I enter Ravi's ID and password and wait. Even though the phone is off, the app should still be able to report its last known location, which would reveal where the last text had been sent from. That will give me a lead.

An eternity passes while the app processes the request, but then the little locator icon appears on the map, and at first, I think I've tracked my own device. According to Apple, the phone is right in front of me. But no, the bubble reads *Ravi's iPhone*, and it sits directly over an aerial outline of the school.

I'm running before my brain finishes processing the information. I slam into the main entrance door, hauling on the handle with all my might. It doesn't budge. I slap at the buzzer, but the main office is

dark, and I know there's no one to let me in. I race around the building, searching for open windows and praying the back entrance will
be pegged and ajar.

The rear parking lot is dark, the quartet of towering lights that
usually glow there standing stark and useless against the night sky. The
light that should mark the rear entrance is also off, but I know where
the door is even in the dark, in the alcove beyond the tree, and I yank
it with all my might. It rattles against its lock. "No, no, no."

I race back around to the front of the building, where it's illumi-
nated enough to find a rock, a branch, anything I can use to smash a
window. I don't care if it sets off alarms. Hell, I hope it does.

I search the ground near the bushes but find nothing big enough
to do the trick. I sprint to The Planet and wrench open the trunk, hoping for a tire iron or a jack stand, but there's nothing but a few wisps
of hay.

I slam the trunk shut, the reverberation juddering up my arm,
and realize I'm looking at my way inside. It will be messy, and it'll
probably hurt, but the walkway to the main entrance is plenty wide
enough to accommodate the car. If I back up, I should be able to get
enough speed to barrel through the door. The parentals will kill me,
and I'll probably get expelled, but I don't care. Every fiber of my being
bellows that Ravi is inside and that he's in danger. It's gut instinct and
logic all tangled up, and I couldn't ignore it if I tried.

I climb behind the wheel, strap the seat belt on as tight as it
can go, and crank the key. The engine, still engaged, grinds in protest.
Something niggles my brain as I shift into reverse. Something about
turning keys. I shift back into park and put my hand on the key in the
ignition, then erupt in a burst of wild, terrified laughter that leaves me
gasping.

I whip the seat belt off and climb through to the back seat. There.
My backpack is on the floor, half under the passenger seat, but it's
there.

I unzip the front compartment and dump it out, the overhead
light illuminating a heap of papers, headphones, and lip balm. I rifle

through it, spreading the contents everywhere until the glint of metal catches my eye. "Oh, fuck yes."

It's the master key, the one we swiped from the custodial suite and used to break into the auditorium. The key I forgot to return. The key to finding Ravi. I turn off The Planet, whirling from how close I just came to willingly crashing the vehicle into a building, and launch myself at the main entrance.

I clutch the key tight in my fist, the serrated edge biting into my palm, and pray to every god I can think of that this will work. I'm terrified that the exterior doors have their own master key, but when I steady my hands, the slim piece of metal slides right into the lock and turns with ease. I almost collapse with relief.

I shoot a text to Priya—*Tell your mom the school right now*—and flick the phone to silent.

I pause in the entryway to give my eyes a chance to adjust to the unlit halls. The empty building was eerie on the day we snuck in after Kylie's death, but that was nothing compared to the utter stillness that surrounds me. The quiet seems to pulse like a living thing in the dark.

I want to shout for Ravi, scream until he reveals himself, but I don't. I can't. Surprise is the only advantage I have.

The main office is dark and silent as I pass. I'll search it if I have to, but I think I know where to find them.

The auditorium doors are locked, the lights off, but I don't trust that to mean anything. Peering through the window, I find a blackness so dense that I can't even see the stage. My heart races as I slip down the hallway, sticking close to the wall, to check the side door. There's no movement, no sign of life at all. I use the master key to let myself in, holding the door so it shuts as softly as possible. The clouds shift and weak moonlight filters through the skylights, offering just enough light to see as I dart up the stage stairs, staying close to the heavy velvet drapes.

I don't want to imagine Kylie's lifeless body on the stage, not when I'm looking for my best friend, but the image intrudes anyway, impossible to ignore. I lean into the horror, give it a moment of full attention, then box it up and set it aside.

There's no evidence on the stage that anyone has been here, no dropped phone or scrap of clothing. I duck behind the curtains into total darkness and creep forward, letting my ears do the work of searching. I hear nothing except the pounding of my own pulse.

Back in the hall, with so many possible places to go, every heartbeat urges me to run, to search everywhere as fast as possible. But I remember searching for Emma and how methodical it was. I have to do the same now. I'll start on the first floor and work my way up.

I start with a sweep of the office and almost scream when I come face-to-face with a tall, shadowy figure that turns out to be nothing more than a coatrack draped with Ms. Larson's long wool coat.

Next, I take the hall between the office and auditorium, looking into every classroom, trying every knob. At the end, I turn left, away from the gym, and ping-pong off the walls as I check rooms on both sides of the hall. I bypass the stairs to the second floor and go down the hall that leads to the cafeteria and the library beyond that.

The change in light is so subtle that I think I'm imagining it—a shifting cloud, perhaps, or my eyes adjusting further to the gloom. But as I creep down the hall, it grows brighter. My stomach clenches with an animal sense of dread.

From beneath a windowless door marked *Boiler Access*, a brilliant wash of light spills across the tiled floor like blood.

Chapter Thirty-three

THE LIGHT coming from under the door wavers, grows dark in patches, and regains its uniform glow.

My heart rattles in its cage of bones as something moves within the room.

I press my ear to the door, the copper taste of fear rising in my throat like bile. A soft sound, like an exhalation of breath, then a low whine turns my knees to noodles.

With shaking hands, I feel for the keyhole. I have no plan for once I get the door open, but the time for dithering is over. I take a deep breath, set the fear aside, and twist the key.

The fluorescent light is blinding after the dimness of the hall, and I blink hard, unable to wrap my head around what I'm seeing.

It's Henry, stretched out on his belly with his head on his paws. His tail thumps a happy hello when he sees me, and he stretches languidly before climbing to his feet and trotting over.

My breath is ragged and far too loud in the echoing room. If Henry's here, that must mean Ms. Larson is too. I sway under the weight of the realization that I now have two lives resting on my shoulders. I pray Priya got word to the Burmans and that help is on the way.

The boiler room is like an alien planet with its rumbling machinery and hulking metal pipes big enough to crawl through snaking along the ceiling. The room is easily twice as long as it is wide, maybe more, and there are countless places for someone to hide.

With my back to the wall, I drop to a crouch and try to get a look under the machines, but too many have parts that are flat on the cement floor to see across the space. Henry tries to stick his head in my lap, but I push him away and stand, searching for something to use as

a weapon. The light should be comforting after so much time searching in the dark, but I feel horribly exposed and have to fight the urge
to duck down as I move.

My eye catches on a small fire extinguisher mounted on the wall
across the room. I run for it, staying on my toes to make less noise,
then hear the machine-gun rattle of Henry's nails as he follows. So
much for stealth. I yank the extinguisher from its bracket and test its
weight. It'll do for bludgeoning.

Henry looks up at me like he's waiting to see what we're doing
next, and I realize he might know more than I do. I lean in close to
his head and whisper, "Where's Mommy, Henry? Where is she? Go
find Mommy."

The dog licks my face, gives a shake that makes his jingling tags
crash like cymbals, and trots off. I trail after him, sticking close to the
machinery and watching for any sign of movement.

Henry keeps glancing back, like he can't figure out what's taking
me so long, and a flash of panic hits me that I could be putting his life
in danger by sending him on ahead like this. I set the thought aside;
there's nothing that can be done about it now.

As we near the end of the room, I wonder if it's possible that
Henry has been locked in here just to get him out of the way. Maybe
Peter has no problem killing people, but hurting animals makes him
squeamish. But the dog disappears around the final machine—some
sort of massive metal tank—and barks twice.

I flatten myself against the side of the tank, certain Peter is about
to emerge, drawn by the barking, but the only sound is the burble of
machinery

I tiptoe around the tank to follow the dog and find him nosing at
the edge of an unmarked door.

"In there?"

He sits and looks at me expectantly. The door is wooden, dark
with age, and bears a simple knob with no keyhole. A closet, then.
That can't bode well.

I steel myself, taking short, sharp breaths in through my nose.
Whatever is in there, I can deal with it. I'll have to.

I turn the knob, and the door opens with a squeal of ungreased hinges. Henry shoots inside.

And promptly vanishes.

Where I had expected to find mops and buckets—and okay, maybe bodies—there's a hallway.

The claustrophobic passage stretches out before me, barely wider than the doorway, with a sloping concrete floor that seems to descend into the very depths of hell. A soft pool of light illuminates the distant end, and I catch a glimpse of Henry's tail as he turns a corner at the bottom.

I adjust my sweaty grip on the fire extinguisher and listen, but it's hard to hear anything over the sound of my own instincts telling me to run. But Henry hasn't yelped pain, hasn't given any indication that there's danger. *Go find Mommy* is a command he knows, and I have to trust him.

I cross the threshold, leaving the door to the boiler room open to provide at least a bit of light, and try to ignore the hammering in my chest.

At the bottom of the ramp, I hesitate, because although the light is brighter here, I'm wary of coming around a blind corner. The urge to turn back is almost overwhelming, like that feeling you get when you turn the light off in the basement and can't help sprinting up the stairs, even though you know there aren't any monsters.

I really need to stop thinking about monsters.

Hefting the fire extinguisher to my shoulder like a club, I take a steadying breath and peek around the corner. All caution evaporates the instant I see Ravi sprawled lifeless in the center of the strange room beyond.

I drop the fire extinguisher with a deafening crash and race forward, screaming his name.

I'm still screaming when a pair of hands grabs me from behind, when a strong arm locks around my windpipe, when I'm wrenched off my feet. I struggle with every ounce of rage and despair in me, but it's futile. I'm still screaming Ravi's name as spots flare at the edges of my vision and the world goes black around me.

Chapter Thirty-four

I **COME** to sitting upright, and the only thing keeping me from falling over when the first wave of dizziness hits is the fact that my hands are tied behind my back around a fat metal pole. *Not a pole, a Lally column*, my brain supplies uselessly. I know without looking that the pole reaches the ceiling and will be impossible to break. That knowledge sets the world to spinning again, and I close my eyes.

Focus. I have to focus.

I start with my feet, staring at them until they stop swaying, then let my eyes crawl up, taking in the sight before me. It's a weird room, with the proportions all wrong. Too long. Way too long. Faded white lines are painted on the scuffed floor. No, not lines. Lanes. Shooting lanes.

So, the range wasn't a myth after all.

I turn my head slowly, taking in the row of metal columns that run the width of the room. Some have small wooden platforms attached to them like waist-high side tables.

There's a rustle of movement behind me, and a disembodied female voice says, "Welcome back."

I whip my head around to find the source and regret it instantly, the dizziness forcing my eyes closed again as my stomach heaves. Slow movements. Slow movements are better.

But something about the motion dislodges the memory of how I got here in the first place, and I throw myself against my bonds like a rabid dog.

"Ravi?" Where is he? Why can't I see him? "Ravi!" I struggle to my knees, ignoring the spinning of the room, and get my feet under me. "Ravi!"

Henry butts his head against my leg, whining softly at my distress, but I ignore him as I struggle to stand. It's awkward, and my shoulders strain like they want to dislocate, but I'm driven by a panic that doesn't care.

Standing, I shuffle my feet, moving around the pole until I'm facing the part of the range that had been at my back. I almost sink back to the ground, weak with relief, because there he is, awake and sitting on a low wooden stage at the end of the room. Shadowy animal shapes that must be targets lurk behind him. The scene makes no sense to my addled brain, but it doesn't matter. He's there, and he's alive, and he's not tied up. I'm so overcome with joy that I can't find words, any words, other than his name.

But something is wrong. He isn't looking at me, even as I shout for him. His gaze is fixed on something beyond my shoulder. "This doesn't involve her," he says, voice harder than I've ever heard it. "Let her go."

I turn to see who he's speaking to and am again struck by a wave of relief that threatens to take my legs away. "Ms. Larson. Oh, thank god." I lean against the column, letting it support me. "When I saw Henry, I thought he'd taken you too. Can you move? We have to get out of here." I shuffle around to get a better look at her but freeze when I see the gun she has pointed at the stage.

At Ravi.

Ms. Larson laughs, a throaty chuckle that sends a chill down my spine. I used to tell Cassidy those shivers mean someone is walking over your grave, and for the first time, I believe it.

My heartbeat is erratic and impossibly loud as Ms. Larson strides down the gun range and positions herself halfway to the stage, where we can each see each other like three points of a triangle. I wonder if I'm still unconscious, if this whole scene is the result of oxygen deprivation, but the pain in my arms is too sharp for a dream.

"What's going on?" I barely recognize my own voice. I have to calm down. I have to breathe. "Where's Peter?"

Ravi opens his mouth to say something, but Ms. Larson waggles the gun at him. "You don't speak yet." She keeps the weapon raised but gives me her full attention. "I'm almost disappointed," she says. "You were so close. I thought if anyone would figure it out, it would be you. It's okay though. You're here now. You're still going to get the scoop first."

I look at Ravi, and he meets my eyes now. His mouth is a hard line, but his eyes are the ones I know better than my own, even across this distance, and I make him my anchor. He takes an exaggerated breath, and I mirror it. Acknowledge the fear, set it aside. Panic will not get us out of this.

"Do you want to take one more crack at it?" Ms. Larson asks, drawing my gaze back around.

I don't let my eyes linger on the gun this time but look straight at her. "A crack at what?"

"Solving the mystery, of course. You do have all the pieces, after all. C'mon, puzzle it out."

I hesitate, trying to assemble what I know, but I take too long.

"Okay, never mind." Ms. Larson's voice is disconcertingly upbeat, like she's addressing a classroom full of inattentive kindergartners. "You were never meant to be a part of this, but I'm going to give you a gift. I'm going to tell you a story—a story about how someone winds up with this much blood on their hands and why it's all so very worth it. You're going to get the whole scoop, straight from the horse's mouth.

"See, the thing no one tells you about real vengeance is how much self-control it takes. It's worth it though, in the end. I think that's a story people need to hear. Just how much it's worth it.

"To make you understand, I need to start at the beginning.

"This isn't the story about who I am today—the one with the power, the one with blood on my hands. It's the story of a boy who grew up in a world that ground him down.

"It's the origin story of a monster."

I DON'T know how long I stand there listening to Ms. Larson recount her and her brother's childhood, but it's longer than I need for the missing piece to slot into place.

James Henry Blackwell. Namesake of Henry the golden retriever, who had unwittingly led me to this very room.

"You're Jennifer Blackwell, the sister," I say. "But how? How has no one known who you really are?"

She laughs, but there's no humor in it, only scorn. "It's amazing how far a little hair dye and makeup will get you if you want to hide in plain sight. Everyone's memories have qualifiers, shortcuts for the people they catalog, and they're not the pithy sayings you've had students writing on whiteboards. They're shorter, more honest. For example, I was the freckled, frizzy-headed ginger. But take that away, and I could be anyone. I could change my last name and disappear even further. Add a job where everyone is programmed to trust you, and the world becomes your oyster."

As Ms. Larson talks, I twist my wrists this way and that, trying to loosen the stranglehold of the ropes, but the struggle only increases the numbness in my hands.

"And I deserved an oyster," Ms. Larson says. "Losing James shattered us. I stopped sleeping because the only thing I saw when I closed my eyes was his body. It's like I was haunted by him as punishment for not being there to save him. I stopped going to school, which my mother never even noticed." She snorts, lips pulled back in a vicious sneer. "She disappeared. James was barely in the ground, and she was gone. My father said she ran away, and we never found a body, but I will believe until I die that she chose to go with James. She chose him over the family she still had left. My father couldn't take it. I had to watch as he withered before my eyes. At first, he still went to work and only drank on the way home. Then it was a drink in the morning to get going, and eventually, he just made drinking his job. He'd start fights at the bar with anyone he could. He never hit me, but he had all this rage coiled up inside him like a snake."

I wonder if Ms. Larson realizes that she fits that description too, but I don't ask. The ropes bite into my wrists as I search for the knot.

"One night, he went after the wrong guy—an off-duty cop—and landed in prison. I was seventeen. No one wanted to foster a kid that age, especially one with a 'troubled background' as they put it."

Ms. Larson flicks the gun up like she's shooing the phrase away, as if it were an annoying fly. "I ended up in care. A group home in Lawrence. I was there for less than a month when I was told my father had died. Official cause of death was a heart attack, but I think he just gave up.

"And just like that, in the space of a single phone call, I became an orphan. I was adrift. I was no longer anyone's twin or anyone's daughter. I could be anything. I could be the avenging angel my family needed."

"Bull. Shit," Ravi growls from the stage.

Ms. Larson whirls, gun raised, and storms across the room.

I throw myself against the ropes, screaming, "No! Please don't. Please don't."

Even Henry scrambles to his feet, but Ms. Larson advances on Ravi with the inexorable force of a tidal wave and levels the gun at his chest. He glowers at her and refuses to shrink back.

"This is not how it goes," Ms. Larson says. "I'm sorry we have to do it this way, but this story is for her." She stabs a finger in my direction without turning around. "She's going to need it. It's the only thing I can give her. If you interrupt me again, I will make you regret it."

"Please," I beg, not sure if I'm talking to Ms. Larson or Ravi.

Ravi's mouth twitches, but he swallows whatever words were there, his teeth bared in a silent snarl. The air crackles with tension as Ms. Larson backs away, returning to a midpoint in the room.

"As I was saying, I could become anything. I wasn't going to give up like my father did. I started going back to school. I graduated on time, with good grades. I became a chameleon, fading into the background so no one would notice the rage that fueled my every action.

"The Fucking Four never left my mind. I used them to write the essay that earned me a full ride to UMass Amherst, where I promptly stopped referring to my past and created an idyllic fictional family that had moved across country for my father's job, leaving me alone on the East Coast, and while my classmates were freaking out over Y2K and presidential blow jobs, I was planning a long game."

An irrational bubble of laughter boils at the sound of Ms. Larson saying *blow job*, but I bite it back. This isn't my principal anymore. It's a monster wearing a principal-shaped mask.

"It took a frat boy, of all things, to make me see my full potential. Jared, his name was, and he enjoyed spiking the drinks of unsuspecting freshman girls. I watched him do it four times before I planted myself in his path, deliberately acting younger than I was, and let nature take its course. I didn't drink the roofied drink, but swapped it for his and led him back to his room—a trick that shouldn't have worked, but did, like a charm. While he was passed out on his bed, I realized I could do the world a favor and end him then and there. All it took was a grocery bag and about six minutes, and I saved countless girls from being raped. It was intoxicating."

The relish with which Ms. Larson makes this final proclamation turns my blood to ice.

"It was ruled accidental thanks to the drugs in his system," she continues, "and I realized that there was no reason why I couldn't do it again on a larger scale. The next day, I switched my major from psychology to education and later graduated with honors. At that point, Facebook was in its infancy, but a fake profile and some phony details were all it took to start keeping tabs on the Fucking Four. I taught for two years before—"

I freeze as Ms. Larson suddenly turns to me. The gun is still pointed at Ravi, but her eyes bore into mine.

"Stop. Wiggling. Pay. Attention." She punctuates each word with a shake of the gun. "This is a once-in-a-lifetime scoop, and I'm giving it to you."

I nod and let my arms relax.

"Sit," Ms. Larson commands.

"I'm fi—"

"Sit."

I do. Henry wanders over to me, circles once, and lies down with a sigh. The basement scene from *The Silence of the Lambs* flashes through my mind, but even if I could get him, I don't think I could hurt Henry for leverage.

"I taught for two years before I enrolled in a graduate program for educational leadership, and I kept up with the news in Maplefield while I bided my time. I changed my hair and learned how to alter my face with makeup. I would be ready. I only allowed myself one kill at that first high school, just to see if I could still do it. He was a proper little shit—homophobic and racist, with Confederate flags flying from his pickup. I offered him a spiked soda after detention, and he was easy as pie after that. No one was upset when he stopped showing up to school, and his victims all walked a little taller in his absence."

I rock side to side, trying to feel if my phone is still in my back pocket, but it's not. Of course it's not. I doubt there's a signal down here anyway, but I wish I could at least be recording this monologue. If we don't make it out alive, at least a recording could be a legacy, proof of the madness that had infected Maplefield.

If Ms. Larson notices the movement, she doesn't let on. "It would've been too hard as a teacher," she says. "While you have access to the building, it isn't unfettered. I'd been right to get the principal's license. I accepted a promotion to assistant principal at the first school and waited. I monitored the Four through Facebook. I couldn't believe how easy they made it. Not a single one left Maplefield, except for Lisa's little stint in Boston, but even she returned, with a husband and baby in tow." She looks at Ravi the way a raptor eyes a field mouse.

Ravi glares back, defiance clouding his dark features.

Ms. Larson turns to me, a wistful smile on her face. "And then, finally, a principalship opened up, and I was able to come home."

Chapter Thirty-five

"**WHY ARE** you telling me this?" I ask.

"Because people will want to know. You need to understand."

"Does it really matter if I understand *why* you're killing my classmates? My best friend?" I try not to choke on those last words.

Ms. Larson offers me a smug Cheshire cat grin that screams de-
ceit. "It does to me."

"Why?"

"So everyone will know the truth. The truth is important. Do you
understand yet?"

I don't want to play Ms. Larson's games, but the desperation to
keep her talking is real. As long as she's talking, she's not putting bullets in anyone. So I play, starting with the obvious, giving myself room
to disassociate. "The Four—their proxies are Emma, Kylie, Liam, and
Ravi." I need to shut the feeling part of my brain off to do this. It's not
enough to acknowledge and set aside; I have to be the epitome of objectivity. "You don't want to harm the actual people who wronged you,
but their children."

"And why might that be?" Ms. Larson sounds like she's leading a
Socratic seminar.

I direct the answer to Ravi, unable to keep from proving the
point. "Because it hurts more when it's someone you care about. It's
worse than dying yourself."

There's a tightening of his posture, barely noticeable, but I know
him well enough to see it. Goose bumps erupt up my arms.

"Very good," Ms. Larson says. "Keep going."

"You want the original four to suffer like you did. Exactly like you did. So you make it look like suicide."

Ms. Larson purses her lips and tilts her head, a *You were so close, have an A for effort* expression on her face. "Not look like." She says it like a hint, a blank waiting to be filled in.

A cold sweat breaks out across my whole body, and the room tips on its axis. I close my eyes against a wave of vertigo.

It's not possible. There's no way to convince three vibrant, mentally stable teenagers to do something so monstrous.

Unless there is.

"Go on," she prompts.

The words lodge in my throat, my larynx paralyzed by the horror. "You make them kill themselves. Somehow, you make them."

"Not this time," Ravi says. His fingers grip the edge of the stage like he wants to pry up a board with his bare hands.

"That's where you're wrong," Ms. Larson says, sounding almost sad.

I renew my struggle with the ropes, knowing that time is running out. Something gives, just a fraction of an inch, a result of either the loosening ropes or millimeters of skin scraping off. I don't care which, so long as it leads to freedom.

"You both need to pay attention now," Ms. Larson says. "Kennedy, you're all caught up. I know it's not going to be enough, but I hope the story can be something of a consolation. You were never meant to be part of this."

"Ms. Larson, you don't have to do this." I try to sound reasonable, try to channel every hostage negotiation cliché I can think of. "What happened to you was awful, but that doesn't mean you need to keep hurting people."

Ms. Larson turns to Ravi as if I hadn't spoken, turns so completely that if I could only free myself, I could ambush her, wrestle the gun free, turn the tables.

But the ropes hold.

"This is the part neither of you knows," she says. "This is the how. This part isn't easy, not for anyone. But it's the price that has to be paid."

She keeps the gun trained on Ravi, who is practically vibrating with pent-up rage.

"You're like Liam," she tells him. "Collateral damage. Kylie was so much like her mother that it was like traveling back in time. It was almost like getting two for one. And Emma, well, Emma was a lot like your mom, Ravi. Smart, but with a mean streak.

"Don't talk about my mother." His eyes are on the gun, but his muscles twitch with the desire to fight.

"The sins of the mother are the worst of all." Ms. Larson prowls the front of the stage like a caged panther. "Your mother, she was the final nail in his coffin. The last stab of the needle."

I know the story, but I doubt Ravi does, and I want to protect him from that version of his mother. "But that wasn't Ravi," I say before she can go on. "Ravi didn't do anything. He doesn't deserve this."

"No, he doesn't," Ms. Larson agrees, then addresses him directly. "You don't. But neither did James. Neither did I. The universe doesn't always give us what we deserve, but it always keeps its balance."

"This isn't balance," I say.

She ignores me. Ravi is the only thing that matters to her now. "When you're ready, you're going to find a syringe behind you on your right. The first dose is already drawn. All you have to do is insert it into your leg and press. It's not painful. I promise."

Ravi looks over his shoulder, and the caged energy in him goes still. "You're insane. I'm not poisoning myself."

"You're going to die no matter what. I believe that's been made abundantly clear. How you go is up to you."

I twist in my ropes, and something small and vital pops in my hand. A searing pain lights up my arm. The swelling is instant, and it fills any slack I earned in the ropes. The room swims dangerously, and for the briefest of instants, I wonder if passing out wouldn't be better.

But Ms. Larson's voice cuts through the encroaching darkness. "Option one is to take the syringe and be done with it. I promise you, it will be quick. The other option is the gun." Ravi looks like he's about to speak, but Ms. Larson cuts him off. "Before you think you can make a play for it, let me remind you that everyone else was given the same second option, and no one took it."

My stomach seizes with a visceral terror.

"If you choose the gun—and that choice will be indicated by any refusal to comply precisely with the first option—you will be shot, and your family will be as well."

Ravi wears a mask of rage, but his skin has gone ashen. He meets my eyes, finally, and his are wide with fear and disbelief.

"Do not think for an instant that I am bluffing," Ms. Larson says. "Remember that it is your mother I truly wish to punish, and I will not hesitate to kill her if you make me go that route." She holds up a hand to forestall any protest. "Your father and your sister will just be more collateral damage."

"You wouldn't," he says.

"I assure you, I would. It would be easy. I could bring them to this very room. I could use your phone to do it, or I could simply use my authority as principal of this school. If I asked your parents to come in for a meeting, and to bring your sister, of course they would. They would have no reason not to. Now, because it's the anniversary, after all, I would like this settled before midnight. To help you decide, refusal of option one will also result in Kennedy's death. Immediately. And you will watch it happen."

The air rushes out of me like I've been kicked in the stomach. I scramble to my feet, adrenaline numbing the pain in my arm. I can't run—I know that—but I can't sit here and wait for death either. If nothing else, I'll be standing when it comes.

"I don't want to have to do that," Ms. Larson says. "But I will."

"You're gonna kill her anyway."

My head snaps to him, but he's right. I know too much. I'm about to be an eyewitness to murder. There's no way Ms. Larson can let me live.

"No," she says. "Kennedy only dies if you make it so. If you choose option one, she will be free to go at the end of the night."

"She can identify you."

"She can tell my story. James's story. That's important. We're in the final chapter now."

I can't explain it, but something in Ms. Larson's tone sounds sincere. "You want to get caught?"

"It's time to end this," she says.

Silence settles over the room, louder than the rushing of blood in my ears.

"Ravi, it's time to decide."

He looks at me, eyes huge, and his life flashes before my eyes. I see him as he was on the first day of kindergarten, those same wide eyes searching for mine in the crowded classroom. Even then, it was the two of us against the world. I see the countless recesses tucked beneath the climbing fort, happy with just each other. I see him with a broken leg, earned in a tree-climbing contest I won, and how he'd worn the grubby red cast like a badge of honor. I see middle school, that first day in the cafeteria, when we both pretended not to be completely overwhelmed by the sea of unfamiliar faces that had shown up from East Maplefield Elementary. I see the birthdays and snow days and summer nights camping in each other's backyards, and the thousands of regular days where he was my constant, as much a part of me as my lungs or my knees. I see the first time he had his heart broken and how those wide eyes had filled with tears, first from sorrow and then from laughing so hard as I described the ways I would make the girl pay. I see his elation and his anger and his passion. I see the best and the worst, and I love it all. I see him, and I see myself, because it doesn't make sense any other way.

And he sees me see it all, and I know before he stands up that he's going to do it. He's going to save me, because that's who he is. That's who we are.

He smiles at me, and it's a smile that rends my heart into a million pieces. I howl, or I try to, but the sound wraps around my heart like a fist, and I can't get enough air to even whimper.

"Get the needle," Ms. Larson says gently. "You're making the right choice."

I watch, paralyzed, as he stoops to pick up the syringe. He holds it like it's a scorpion, something dangerous and alive. The roar in my ears is deafening. I'm speaking before I realize I'm going to. I can barely even hear the words, but they tumble over each other in a desperate need to be first. "I'll do it instead. I'll do it instead. Please. I'll take his place. Please don't make him do this."

"He has to," she says. "It's balance."

"It's madness." I moan. I can't help it. There's no such thing as objectivity now. A keening sound pierces my ears, and I realize it's coming from my own throat. I bite my tongue to make it stop and taste blood. Henry whines behind me.

"Kennedy." Ravi's chin quivers for a horrible moment, then he clears his throat. "Ken. It's okay."

I shake my head, because there's nothing okay about anything anymore. Nothing at all.

"Ken," he says again, his voice thick. "Look, I'm gonna need you to do some things for me. If you can." He squeezes his eyes shut and sucks hard, fast breaths through his nose. The tendons jump in his shaking hands.

When he opens his eyes, he doesn't have to search for mine. "I need you to take care of my family. Tell them the truth. Don't let them think I did this. You can't let them think I would ever do this on purpose. Tell them I didn't want to go. Tell them I loved them—even Priya, even though she's a spoiled brat. Help Dad at the shop for me, yeah? He wouldn't know what to do if we both disappeared. And Ma loves you like her own, so don't be a stranger at the house either. She cooks better than your mom anyway, so can you at least show up for dinner sometimes? Don't go away on them, Ken. Please, don't go away. I need you to be there when I can't."

His face contorts, a thousand emotions vying for control, but he closes his eyes and swallows hard. He's not done.

"And don't forget me. We were supposed to make our mark on this world, but it's gonna be up to you now. You have to do it for both of us. Go on all the adventures we talked about. Bring my camera and take the pictures of everything you think I'd want to see. You're my very favorite human, and I need you to keep being that for the rest of your life. I need you to do that for me. You're fucking incredible, Ken, and I will love you for eternity. Remember that. Just that. Don't let the rest of this be our defining moment. I love you. Always have, always will."

"I love you too," I tell him. Although the words are woefully inadequate, he knows. Of course he knows.

Chapter Thirty-six

MS. LARSON walks him through it.

She keeps the gun trained on him while explaining that the first dose will go in the meaty part of his right thigh like an EpiPen. A second dose for the second leg, and then it will be fast. The instructions are dispatched without emotion, the flat recitation of something she's said too many times to care about anymore.

An abyss opens itself in my chest, right where my heart should be—or maybe my soul. I thrash against the ropes, the pain in my arm a distant memory. If this were a movie, I would've already freed myself and overpowered Ms. Larson. I would've saved the day.

As I struggle, my eyes never leave Ravi's. I want to look at Ms. Larson, make her see the error of her ways, but I can't. I want to search for Henry, to use him, somehow, for leverage, but I can't. I can't risk tearing my eyes from Ravi's, lest we lose a single second of the time we have left.

Ravi stands at the edge of the abyss and holds the syringe, eyes boring into mine as if waiting for salvation. I slam myself against the column, not caring about the damage to my arms, wanting only to break every bone in my hands so they might slip their shackles and set me free. I'm shaking my head without meaning to, without even knowing what I mean. Some variation of *no, don't do it; no, don't let this happen; no, I can't save you.*

No, don't let this be real.

Ms. Larson appears at my side, but I refuse to take my eyes from Ravi to acknowledge her presence. And then he's the one shaking his head—*no, don't do it; don't let this happen.* Cold metal bites into my temple. I shrink away instinctively, the way you would from a wall of fire or the swarm of bees, but still, my eyes never leave his.

Ravi raises the syringe, mouth moving with words I can't hear, and jabs it into his leg. He depresses the plunger, and I convulse against my bindings, heedless of the gun at my head or the hands holding it.

I wail, and from far away, a siren does too.

"Again," Ms. Larson says.

Objectivity comes then, as swift and sweeping as a guillotine blade, and I'm outside of myself, watching the tragedy being played out from balcony seats. It's a relief, in a way, because there's no way to survive inside the girl screaming against her bonds, no way to watch the boy she loves die, no way that this could be real.

My ghost watches as Ms. Larson holds the gun to my body's head, watches Ravi draw the second dose, watches Henry disappear through the door that leads away from this hell, because apparently, even dogs can only take so much heartbreak.

And I watch, from so far away, as Ravi brings the needle to his other leg. I want to scream at him to look at me, to stop wasting our last moments, but how can I, when I'm floating near the ceiling, outside the madness?

But he finds me anyway, and I slam back into my body with the force of a thousand trains. It's like being torn apart, but I don't care. I have to be here. I can't let him do this alone. We don't do anything alone, at least not until whatever comes next.

So I still myself.

I hold his eyes.

It's the last thing I can do for him, my very favorite human.

And he is steady. He looks at me with the conviction of someone saving the only thing that matters in the world. His sacrifice will mean the survival of everything he holds dear.

He raises his chin, and he smiles a final, beautiful smile. He doesn't look at Ms. Larson; he only looks at me, and it's okay, because we're going together. We're going to jump into that abyss holding hands, and I will see him through to the other side.

And that matters.

It matters more than anything, and I do not waver. As Ravi delivers the final dose, I go with him. I follow him down, and I don't even notice the barking or the pounding feet that swell around me or the gun going off. I stay with him, in my mind, even as he collapses to the stage, even as his body twitches, even as I scream until my throat is raw.

I'M STILL screaming when they cut me free.

They. The police.

Finally.

I barely register it.

All I see is Ravi, sprawled unmoving at the feet of the deer-shaped targets out on the platform.

I don't register the other body.

I don't acknowledge the stretchers being brought in, the commands being shouted, or the questions being hurled at me like grenades.

All I can process is the unmoving body of the person I love most in all the world, and eventually, vaguely, incongruously, Henry pressing against my legs like he's as adrift as I am.

My swollen hand rests in my lap like a thing that isn't mine. I don't remember sitting down. Part of me knows I'll have to surrender to the frantic attention of the uniformed workers, but not yet.

Not until I can set aside some of the raw emotion gnawing at my sanity. But I can't. Maybe not ever. Especially not with the people swarming the stage, keeping me from him. I want to scream at them to go away, to let me have this space and him for as long as I need, but I've gone mute.

The metallic reek of blood and smoke hangs in the air, but I don't acknowledge that either. I can't. Not yet.

I drop my uninjured hand onto Henry's back and dig my fingers into his fur. He lays his head on my knee and whines once before falling silent.

Officers try to coax me up, ask me questions, but I'm gone again. I'm in the abyss.

It's Mr. Burman, of all people, who brings me back.

The calculations were off.

Ravi hadn't died as quickly as Ms. Larson promised.

In fact, he hadn't died at all.

He'd slipped to the ground only unconscious, not dead, just as the police—summoned and flanked by the Burmans—stormed the room after Henry traitorously met them and led them into the bowels of the building.

Ms. Larson had turned the gun on herself the moment she saw the uniformed officers. Her story is finished.

But Ravi's isn't.

Ravi is alive.

It's the only thing that matters in the world.

Chapter Thirty-seven

BY THE time Ravi is released from the hospital after spending three days in a hypoglycemic coma, Maplefield has gone from a town that people didn't even notice passing through to the most talked about place in America.

Ms. Larson died instantly when she shot herself in the head, and I can't help wondering if that had been the plan all along—to get her revenge, then go off to join her brother. Maybe she really was going to let me go when it was all over, but I'll never know. The not knowing bothers me more than I care to admit.

What I do know is that Ms. Larson gave me more than just her "origin story." During the rescue, the police dogs had gone into such a frenzy in the basement, digging at the ground near the target platform, that the police had shifted the entire structure. When it was dragged away, the truth about the senior curse was finally uncovered.

It had been real all along.

Seven bodies were uncovered from the basement shooting range. All were identified as seniors who'd supposedly run away, including Madeline Archer, the circus girl. A cache of cell phones, along with a bag of SIM cards, was found in Ms. Larson's house, and the theory is that she'd used them to gain access to her victims' email and social media accounts, where she posted just enough to convince everyone, including their parents, that they were alive and well somewhere far away. If practice makes perfect, Ms. Larson proved that she could've gotten away with all the murders, including the four that mattered most. That may have been her plan when she started, but after what she said in the basement, I think she wanted to get caught. She wanted credit for avenging her brother's death.

She might've been the curse, but she was cursed too.

The first thing the new principal, Mr. Quinones, does when he takes over is overhaul the school's security. He makes a big show of it, but it wasn't a lack of cameras that had led to the horrors we faced. That kind of terror will find its way around the best locks and the loudest alarms if it really wants to. But I let Mr. Quinones think the upgrades make things safe, even though I know it's the blood that ended the curse for good.

The community loses its collective mind in the aftermath of everything that happened, and Ravi and I are courted by every major news outlet there is. The world doesn't want answers though; they want gory details. They want the rasp of Ravi's voice, hoarse from breathing tubes, and the cast encasing my hand. I broke a trio of small bones in the struggle to free myself and am now convinced that the whole dislocate-your-thumb-to-escape-handcuffs thing is a lie.

We surprise everyone by turning down the interviews.

My thumb is completely immobilized by plaster, but my fingers are free, which makes typing awkward but not impossible. That's important. Before we can do any interviews, I have to tell the story myself.

And I do.

I write like I'm possessed, pages and pages detailing Ms. Larson's story, our own ordeal, and the curse while Henry sleeps at my feet. I write in-depth profiles on all the victims, including the seven from the basement. Ravi films interviews with the families—not about their children's deaths, but about their lives. Of course, there are tears, but there's laughter too. With so many stories to tell, it takes hours of video to get it all, but we do. We sit in living rooms and kitchens, and we bear witness to lives lived and lost and vow to honor them. We caught the killer, and while we can't bring back the victims, we can do this. We can let the world know who they were.

Jennifer Larson becomes a household name—a rare serial killer in a time when mass murderers rule the headlines, and a female one at that. The notoriety is instant, and I have no doubt she'll go down in history as one of the country's worst killers.

We make it our mission to ensure the victims are remembered as well.

Our parents worry that we're working too hard and think we should try to forget, put the trauma behind us, and focus on healing. But there is no forgetting, and there shouldn't be. This isn't something to acknowledge and set aside, no matter how much easier that would be.

It takes days to organize all the parts of the story into a state of coherence. We spend these hours hunched over laptops at The Donut Hole or in each other's rooms. It's become physically difficult to part ways at the end of the night, and scenes from the basement plague my dreams, but I remember what Ravi said: I won't let that experience be our defining moment. We're more than that one night.

And Maplefield is more than its murders.

We stagger the release of the stories over a week, starting with *The Making of a Monster*, Ms. Larson's background in her own words—which is what everyone is clamoring for—and ending with victim profiles. I want those final stories to be the ones that people remember most vividly.

Every single post goes viral.

We grant the interviews after that. We have to.

It's strange being on the opposite side of a story, as the ones being reported on rather than doing the reporting, but we use the platform to send the stories of the victims into even wider spheres. They might not have been perfect people when they were alive, but who is? They should've had more time to get it right.

We bring Henry for the TV interviews because he deserves as much credit as anyone for ending the Maplefield curse, and his popularity risks eclipsing the victims when he becomes the internet's new favorite dog. Sherlock was right: dogs don't make mistakes.

Mr. Monroe insists that, in addition to the New England Excellence in Emerging Journalism contest, I also assemble and submit a portfolio for the National High School Journalist of the Year award, a two-stage process that requires judging at first the state, then national level. I agree on two conditions: that it can wait until the capstone piece of the project is finished and that I can submit with Ravi as a team. He agrees to the first and balks hard at the second, insisting that it's a very prestigious individual award and one I have a real chance of winning.

I don't care. It's both of us or neither of us.

In the end, he gives in and writes the required recommendation letter, which focuses on the importance of teamwork and how we each make the other a better journalist. And who can guess how it will be received? In an industry where careers are made by pushing boundaries, perhaps our unorthodox application will start a trend.

Either way, we don't need an award to validate us.

There's only one more story to complete, and Mr. Quinones is waiting, as promised, when we arrive at school on Sunday afternoon to get started.

It takes hours.

Mr. Quinones offers to help but isn't offended when we turn him down.

We work late into the night and are the first ones in the door Monday morning. We haven't told anyone what we were doing, not even Cassidy or Priya, and Mr. Quinones promised to keep it a secret from the staff as well. He might be new to the school, but he understands what we're trying to do.

The world needs to remember that Maplefield is not synonymous with serial killing. But more importantly, Maplefield needs to remember it.

So, from now on, everyone who walks the halls of Maplefield High will be reminded of that every day, in over six hundred ways.

Every single *I Am Maplefield* portrait has been printed, framed, and hung at eye level throughout the building. Each hall holds dozens of reminders that Maplefield is more than its murders. The last two pictures, our own, were taken in the days immediately following the attack, when Ravi's throat was ringed with purple and my own was raw from screaming. We set up a makeshift studio in Ravi's kitchen, using a sheet for a backdrop, and took turns snapping the photos.

We hung them on either side of the boiler access door, Ravi's on the left, his sign at chest height, and mine, with my sign balanced on the plaster thumb of my cast, on the right.

Our signs are deliberately linked, a paired statement that we settled on together over late-night donuts, the thesis of the project itself.

His says *I Am Not Defined By What Happens To Me.*

Mine says *I Am Defined By What I Do About It.*

Epilogue

I'M PRETTY sure the organizers of the New England Journalism Awards secretly want to be wedding planners.

Their invitation and tickets arrive in stiff linen envelopes that are sealed with an elaborate wax stamp. The event is being held at Mechanics Hall, a nineteenth-century concert hall in Worcester, and is set to include a keynote address by the president of the association, followed by dinner, awards, and dancing. A business card-sized insert indicates that attire is black tie optional, and a separate RSVP card asks us to disclose any special dietary restrictions.

Between the two of us, Ravi and I have enough tickets to cover parents, siblings, and still have two tickets left over. I offer mine to Bryce, and Ravi's extra goes to Mr. Monroe.

I let Cassidy talk me into dress shopping, and we spend a day at the mall with Mom, trying on an endless parade of gowns. Cassidy appoints herself director of the trip, and after she settles on a sleek and shimmering purple dress that hugs her athletic frame and flares into a trumpet shape below her knees, she turns her attention to dressing me.

I try to convince myself that I don't care what I wear, but it's a lie. I also have to concede that Cassidy has a knack for picking dresses that look good on me, even if they're not the simple black ones I would have chosen on my own.

In the end, it's still a black dress I leave with. Though according to Cassidy, there's nothing simple about it, because the boatneck, lace sleeves, and flared skirt make it something straight out of Meghan Markle's closet.

I can live with that.

I go with Ravi while he upgrades his funeral suit to something that actually fits, and we make it our mission to find the most ridiculous bow tie available, which still ends up being stylish and formal, all things considered, with small white flamingo skeletons set against a black background.

We drive together, him and I, leaving my parents to chauffeur Cassidy and Bryce and the Burmans with Priya. We park in the garage near the concert hall and follow the flow of formal wear to the entrance. Everyone is decades older than us, but we don't care. We stop at the New England Journalism Association backdrop and pose for photos like everyone else. We belong here as much as anyone.

Both families and Mr. Monroe are seated at a single table, the ten of us leaving no room for random add-ons. Mr. Burman and Mr. Monroe hit it off, and they even draw my father into easy conversation. The evening passes in a pleasant blur of faces and speeches and a mediocre dinner.

When the host of the evening takes the podium at the end of the program to announce that the final award will be the first of its kind, I reach for Ravi's hand and find it already seeking mine. Our fingers clasp beneath the table.

"This year," the MC says, "we are pleased to present a new category for the New England Journalism Awards. The Excellence in Emerging Journalism will be presented each year to a deserving student member of our profession. This year, I am pleased to present the inaugural award to Kennedy Carter and Ravi Burman, a pair of intrepid journalists from Maplefield High who exemplify the commitment, integrity, and professionalism that mark a true journalist."

On the screen behind him, a series of images from the *Monitor* plays across the projection screen.

"Since founding their own online newspaper, Ms. Carter and Mr. Burman have proven to be balanced and insightful in their reporting and have become a trusted source of information in their community. These past few months, that community—as many of you have reported on—has been rocked by tragedies, but these two have kept the light of the story shining on what matters most: the people affected."

The screen shifts from still images of articles to captioned video of the interviews we did with the Larson victims' families.

"They covered the news that mattered to the community in a way that kept the community first," the presenter says. "And in the face of overwhelming media coverage, they kept the town from being defined by tragedy."

The film shifts again, this time to the coverage of the *I Am Maplefield* reveal. There are scenes of student and faculty reactions—the surprise, the delight, the tears—followed by a narrated tour of the exhibit, where a crew follows Ravi and I and a reporter speaks off camera about the importance of moving forward while the faces of Maplefield fill the screen.

When the clip finishes playing, applause thunders around us, and the announcer has to raise his voice to be heard. "It is with great pleasure that I welcome Kennedy Carter and Ravi Burman to the stage."

We walk, hand in hand, through the clapping crowd and accept our awards: small granite plaques and stiff white envelopes that contain $5,000 each—money that was meant to fund our quest to find the stories that mattered.

But that plan, along with everything else, changed in the basement.

We don't have to trek to some far-flung land to find stories worth telling. The stories worth telling were all around us all along. They always will be, no matter where we end up.

It's with that knowledge that I return to the table, high on the applause, and drop my envelope into Cassidy's lap. She looks up, confusion on her face.

I speak close to her ear, because it isn't an announcement for everyone—just her. "For Mudd. It's not enough to buy him outright, but it will help."

Cassidy claps a hand over her mouth, and I grin.

I turn to Ravi as the music starts and the announcer invites everyone to the dance floor. "Shall we?"

He holds an arm out. "I believe we shall."

And we walk, arm in arm, straight out of the banquet hall, down four city blocks, and through the door of Noodz, where we order scandalous amounts of ramen and stay for hours, talking and laughing into the night.

About the Author

MISCHA THRACE enjoys writing fiction for young adults and is the author of *Bury the Lead* and *My Whole Truth*. She has worked as an English teacher, a horse trainer, a baker, and a librarian and has amassed enough random skills to survive most apocalypses.

She loves tea, all things geek, and not getting ax-murdered on long walks in the woods. She lives in Massachusetts with her husband and the best one-eyed dog in the world.

CPSIA information can be obtained
at www.ICGtesting.com
Printed in the USA
LVHW091634310521
688960LV00013B/324/J